MAKEDA

MAKEDA

BY **Randall Robinson**

AKASHIC
BOOKS

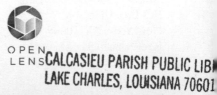

OPEN LENS

This is a work of fiction. All names, characters, places, and incidents are the product of the author's imagination. Any resemblance to real events or persons, living or dead, is entirely coincidental.

Published by Akashic Books/Open Lens
©2011 Randall Robinson

ISBN-13: 978-1-61775-022-9
Library of Congress Control Number: 2011923178

Akashic Books/Open Lens
PO Box 1456
New York, NY 10009
info@akashicbooks.com
www.akashicbooks.com

Also by Randall Robinson

Nonfiction

The Debt: What America Owes to Blacks
The Reckoning: What Blacks Owe to Each Other
An Unbroken Agony: Haiti, from Revolution to the Kidnapping of a President
Quitting America: The Departure of a Black Man from His Native Land
Defending the Spirit: A Black Life in America

Fiction

The Emancipation of Wakefield Clay

For Hazel, ever and always

The story that follows is fiction.
The scientific and historical details are factual.

But again and again there comes a time in history when the man who dares to say that two and two make four is punished with death.
—Albert Camus

PART ONE

PART ONE

CHAPTER ONE

Her voice breaking with the joy of adolescent enterprise, the highborn pretty girl leaned over the stone parapet and called down to a friend who was watching the oncoming procession from the winding ramp below.

"Meron! Meron! Look, Meron!" the pretty girl—a royal—called down, rolling and trilling the *r* in her friend's name—sounding it Mar-r-ron—as one would the soft melodic phrase of a lullaby.

"Isn't it the most beautiful sight you've ever seen? Isn't it, Meron? Isn't it?"

The two girls, both thirteen and dressed in long white *shammas*, raised their gaze to the towering volcanic rock peaks of Mount Abune Yosef. The mountain looked to have been set ablaze by the Sabbath morning sun. It was for the girls still another sign that theirs—Africa's Abyssinia, one of the first Christian kingdoms in the world—was a special place.

"Come up here," the child, second in line to the throne, called out. "You can see the whole world from here."

It was the day of Fasika, the anniversary celebration of the Savior's resurrection in the North 1,186 years before.

Meron climbed the steps up to the parapet where her friend leaned out against the waist-high wall. They looked out together from a natural rock terrace that stood 8,500 feet above the sea.

Far below, they saw a long procession of the faithful

moving slowly away from the banks of the River Jordan and up along the sinuous mountain pathway that would lead the worshippers to the Beta Medhane Alem—House of the Savior of the World—the church that was to be consecrated that morning. The church was one of eleven recently completed on the authority of King Lalibela. The churches—interconnected by tunnels—were perhaps only in some ontological sense *new*, and had not in any case been *built*, so to speak, but rather intricately carved in one piece out of the mountain's solid volcanic rock. With their keel-arched windows and their elaborately decorated portals, the cruciform stone churches were to remain a wonder of the ancient world hidden from foreign eyes for nearly 400 years until Francisco Álvarez, a Portuguese friar, arrived in Lalibela sometime during the 1520s.

Over the course of her childhood, the royal child's mother tutored her daughter that their storied lands, according to the early texts, were sacred and that their kingdom was the biblical birthplace of the human race. Her mother had taken her through all of the tunnels and to all of the carved-stone Lalibela churches connected by them. She also had taken her deeper into the mountain beneath the churches to the Tomb of Adam and to the Tomb of Eve that lay beneath it.

A bright ray of sunlight caught the face of the procession's leader, an elderly deacon in the Beta Medhane Alem church, and tinctured his burnt-umber skin to a startling brilliance. The deacon wore a jeweled gold filigree crown and a long embroidered velvet burgundy cape that opened into the shape of a cross. Climbing toward the church along the mountain's stone path, the deacon held with both hands high above his head the staff of a large smithed-bronze cross.

Behind the deacon walked a line of robed senior priests

bearing upon their heads the sacred *tabots* wrapped in embroidered silks, gold and silver brocades.

With her father preoccupied by affairs of state, the pretty girl had learned from her mother most of what she knew about the *tabots*, the ancient engraved stone tablets that had been brought back by King Menelik from Jerusalem more than a thousand years before in the Ark of the Covenant. Another deacon, younger by a generation than the cross bearer, carried in both arms a heavy and very large old Bible that was clad in leather and wood. The Bible had been handwritten in the old language, Ge'ez, the Semitic linguistic cousin of Galilean Aramaic, the Semitic tongue the Savior had spoken during his brief life in the North. Following behind the lead group of icon bearers were hundreds of worshippers making their way up the mountain to the Beta Medhane Alem church to attend the long-anticipated consecration ceremony.

The two girls watched mesmerized by the eddying sea of colors—robes and capes and crowns and exquisitely worked bronze crosses—swimming upward toward them under the brightening sun. Their nostrils filled with the bouquet of frankincense and myrrh spent onto the soaring mountain currents by swinging bronze censors. Trumpets sounded. Hand bells rang. The jingle of sistra floated up from the banks of the Jordan to the doors of the eleven churches that had been hewn with artisanal precision from a mountain of solid rock with simple twelfth-century tools. The awe-inspiring project, the work of thousands of hands, had taken twenty-four years to complete.

The girls were all but surpassingly proud, proud of their ancient country, proud of their much-admired kingdom, proud of their people's well-chronicled age-old history, proud of their signal role in the foundation story of Christianity.

As the procession neared the church, the girls hugged each other and shook with euphoria.

The royal, beaming, said to her friend, "Oh, Meron! Isn't this the greatest of days?"

Meron answered, "Oh, yes, Li'ilt (*Princess*). This may be one of the happiest days of my life."

The princess had been thinking much the same thing. She couldn't remember at that moment ever having been happier.

"Look, Li'ilt!" called Meron.

As Meron was speaking, the princess felt in her ears a pulsating rush of blood and heard an unfamiliar interior voice that was not her own. The voice seemed to be coming from far away and inside her head at the same time. The princess made an effort to ignore the voice and tried to push it away from her. But the voice came again, this time more insistent. It frightened the princess, not least because the one word the voice had sounded inside her head and in the back of her mind was not of her language, Amharic, but of a strange language she'd never heard before and could not understand.

"W-where, Meron?"

But the voice inside her head had by now gained purchase. With the small soiling undertow of an unwelcome memory, the little voice spoke again. Childlike. Lovingly. The princess had been happy on that Fasika morning, even as something warned her that she oughtn't have been, something in the back of her mind that kept pushing itself into her thoughts.

Then she heard the strange foreign word again. The word seemed to have been spoken by a child, a boy child.

Grandma.

Her eyes came open. Fully open. But she could no longer see the Abyssinian mountain that the Sabbath sun had turned red like fire. She could no longer see the calm waters of the River Jordan. Or the church faithful in their ceremonial finery. Or the magnificent stone worship houses her people had carved from solid rock.

She could no longer see anything. She was blind.

For a long and disconcerting moment, she did not know who she was or where she was. Only five to eight seconds later did she begin to realize that she had been dreaming.

She was believed to have been blind from birth. From the beginning, as I her youngest grandson would remember it, my grandmother's blindness seemed to reveal something colorfully anomalous and mysterious about her. When I was seven or eight she told me, as if she were sharing a delicious secret, that she dreamed in pictures—color pictures, pictures of people, pictures of odd places—though she had never in her life seen a human soul. It was not only that she possessed an inborn grace that belied her social station. She had an imagination of near mystical reach that was unexplained by the provincial small space of her experience. To my knowledge, during her adult life she had never ventured out of Richmond, and if she had, not out of the state of Virginia, I was all but certain.

Imaginative as she was, she never betrayed the smallest curiosity about what she looked like, though once, curiously, she had been heard to say, somewhat matter-of-factly, to her family that her skin was dark like "Ghanaian cocoa." But no one seemed to know how she had come to learn this.

When and where she was born also remained something of a mystery. She seldom spoke of her early life, not even to her son David, my father, who believed she'd been born on a small scratch farm on one side or the other of the Virginia–North Carolina border. She kept an old nineteenth-century family portrait in her downstairs front parlor and revealed to no one, save me, the portrait's provenance. Absolving her, my father ascribed her penchant for secrecy to a natural eccentricity that seemingly marked every social belief she voiced and every social behavior she practiced.

No detectable artifice, no affectation marked her bearing. In the most effortless way, she'd seemed to glide above time and space, unaware of, apparently, and uninfluenced by any obeisance to anything much contemporary in taste or fashion. Most of the few who knew her attributed this "queerness" to her never having seen anything through the watery gray fog of her lightless eyes.

Having toiled virtually all of her working life as a hand laundress for six wealthy white families up on Monument Avenue, she was, when I as a small boy came to know and treasure her in the early 1950s, all but penniless.

Everyone but she said that her name was Mattie Gee Florida Harris March. March was my biological grandfather's name, my father's father. Mama had met him once before he died in Baltimore some years ago. But Gordon and I never did. When he knew that he was dying, he'd asked my father's permission to see his only grandchildren. My father had refused his request. At that time I thought this uncharitable of Daddy, but Gordon, who was fifteen and three years older than I, seemed to understand Daddy's reasons for despising his father, who had, from the little I could gather, left my father and grandmother to fend for themselves shortly after he and my grandmother married at the age of sixteen, somewhere near Richmond.

It is fair to say that I began preparing to give this account of the fascinating events of my grandmother's life when I was little more than ten years old. By then her arthritic hands could no longer wash the clothes of the rich white families in the big stone-clad houses up on Monument Avenue. It may have been that I spent more time with her then than with anyone else in the world. She told me things she told to no other living person. In turn, I told her things I had told neither my brother Gordon nor Mama nor Daddy, things I thought they might not know how to take. For instance, I remember telling Grandma during a week-end spent with her when I was about five that I believed God was sleeping and that people existed inside the sleep as figments of God's dreams, figments that would disappear when God woke.

"All of us, Grandma, everybody in the world."

She gave me a bemused look that turned slowly into a smile. I took this to mean that I had impressed her. I remember at that point she said to me, "Things are almost never what you, with your two eyes, can see them being. Sometimes they are less, but most times they are more. Worlds and worlds more, son." Saying this, she'd tilted her head slightly to the left. It was an attractive manner-ism of hers that usually meant she was sharing some spe-cial portent with me—a portent I was being challenged to puzzle out the meaning of on my own.

Even when I was very small, several of her cryptic re-joinders made near perfect sense to me. She seemed to know this without saying so. Early on, I sensed that she had chosen me as a confidante because she believed I was spiri-tually endowed in somewhat the same way that she was.

From time to time, I'd hear my father, however, say that he did not understand her much at all. "She always seems to be here and somewhere else at the same time."

Yet there was no doubt at all that he loved her—loved her as deeply as any son could love a mother. From a back-breaking summer job in an ice house where he'd worked when he was fifteen, he'd used almost all that he'd earned to pay for her Braille lessons which were taught in defiance of Richmond's race segregation policies at a white Unitar-ian church.

The streets of Richmond were still safe to walk in the early 1950s. From the age of six, I would walk every morning the ten-block distance to Baker Street Elementary School. Usually, Gordon and I would walk together. Gordon was older than I, and his school day as a result was two hours longer than mine. This meant that I would have to walk home alone in the afternoons. Nearly every day, I would detour a block or so along Duvall Street for a visit with my grandmother, whose house from school was about half the distance to ours.

In the early years, she was the only grown-up I knew who did not relate to me in child-speak. I was inflated by this. Still, much of what she said to me flew swiftly over my head. In some intuitive way, however, both of us recognized, I think, that we were joined by some special age-neutral medium of kinship that was paramount to all others and had little to do with blood.

She once said to me during one of my after-school visits, "Son, most people, and I mean *most* people"—she usually referred to this massive chunk of humanity as the *counters*—"have eyes but cannot see. Oh, they look at things, but the things they look at get in the way of the worlds they cannot see. Do you understand, Gray?"

Had she been sighted, she'd have known from the look on my face that I was uncertain of what she meant by this.

"I think I do, Grandma."

She'd laughed then. It was a deep round laugh that originated low in her chest.

"Of course you don't, but you will."

She would then stretch out into one of her easy silences that I had long since learned to rest in. Then, she would start again as if I had been listening somehow to her ruminations.

"They think that if you can't feel it, touch it, count it, it's not there. But what do the counters know, Gray?"

I had tried to feign comprehension, the failed attempt at which she'd laughed rosily, and I had joined her.

"*They're* the ones that are blind. Not me. How's that, Gray?"

We had then laughed louder than before.

"Just the other night I was listening to WRVA on the radio. They had a professor on there from the University of Richmond who said he was a Christian, talking about philosophy. The man said that 'the problem with life is the destination,' as if he knew what he was talkin' about, tryin' to be funny. He was just another counter, blind as a bat."

She'd paused then and raised her face to the room's ceiling as though she could see through to the sky above. Then she smiled from far away and said, "But you're different, son. You're my spirit child."

I had no complete idea at the time just what it was I would come to understand, or, for that matter, what it was she had been talking about that day. Still, I felt that I had been *selected*. This, though I was still very young, made me feel quite special. I had felt, even then, her spiritual force and sensed its compatibility with my own.

Quite a few people in our small black church community, despite liking my grandmother, thought she was, to put it generously, *different*. Mama and Daddy, and maybe even Gordon as well, may have felt this way. But I never did.

There were occasions, however, when I thought her unrealistically virtuous. Much of this instinct I had mistakenly ascribed to her blindness. In any case, virtue alone would have been too simplistic a basis for her strong views. Unlike others, I knew even then that she was more than the sum of her platitudes and sayings. I was thirteen at the time of the discussion about the University of Richmond professor, and I had just become interested in girls. Claudette Benson, two months younger than me, went to our church and came from a good family. She was very sweet and my grandmother liked her very much.

During one of my visits, my grandmother asked me, "How do you like the Benson girl?"

"She's nice, Grandma."

"But I mean how do you *like* her?"

"You mean like a girlfriend?"

My grandmother smiled as if she were teasing me.

"She's not too pretty, Grandma."

"Hmm. Well you know, boy, pretty is as pretty does. Look beyond what you can see with your eyes. Do you understand, Gray?"

"Yes, Grandma." By the age of thirteen, despite not always following her cryptic advice, I had come to believe most of what she told me.

Somehow, I could never imagine my grandmother in the waitress-like costume she'd worn to work, leaving home in the early light to catch the number 27 bus and then the number 43 bus that would get her to the first of her day's washing stops by seven. She'd worked every day save Thursdays and Sundays. She'd refused to work on Thursdays and had gotten away with it. Why Thursday was so important to her I would wait to learn many years later.

Whenever I'd tried to picture her in a washerwoman's role, I would have to rive her into two completely and incongruously different people: the transcendent pillar of vision that I knew as no one else did, and the subservient menial who answered to an impersonal bell on a big house laundry room wall. I knew a lot of people who'd had to live like this for all of their working lives. But only in my grandmother's case had I gotten to see with my own eyes the higher face of a double persona.

Mr. George C. Crump, for instance, was chairman of

the deacons board at our church, First African Baptist. On Sundays, in his three-piece black serge suit and stormy style, he would cut a figure of considerable notice, second in line only to the Reverend C.C. Boynton whose great-grandfather had founded the big church on St. Peter Street. Everybody knew that on weekdays, Mr. Crump, who was light-skinned enough to be mistaken for white, wore a barber's tunic and cut white folk's hair in a way-off neighborhood that no one else in the church had ever seen. Though such was hard to visualize, much the same sort of duality would have described well enough the existence of most of the members of the church.

Still, with my grandmother it was different. The space between what she *was* and what she had done for a living was a thousand-fold larger than it was with Mr. Crump or anybody else that I knew.

I am twenty-five as I write this and have scarcely begun to understand my relationship with my father. We have been estranged a good while. There is more. He himself had suffered a rough draw of fathers. His natural father, he believed, had abandoned him in his infancy, although the truth was a bit more complicated than that. Or so it seemed to me. I couldn't really be sure, inasmuch as my father never talked about his childhood, and what little I came to know of it I'd had to extract from my mother who was chronically phobic about conveying the smallest information that may have seemed unpleasant. My father, when he did speak, spoke forth opinions that often landed like boulders on new grass. He was indeed something of a categorical man who erred with his certainties usually toward the general good and away from the varietal risks of gray. His childhood had been very nearly too complicated for him to survive. To do so, he'd had to simplify the world. To flatten out or make uncomplicated those against whom he had too few resources to spend in routine defense. Thus, he deemed people good or bad. Done. This worked quite well enough for him.

My mother, however, was smarter, and in some interior way more secure, but otherwise less brave than my father. She liked peace and always looked for it somewhere in the middle of all disagreements, real and theoretical.

"Your grandmother says that she needs to see you. That she needs to talk to you about her recent travels." She paused. "We also need to talk about whether at her age and disability we should let her continue on by herself in the house on Duvall Street."

I thought my mother's view here may have been colored by what my grandmother had said about needing to talk to me about "her travels." My mother hadn't understood, but nonetheless had reason to suspect what my grandmother meant by this and, consequently, may have taken it as a sign that my grandmother was becoming senile, which, I suppose, was a reasonable assumption since my grandmother had not traveled anywhere to speak of in the seventy-two years of her life.

Only I knew what my grandmother meant by "travels," and I was greatly interested in hearing about them. My grandmother had never owned a telephone and had steadfastly resisted our entreaties to have one installed, even after we insisted upon a phone as a safety device. She had always believed that the telephone and what she called "other needless modern things" were among the blinding distractions that "shrank the souls of the counters." I would just have to wait or reach her through Mrs. Grier, a next door neighbor and friend of my grandmother's who owned a phone.

"Tell her that I'll be there by tomorrow evening."

CHAPTER TWO

I n 1955, 15 years ago, when I was ten, my grandmother said to me in a quiet voice, "My name is not Mattie Gee Florida Harris March. My real name is Makeda Gee Florida Harris March."

The discussions I had with her upon which she would intently train her attention are fixed clearly in my memory from the age of five. Daddy would drop me off at her house on Saturday evenings and she would bring me with her to church on Sunday mornings. Gordon would visit her as well, but not nearly as regularly as I. My conversations with my grandmother always took place in the downstairs parlor at the front of her little row house. The room was usually dark, even at midday. The furniture was baroque and heavy. What little natural light the narrow space afforded could not overcome the dark velvet drapes that crowded across the room's two small windows. Doilies and bric-a-brac coated every horizontal surface except the top of the big oil space heater that dominated everything around it. The bric-a-brac had been given to her years ago by a church member. While it may have seemed an inappropriate gift for a blind person, my grandmother liked to run her fingers over the smooth soft-paste porcelain figures. She always sat in her wine-red upholstered rocking chair by the window. I always sat in a side chair which I positioned four feet or so away from the front wall and into the room toward the middle. In a corner across from my grandmother's chair was an ageless Emerson radio with a big circle dial that was housed in a waist-high oak wood console. Save for a picture of my father as a boy posing on a spotted pony, the cloudy photographs that sat about hickly-pickly were all of distant relatives who had died long before I was born and whose names meant nothing to me. Although she could not see the photographs, she wanted them there, she said, to keep her company.

After I turned fifteen, something conspicuously different was added to the little parlor's generally cheerless décor. On the long interior wall of the room that ran along the other side of the hall that carried through the house from front to back, hung a huge cream-colored coarse-weave cloth on which a symbol of some sort had been printed from a woodcut. I had been with her the day she was given the hanging by a man we met at a market, but I hadn't gotten a very good look at it then. The natural fiber weave had several rents in it and appeared to be very old. The thick-membered design seemed to be printed on the cloth with what looked like a natural pigment of red ochre that over time had grown dark and veined with razor-thin crisscrossing fissures. The handcrafted design was perfectly symmetrical with quadrants of roundish loops which joined in the center of the symbol to a single straight line that assembled the design's four elements into a unified statement.

It was stunningly out of place in the little room. At the same time, it was its very incongruousness that seemed to give the exotic hanging its light, lift, and power over what was otherwise a dreary and tenebrous space.

Riveted by the old painting, I asked my grandmother what it meant.

"Sometimes it's best to simply feel," she had said cryptically.

The happiest times of my life were spent with her in

the little front parlor on Duvall Street with the mysteriously exotic wall hanging.

"Why did your mother name you Makeda?" I once inquired of her.

"I asked my mother that very question and all she would say to me was, 'You *are* Makeda,' and that was the end of it."

"Where did the name Mattie come from?"

"My mother said that folks would not hire someone named Makeda, even to wash their clothes, and that I should call myself Mattie, but that I was never to forget that I was really Makeda."

It was the only time that she ever spoke of her mother to me.

On Sundays my grandmother wore to Reverend Boynton's First African Baptist Church the frill-free white dress of the deaconess that she had been wearing virtually all of my life. But the decorous deaconess who toiled during the week in a laundress's uniform wore flowing colorful tie-dyed muumuus of African inspiration at home. The muumuus had been acquired at my grandmother's request from a Nigerian woman who served with her on the church deaconess board. This—the wearing of muumuus, that is—was quite unusual in the 1950s for black women of late middle years in a place like Richmond, Virginia. Indeed, it was more than unusual. It was all but unheard of. My grandmother, who seemed not two but three people, unsurprisingly had more than her share of detractors, blithely ignoring convention, as she faithfully did, as often as not.

Though she would never have confessed to it, I suspect that my unremarkably conventional mother did not always approve of my grandmother who in any case would hardly have noticed.

It was from that chair in the little poorly lit parlor that I confided to my grandmother when I was fifteen that I wanted to be a writer. She had not washed other people's clothes for five years by then. She turned her face toward the window so that she could feel the warm bath of the early-autumn sun and answered as if she had not heard what I said.

"Do you ever talk to your mother or father about Gordon?" I did not answer and we sat together in silence for a time. "How is Gordon? Is he all right?"

"Yes, Grandma. Gordon is fine." Questions about Gordon were always asked with an urgency that I did not understand.

Moments passed.

"So, you want to be a writer."

In the early days, we would sit much as we were sitting now and discuss the progress of our lives. Even then she appeared to be looking without seeing, as if she were watching in her thoughts a screen of past experiences. The movement of her occluded irises would tell me when they were off to some far place, when she had divided herself between here and there. Owing, I think, to her ability to perform this trick of simultaneous presences, her irises would move in small lateral darts as if they were being operated by two separate selves.

Upon greeting me and others, she would bow slightly in a most uncommon fashion, as if she were not offering a courtesy but responding to a courtesy a lesser had rendered first to her.

Some twelve years or so ago, around 1958 or 1959, I calculatedly asked her the question I thought would stir in her the fascinating otherworldliness that I found so compelling.

"How old are you, Grandma?" Her eyes were wide, seeing virtually nothing. She seemed not put off by the question but rather to be waiting along with me for the answer.

"I think I was born around the turn of the century. I suppose you will calculate that to make me about sixty years old." A vague smile followed. "But who knows how old one really is."

Once she told me that she thought she and her family had "come from the Moores." When I asked my father about this, he said he knew of the Harrises, but not of any Moores that we had come from. When I told my grandmother what my father had said, she replied in what I thought to be her deaconess voice, "Well, young man, by and by, we all come to know that the soul travels light." As with much of what she said, I did not know what she meant by that. I was very young and she was very strange. But wonderful still, and I loved her more than I did anyone in the world.

"So you wish to become a writer. Well, I suspect that you will have somethin' to say. That is the most important thing. Now all you have to do is learn to write."

I had come to the house on Duvall Street after school that day in 1960. It was chilly in the parlor. Late-autumn shadows lengthened across the darkening room. A single thin shaft of gold light cut diagonally through the symbol on the wall hanging, making it resemble a sun dial.

"What time is it?" she asked.

"Almost half past four."

"You'll have to run along home soon. I know you got your work to do."

"I've got some time, Grandma. What is it? Is something wrong?"

"No, Gray, nothin's wrong." She paused and turned her face away from the low sun and toward me. She seemed to see me, just briefly. It startled me.

"Gray," she began, and stopped.

"Yes, Grandma."

"Do you have pen and paper with you?" Her voice was flat, uninflected.

"Yes." I retrieved a black-and-white-speckled notebook from my book bag and took a pen from my inside coat pocket. "I have a pen and paper now, Grandma."

"I want you to take down what I tell you and do what you see fit with it later. Do you understand?"

"Yes, Grandma."

"But never let the record of what I'm goin' to tell you out of your possession. Do you understand?" Her usually soft voice rose and hoarsened slightly.

"Y-yes, Grandma, I understand."

"You will not understand what I am goin' to tell you. Just take it down and put it away until you are grown. You will come to understand later. Will you promise to do this for me?"

"Yes, Grandma."

"I know things that have been lost to us." I did not know what she was referring to. Nonetheless, I began to write. Her eyelids flickered once and then closed slowly.

The blood appeared to drain from her face which took on the starched, untroubled countenance of a pale death mask. I was frightened by the look of her and became as still as she. Not knowing what to do, I remained motionless, fearing that the smallest movement from me would worsen matters. My thoughts raced themselves into a maddening tangle. Panicked, I began to cry silently. I looked at her. For how long I can only guess. I prayed. Even though, unlike my grandmother, I did not believe in the efficacy of prayer, I whispered, "Please, God, don't let her die." Her right foot jerked ever so slightly in its sandal. Then she was still again. Involuntarily, as if they belonged to someone else, my lungs emptied themselves of air. In desperation, I glanced around the room for something—anything—that would help me. For a brief moment, I raged at the telephone that she would not have. I feared to leave her, even though I recognized that leaving would be the only way to get help. I thought she might already have died. I considered trying to feel for a pulse, but I had no notion of how to do that. I looked up with terrified eyes at the large symmetrical symbol on the wall hanging to appeal to it for help.

CHAPTER THREE

A charge seemed to arise in what little air there was left in the shadowy parlor.

It was then that her eyelids again flickered—once, twice—before closing again slowly. Her chest rose and fell beneath her elaborately embroidered gown.

When she spoke she seemed a different person.

At first she spoke softly in her own voice and idiom. "I have lived in many places."

"Grandma, I—"

"Please, Gray, have patience and listen. I was there."

"Where, Grandma?"

"Gray, you are a smart boy. One day you will have a chance to study and prove what I tell you. That's why I want you to write it all down now. Just hold your horses for now. You'll see in time."

I said nothing to this and she continued. I would not interrupt her again. I would suspend judgment and write down in my notebook as much of what she said as I could. She helped me to do this by speaking slowly, although I am sure that had nothing to do with why she spoke so. Her English now bore an accent I had never heard before and was marked by an inventiveness that did not mark her normal speech.

I only knew that she was still aware of my presence when she said, "I have dreams that are different from ordinary dreams, dreams that are as real as the life we are living now, Gray, dreams in which I travel to far-off times and places. The dreams are of people I seem to know. People of all stripes. Dreams of past mothers and past fathers. Members of foreign villages and towns and courts. Law-givers, tin-makers, filigree artisans, muezzins, scribes, goat herders. And loves. My children's, theirs and their children's.

"These are dreams like none other. Dreams of vivid colors, shapes, and dimensions, dreams of all manner of tangible appointment in which I turn as I would in this world to discover a glorious manifest of nature's art wrapped around me, the breathing Earth alive beneath my feet, the sky a soaring blue dome pearled by floating cumulus sculptures. Sounds and scents whither to bathe amidst palm fronds clicking in the wind, mimicking the voice of light rain. The feel on my fingers of the textured, long, oval hanging fruit of the giant baobab tree. The taste of tea from the leaf the Berbers call *adil-ououchchn*.

"It is so different from an ordinary dream which is flat, half-rendered, and knows itself to be just a dream. No. What I have seen, where I have been, is different. So you see, I call these experiences that are mysterious even to me *dreams*, but nothing so real could be dreams, nothing so indistinguishable from common reality, nothing of such unmistakable meaning in the conscious sense."

I was dumbfounded. This was my grandmother *with* me, *recognizing* me, but speaking from another realm, and in a grammar I could not recognize as belonging to her.

"In the last dream, over 550 years ago, the year was 1394 to be exact, I was a Dogon girl of fourteen living in my family's large compound in a small village at the foot of a high stone cliff beside a river. My mother's name was Innekouzou. My father's name was Ongnonlou." The names which were completely foreign to me had rolled off her tongue with a practiced fluency. "I had five sisters and three brothers. But neither they nor my mother were in the dream. Only my father and I and a mammoth old banyan tree that stood on gnarled stilt roots in the middle of our courtyard. My father and I sat on the flat two-foot-high knees of the roots and faced each other in the cool shade of the tree's dense canopy. My father was a holy man and I was the youngest of his nine children. In the dream, it was my day for religious council which was always given weekly by my father to all of his children in the late afternoons in the lee of the family's ancestors' tree, the very same large and ageless banyan tree.

"By then, he was an old man, though I did not know in the dream what his actual age was. His skin was dark and smooth. A small man of handsome countenance, his compelling features counted a mouth that hinted of inner peace and eyes that held in them some great unplumbable wisdom. The only hair he displayed was worn under his chin in a thick white brush that matched in color his long unadorned flowing cotton robe and the soft sock cap that folded against itself in the direction of his left ear. He spoke softly but with great purposefulness.

"*How are you faring, my daughter?*

"*I am faring well, Father,* I said to him.

"*Your teachers tell me that you are quite an able student. Of this, I am very proud.*

"*Thank you, Father. You do me great honor.*

"*May the immortal Amma keep you seated.*"

Without comprehension I wrote this down much as I would the sound of a foreign language. I asked her to explain. Her eyelids remained drawn. The interval between my question and her answer was longer than it would have been under normal circumstances.

She said, "Amma is the Creator God, the most important god of the Dogon people. To be seated is to be stable and safe and at peace with the immortal god Amma.

"My father was a village priest who served under the high priest, the *hogon*, who lived high up on the cliff face, separated from the village. My father was bound to secrecy by our customs from sharing much of what he knew. Nonetheless, he began my religious education early. At the very foundation of Dogon religious knowledge is a far-reaching understanding of the role in our lives of the stellar world."

"Stellar?"

"The stars, son, the stars."

It was growing dark in the little parlor. The sun had fallen behind the dingy line of row houses to the west. I chose not to turn on the floor lamp standing beside my grandmother's chair. I remained still. Waiting for her. A police siren sounded and died away in the distance. Joined to me only by a slender filament of trust, she appeared pressed by some great duty to unburden herself of her strange vision.

I could scarcely see to write. She began again: "In the dream, my father began his council talking generally about Dogon knowledge of the stellar world. Yalu Ulo, or what you call the Milky Way galaxy, is the constellation of heavenly bodies in which the Earth turns on its axis. It does this as it moves around the sun in an orbit the Dogon call the Earth's space. My father likened the movement of these bodies to the circulation of blood in the human body.

"I remember him speaking to me of Dana Tolo and Dana Tolo's four children."

"What did he mean?"

"Dana Tolo is Jupiter and the children are its four moons. Using the Dogon names, my father also described how Venus follows Jupiter around the sun. He then withdrew several Dogon drawings from a goat-skin bag at his feet and showed me one of Saturn with a ring around it.

"Amma, my father said, created everything, the universe, the Earth, its movements, and its living creatures. Amma created as well the living creatures that dwell on other earths.

"My father then did not speak for what appeared to be a long period. I knew well to remain silent until he was ready to speak again. After a time he took from his bag another drawing which was that of a stretched circle. The stretched circle enclosed five small distinctly irregular figures of some kind.

"I asked him, *What is that, father?* He said, *It is the pure place of stars from which Nommo on the Day of the Fish came to Earth to purify it and initiate society. Humans rebelled on Earth at creation and remained impure. Nommo came in a sacrifice of himself to cleanse the Earth. He was crucified on a tree. A star will one day appear in the sky to herald his resurrection and return to us.*

"I pointed to the drawing of the stretched circle and asked my father, *Where is this place that Nommo came from to Earth?* He placed his finger on the crossed line-and-sickle figure in the lower right quadrant of the stretched circle. *This is the brightest star in the sky. It is larger than the sun. Tonight you will see it there.* He pointed to an area in the northern sky. *It wobbles as it turns.*

"*Is that where Nommo came from?*

"*No, my daughter, Nommo's star, the star of all creation, is Po Tolo, the little star that orbits around the big star along the outline of the drawing. See here?*

"He traced his finger along the line of the stretched circle and said, *Po Tolo revolves such. It requires fifty years to go all the way around the big star which wobbles because Po Tolo is made of sagala which is the heaviest substance in the universe and not found on Earth. It is so heavy that nothing on Earth can lift it.*"

The little parlor fell silent. "Grandma."

"Yes." The voice was raspy and low and did not sound like my grandmother's.

"I can't see anymore. May I turn on the lamp?" I asked. Again, a space, a silent space, longer than normal.

"Yes, son."

I turned on the floor lamp and said, "Grandma, I'm trying to understand."

"Yes?"

"You think you could draw what your fa— the priest showed you in the dream if I put paper in your lap?" I took a sheet of typing paper from my bag and fastened it to a clipboard. I put it on her lap and placed in her right hand a marker and positioned it in the center of the paper. "Try to draw the stretched circle, Grandma." She pulled the marker around the paper in the line of a rough ellipse. "Try to draw the five figures." I placed her marker within the quadrants of the ellipse as she instructed.

"Label this one *bright star*," she said, "and this one down toward the right bottom *Po Tolo*. Here, place the star, Emme Ya. It is, my father said, larger than Po Tolo but four times lighter. The Dogon call it the sun of women. The fifth figure in his drawing is not a star but a planet. Place my hand inside the left line toward the bottom . . . There. There. I hope that this looks like what I picture in my head from the dream."

She rested her head against the high curved back of the rocking chair. "You must be running along now. But remember what I told you. Tell no one and never let what you have written down out of your possession."

"Why, Grandma, did the priest and the Dogon people call the heavy little star Po Tolo?" I asked.

"In Dogon, *tolo* means *star* and *po* is a cereal grain, the smallest known to the Dogon. In the dream, my father said that the heavy little star rotated on its axis in a period of one year and that the Dogon celebrate the rotation in what is called the *bado* rite. The Dogon believe the little star is the starting point of all creation."

"Grandma, who were the Dogon people, and if they existed, where did they live?"

My grandmother raised her eyelids. "I don't know, Gray. I don't know. I don't remember that from the dream."

Now she sounded like my grandmother again.

Chapter Four

Looking back now on that strange afternoon of ten years ago in my grandmother's parlor, it is clear enough that what she divulged to me there, as well as the place of trust she accorded me, had a considerable impact on me, a midterm adolescent of unsuspected merit. She had *seen* something of value in me, if nothing more than a curious and open mind, and perhaps a certain congenital appreciation of the metaphysical. The bond between us, sealed forever in the tidy little over-furnished sitting room, was one of the two major watershed events in my life. The second event which lay just ahead, I could not have withstood had my grandmother not made me the sole caretaker of her great and improbable secret.

Something else happened on the bus ride home from Duvall Street that day, which I took, in the unusual context of things, to have more significance perhaps than it warranted. I had turned fifteen on May 1, 1960, five months before my grandmother told me the Dogon story. This was a month or so after my family moved from our flat in the Jackson Ward section near my grandmother's house to a block in the Church Hill section of Richmond that changed from all white to all black within months of our moving there. That night, I took the East End 30 bus on Broad five blocks south of my Grandmother's house and got off at 37th and M, two short blocks from my house on the corner of 39th and M. My stop was only minutes from the end of the line and no one was on board save the driver and me by the time we reached the next-to-last stop at 35th and M. It was after six o'clock and dark when the bus pulled away from the curb. Just as it was doing so, I heard someone cry out, "Hold up! Hold up!" I called ahead to the driver to stop, which was something drivers, as often as not, refused to do. Business that night, however, was slow and unhurried. The driver stopped. The door hissed and opened to an elderly black man who appeared winded from running alongside the moving bus. The man heaved twice, caught his breath, smiled at the driver, and said, "Thank you so much. I guess tonight is my lucky night." He smiled as he walked past me and took a seat in the middle of the empty rear bench seat. The bus rolled two blocks before it turned left and pulled to a stop with its big air brakes wheezing in front of the all-white East End Junior High School. The school had remained open after our arrival in the neighborhood. Within months, however, the school's student body would be all black.

I got up to exit by the rear door and noticed the pleasant elderly man slumped on his seat with a narrow rivulet of blood negotiating a path from his left ear across the rise of his dark face and into his nose. "Driver! Something's wrong with this man!" But by then I knew that the man, without having made a sound, was dead.

From that day on, whenever I thought of the dream my grandmother had described to me, I would think of the old man who had vanished from the realm of the living without whirl or whisper.

My grandmother seemed to believe that she had visited the dead that the old man had silently joined. Perhaps that was what she meant by souls traveling light.

We lived in a modest redbrick colonial at the edge of a wood on the last street in Church Hill. I did not have a house key. My mother was at home, as she almost always was. She did not work, or at least outside our home she did not work. This was not as she wished it, but my father was strongly opposed to the idea of her having a job outside our home.

"You're late," she said absently.

"I stopped by Grandma's."

"Is she all right?"

"She's fine. Is Gordon home yet?"

"No, he had football practice but he should be along in a few minutes. Your father too. We'll eat at seven."

I went upstairs to my room, the smallest of the three small bedrooms in the house, and closed the door. From the top shelf in my closet, I took a battered tin tongue-lock strong box that my father had discarded to me as a toy when I was ten. I tore the three pages from my notebook on which I had written what my grandmother told me and inserted them along with the drawing she had made into a page-sized plastic sleeve. I placed the package in the strong box, locked it, and returned it to a place at the back of the highest closet shelf where it could not be seen from the floor by my mother, who, when no longer able to bear the room's usual dishevelment, sometimes waded in to restore a semblance of order.

I sat on my bed and attempted to gather my thoughts about what I had learned. Unbidden, the names my grandmother had recited to me—Innekouzou and Ongnonlou—sounded in my head. I had never before heard an African name said aloud before my grandmother told me an hour ago that they had been her Dogon parents in the dream. Staring now at the dark brown skin on my arms, I wondered why. And why such had never before occurred to me. I'd heard around all sorts of foreign, even ancient, maybe antediluvian names without it occurring to me that I'd never heard any African names at all. Not one. Not a single one. I knew from school a Hezekiah who'd been named by his parents after the King of Judah. I even knew from my third period English class a Mordecai who'd been named for the Bible's Mordecai who someone told me was a relative of Esther's. A Moses played on the football team with Gordon. Just that morning in history class, our teacher Mr. Brown had taken up most of the hour telling us about Agamemnon and the Trojan War before allowing that both the king and his war may have been a myth. No one that I knew outside my family ever spoke about Africa without disparagement. That is, if they mentioned Africa at all.

I went downstairs and into the kitchen where I found my mother removing a casserole of baked lasagna from the oven. I started down the steps which led to a tiny utility room and the back door of the house.

"Where are you going, Virgil?"

My mother was the only person in the world who called me by my first name, Virgil. Everyone else called me by my middle name, Graylon.

"Outside for a minute to catch some air."

"You just got home."

"I know. I'll only be a minute."

"In the cold?"

I did not answer and opened the back door. My mother called after me, "You're acting mighty strangely, son," but she was by then already distracted by what she was doing.

My mother kept a beautiful flower garden of rosebush beds and evergreen shrubs; perennials that had all but finished the stagger of their summer show; annuals that smiled colorfully from early spring bravely onward into the teeth of the oncoming frost. Verbenas, snapdragons, periwinkle, marigolds, daylilies, touch-me-nots, all showing their fading wares in well-weeded beds that wended this way and that full around the green central lawn of the large yard.

I walked to the center of the yard. There was little light from the house and a corner streetlamp to mitigate the yard's inky darkness. I had come out without a coat. I shook myself to preempt shivering as I began to search the north sky.

The star was big and brilliant and easy to find. It stood well out from the thousands that shone in the black night sky, a luminous bluish globe hanging just above the horizon where the old Dogon priest in the dream had told my grandmother it would be.

I hugged myself against the cold and stared into the sky, searching the neighborhood of the big star for the little one that the priest had called Po Tolo. I found nothing. I looked again, hard and longer, but with the same result. I then surveyed the full stunning immensity of the shimmering blackness, as if I were looking upon the grand and mysterious beauty of the night sky for the first time. And with a point of reference. Strange, what a difference this alone made. Could it be that anything up *there*, near that shining light, could have something directly to do with us, me? Somehow I felt oddly, with the mere contemplation of such a question—what?—changed.

My grandmother used to say to me, "You're my late bloomer. My spirit child. Your mother and father love you but they just don't know who you are yet. You don't either, I suppose, but you will soon enough. Just you wait."

Gordon was the hope-star of my family. He was more handsome than I, more athletic than I, smarter than I. He was even pleasant and generous and social of temperament. That I was jealous of him seemed to demonstrate that he was, well, kinder than I as well. These were the facts. My father's hopes revolved largely around Gordon, who was "going somewhere," language no one used to measure my long-term prospects. My mother, for her part, was captured by the energy of my father's pride in Gordon, the grand prize that my father, an ordinary insurance salesman, and my mother, an ordinary housewife, had won in nature's lottery of small miracles. One hardly expects fortune of such magnitude to smile twice upon the same household. Indeed, I was loved. That, I never questioned. Otherwise, though, I was largely and benignly ignored.

All that said, as I remember it, I had not been an unhappy child, but rather one who ate, slept, and spun in a bubble of aimless spiritual and intellectual indifference. I hadn't known what I would be, or was even supposed to be. I only knew that I was supposed to be *something*. Gordon would be a doctor. This seemed all but assured. This had been known to him for years and he was only eighteen. Gordon and my parents approached this as if a career in medicine were little different from a big-ticket item of merchandise toward which one simply planned for years and saved to obtain. They were solid north-south straight-line flat-plane people. Unfortunately, I was not like them. I was a muddle of questions that wound around themselves. It wasn't that I did not want to *go somewhere*. Indeed I did. But my *somewhere* required a measure of passion to reach, passion I could not generate before *somewhere* chose to reveal its elusive face to me.

When I look at Gordon, I guess I can understand why people would say that we favor one another, but most of the time I can't see it at all. Perhaps this is because I know in every other way how very different we are. What I am about to say is not to disparage Gordon at all, or at least I earnestly think not, because I love him, but Gordon is not at all, from what I can see, a complicated person. He is very smart, but he labors under no psychological compulsion to dice every unimportant social issue into an incomprehensible hash. Thus, he appears to enjoy a working happiness, or a contentment of sorts at least, that he is not driven to deconstruct into a mess of gloom. He does not despond. I despond—and as instinctively as he does not. I do not enjoy being this way (or perhaps I do), but I cannot help it. I think that I mean this when I say it, but I do not wish to be like Gordon who appears to me happy but flat with an emotional surface that is all but impervious to abrasion. The hide of my psyche is rather more corrugated than his and registers even the most inconsequential of experiences that roll across it. For this reason, it is my guess that I know him better than he knows me. There is less of him to know. Or so it would seem.

Seeming, however, is deceptive. I can only know how Gordon seems. Not how he *is*. For I think that I may *seem* friendly and outgoing. In my heart I am. But the mechanics of engaging people make the entire proposition of doing so, for me, not worth pursuing. Most people who know me think that I am funny and social. I am anything but. I much prefer being alone, or with the very few for whom I feel uncalled to act or perform. When I am introduced to people, I invariably, seconds later, don't remember their names because I never really listen for their names, so unnatural and false is the moving space between us. I don't think this is the case with Gordon, or, at least, this doesn't appear to be the case with Gordon who has no faculty for obsession of any kind. Thus, life for him seems easy, but I cannot know this because teenagers, even brothers, don't talk about such things. Probably no one else does either.

My grandmother had always been something of an unspoken karmic ally to me. Only she seems to see inside my heart. My guess is that when I told her that afternoon that I wanted to be a writer, she knew that what I really meant was that I wanted, really wanted, to *want* to be a writer. Perhaps she believed that I had told her this merely to curry favor with her. But maybe I had only been hoping that destiny primed would provide me in my confusion some small glimpse of itself. Looking back on it, I think now with conviction that it was my grandmother's uncanny *knowing* of me that inspired the timing of her revelations that day. Standing in the frigid dark gazing into the heavens that night, I felt for the first time in my life the sweet force of purpose.

A dark middle-aged four-door sedan rolled slowly to a halt, its headlights washing the yard. "Is that you out there, Gray?" The voice was loud and gritty in the cold night air, jarring me from my reverie.

"Yes, Daddy."

"You all right, boy?"

"I'm fine, Daddy," I said and sighed involuntarily.

"Well, come on in the house," my father said, sounding worried.

My father's father and my grandmother married when they were fifteen, after she became pregnant with my father. Little more than children themselves, the two of them awaited the birth of their child while living in the house of my grandmother's mother, an ill-tempered divorcée of high temperance and small charity who believed the *crime* the boy had committed against her daughter to be unpardonable in the sight of her very own vengeful God. The boy ran off, eventually, in adulthood, making a new life and family 150 miles away in Baltimore. Though he saw my father from time to time before he died of old age and regret in Baltimore, my father never forgave him for leaving his mother at the age of sixteen, months after he was born. My father was not a forgiving man, even during those early years. He had been an only child with no model of a man to copy and a blind mother who worked from dawn to dusk laundering clothes up on Monument Avenue. He had literally *fabricated* himself, which was to mean that Gordon and I would have no need to do the same. I did not understand this when I was growing up. All I could uncharitably see was a distant inflexible man who clanked about in a false girdle of out-rigging armor, while chiseling out immutable laws-for-living on tablets of certainty. With no margin of error to speak of, he had very much needed, so to speak, to keep his lines straight. Gordon intuitively understood this and my father, while I, less mature at the time, somehow childishly found attractive the poet's weakness for philosophical dilemma and practical failure. But here I do myself too much credit. The fact is, though I did not know it at the time, I may have been too much like my father at least in one way, and as a consequence, took no pains, as Gordon had, to try and understand him.

We took our customary seats at the Formica-top kitchen table, and after a toneless recital of grace by my mother (grace that my father did not believe in, in any case), ate our lasagna in silence.

CHAPTER FIVE

The day after my grandmother told me her dream story, I stayed after school to meet with Mr. Garver to find out what I could about the Dogon constellation. He not only taught integrated science, but that particular year, 1960, he served as faculty advisor on the yearbook committee. The yearbook for Armstrong High School was called the *Rabza*. I did not know why it was called that and, to this day, I do not know why. Curiously, no student during my years at Armstrong was ever provoked to investigate the word *Rabza*, which ought to have seemed a conspicuously peculiar name for a yearbook.

Mr. Garver was a big barrel-chested man who wore a big black brush mustache that cast a shadow over his mouth.

"Graylon, why is it that I have the impression you're someplace else when you're in my class? I had Gordon when he was a freshman like you and he was an exemplary student."

Gordon was pictured in the 1960 edition of Mr. Garver's *Rabza* in no fewer than five places: in cap-and-gown with the graduating class, as captain of both the football and basketball teams, in a group photograph of the school's National Honor Society, and as president of the class of 1960.

"Your brother set an example that we all expect you to equal."

I hated Mr. Garver, the only colored man in America,

as far as I knew, who played the *hneh*, a bamboo oboe-like instrument he had picked up during his travels in Burma, travels about which he had recounted insufferably to our fourth period class on numberless occasions.

"I'll try my best to do better."

Mr. Garver was surprised that I'd stopped by but dutifully said all the things that I had heard all too many times before: that I had been gifted with as much ability as anyone, that I was wasting that ability, and, not least, that I was causing my mother and my father a great deal of needless worry and pain.

Hanging over the blackboard from hooks was a large oilcloth illustration of the solar system. Focusing on it, I asked him the question I needed answered about the big star that the Dogon priest had described in my grandmother's dream, the star I had found in the sky the night before.

"Which way were you facing when you saw it?"

"North." I showed him.

"Was it bluish in color and the brightest star in the sky?" I told him yes. "Then the star you saw would be Sirius. It is large and close, only eight and a half light-years from Earth. It is larger even than the sun."

I asked him, "Is it orbited by another tiny star?"

"No, it is not." He looked at me quizzically.

From the door, I asked, "Have you ever heard of the Dogon?"

"No. What is that?"

"They are people, sir."

"Where do these people live?"

"Well, I don't quite know."

The school, built in 1951, was a two-story brick example of the American modern public school minimalist idea, replete with low ceilings and endlessly long hallways lined with vented metal student lockers that deafened at school day's end with the racket of a tool-and-die factory. Near the building's front door were Principal Herbert Bean's office, the auditorium, and the library, my next destination, which was run by Miss Martha Botts who by all appearances was a mirthless woman of bone-straight posture.

"Miss Botts, have you ever heard of the Dogon people?"

She sat behind the counter in the library on a high stool, looking sterner than usual. "No. What are they? An ethnic group? Where do they live?"

"That's the problem. I don't know."

"Well, let's just see, Mr. March. Come with me." She led me to a table in the reference section and ordered me to sit. She then disappeared into the stacks and returned in five minutes with four heavy oversized volumes.

"Look through these. Tell me if you don't find what you're looking for. Then we'll look some more. Okay?" She was nicer than I thought she would be.

"Yes, ma'am."

The first book was *The Butcher Encyclopedia of the World's Peoples*. I searched the index and discovered that the word *Dogon* appeared nowhere in the 2,075-page tome. Second in the stack was a book of maps for which I held out little hope. I turned my attention to the third book, which was titled *Culture and People of the Global Community* by C. T. Hoppes and Vivian Kornegay. I drew my finger down the index entries under D and found halfway down the page, *Dogon Tribe of Peoples, 52–53 passim*.

The sight of the word *Dogon* in print on a page in a book gave me a stir of jittered excitement. I turned quickly to page 52 and there it was, text and pictures. The pictures were of a breathtaking topographical feature and a black family dressed in flowing white robes. The first picture had under it a caption which read: *The Bandiagara escarpment, a 600-foot sandstone wall that runs for 120 miles south of the Niger River.*

I got up and walked to the end of the long table where an unabridged edition of Webster's Dictionary rested on a book stand:

es • carp • ment (*noun*)
a steep slope in the form of a fortification.
a long cliff.

My God. The cliff. The river.
I returned to the book by Hoppes and Kornegay and began reading the text section on the Dogon people.

The Dogon people migrated to an area near Timbuktu in Mali, West Africa, sometime during the fourteenth century. It is not known where they came from. They settled at the foot of the Bandiagara escarpment. The Dogon speak a language of the same name and are believed to place religious significance in the movements of the stars and planets . . .

I reached my grandmother's house before four-thirty. On the bus ride across town, I thought of little else besides the dream. How could she have known such things, things that the well-educated people I knew, knew nothing of? How could she, a retired blind laundress with a grade-school education, possibly have ever heard of any Dogon people at the foot of a cliff beside a river in Africa? Yet I believed her that she had dreamed it. I believed further that she believed what she had dreamed. Climbing the weather-beaten wooden steps to her small front porch, I told myself that I would make notes on all that I had learned (or not learned) from Mr. Garver and from my library researches immediately upon reaching home. I would secret the notes in the plastic sleeve where I'd put the drawing and dream notes yesterday in the locked metal box on the top shelf of my closet.

Recognizing the special antic tempo of my bell ringing, my grandmother called through the door's oval glass window, "Gray, is that you, son?"

"Yes, Grandma. It's me all right."

"Come on in, son. Take off your coat and come sit down so we can talk awhile."

Grandmothers are put on Earth for harmless conspiracies, for telling things, things that cannot be told to parents—parents who are ever woebegone beneath the weight of rules, responsibilities, and a well-understood need to lie to their children about their own adolescent misadventures.

There were flowers in a vase on my grandmother's little mahogany coffee table, yellow carnations standing round-faced on a spray of jasmine that scented the close air.

"Those are pretty flowers, Grandma."

She took this as a request for explanation. "You know Agnes Sally, don't you?"

"You mean the lady from the deaconess board?"

"Yes. Well, she sells vegetables down at the 6th Street market. Got these flowers from a neighbor's stall. Brought them not long before you got here. Sweet of her, don't you think?"

"Y-yes, I guess."

"Oh, son, she knows I can't see them. But I can smell them. That's jasmine you're smellin'. You like it?"

"It's great."

She paused and then said abruptly, "Why are you here today, Gray? You don't usually come two days in a row like your father who, bless his heart, comes just 'bout every day."

When I did not answer immediately, she said, "You want to talk some more about my dream, don't you?"

"My science teacher said that the big star is called Sirius."

Her arms surged with alarm from the wide drape of her exotically embroidered shift. "You didn't tell anybody what I told you, did you, son?"

"No, Grandma. I didn't tell him anything."

"I don't want people thinkin' I'm crazy."

"You're not crazy, Grandma."

"Who *you* tellin'?" she said and laughed.

"Grandma, had you ever read about or heard about the Dogon people anywhere before?"

"No. Where would I?"

"I don't know. This is just all so, you know, strange."

"You found out somethin', didn't you? What is it? What did you find out?"

"There *are* people that are called Dogon."

"I know *that*, Gray. They were in the dream."

"They live in Africa."

"I knew it. I knew it in my bones," she said *sotto voce*.

"West Africa."

"Yes, yes," announced in muted celebration.

"In Mali."

"Where?"

"Mali, Grandma."

"Is that so?"

"At the foot of a huge cliff." My grandmother began to rock slowly. "Along a great winding river called the Niger."

"I knew it. I knew it," my grandmother said, almost whispering. "God be praised. God be praised."

We sat together for a long while saying nothing. My grandmother, Makeda Gee Florida Harris March, head resting against the chair back, rocking in a slow swim, wearing on her smooth brown face the enigmatic smile of one who had gazed full upon the face of time.

It was I who spoke first, disturbing her back into the dark little room.

"Grandma."

She drew in a punctuating breath.

I was reluctant to share with her the other piece of information I had come by that might appear to offset the good news I had brought.

After putting on my coat, I said, "My science teacher said that there was no small star that orbited the big star."

This did not bother her as I had expected.

"Don't worry, son. Your science teacher will learn soon enough about the heavy little star Po Tolo. My father, the priest, knew this in 1394. His people, the Dogon, have known this for 5,000 years. Of this I am certain."

CHAPTER SIX

Nineteen sixty was to be a fateful year for the March family, and for black people generally, to tell the truth. In June, Gordon would graduate from high school with top honors and head off in the fall to one of the four prestigious colleges from which he had won academic scholarships. The letter from Harvard College was the last of the acceptance letters from Gordon's "big four" to arrive at the house on 39th Street. Gordon, well, Gordon and Mama and Daddy, really, would choose from the list of offers that also included Princeton, Stanford, and Columbia University.

Richmond, of course, and the whole of the South, remained riven by race. But the signs of change were all about us. Five years had gone by since thousands of blacks had assembled at the Holt Street Baptist Church in Montgomery, Alabama, to launch a bus boycott after a black seamstress named Rosa Parks was arrested for refusing a white bus driver's order to move to the back of a city bus. The leader of the boycott, a young pastor from the Dexter Avenue Baptist Church named Martin Luther King, Jr. had even come to Richmond to visit our school in 1958. He had become a national figure by then. I had not forgotten meeting him during the brief stop he made at Armstrong.

On February 1, 1960, David Richmond, Franklin Mc-Cain, Ezell Blair, Jr., and Joseph McNeil, freshmen at North Carolina A&T University, an all-black school in Greensboro, North Carolina, had gone downtown and demanded to be served at a segregated lunch counter.

The action the freshmen took had electrified and frightened me all in one stroke. It was three months before my sixteenth birthday. So I saw the brave young men in Greensboro as near peers.

They had thrown down the gauntlet, and not just to the Southern white establishment, but to Southern blacks as well. Looking back on it, I felt a great pressure to *do* something, to follow their lead. It was like they were watching me, and waiting for me to get off my duff.

The sit-in hadn't felt at all like the aftermath of *Brown vs. the Board of Education* six years before. My friends' response to the Supreme Court's decision had been decidedly mixed. The sit-in may have come as a surprise to the white students over at Douglas Freeman High who'd been given the erroneous impression, I think, that we wanted to *be* with them, which was, in my measure, a desire that did not exceed their desire to *be* with us. Surely, the white-imposed *act* of segregation itself was humiliating to us—hate-inducing even—but with respect to the act's sheer administrative result, it could not have been denied that blacks enjoyed the exclusive company of blacks every bit as much as whites enjoyed the exclusive company of whites. At least, this was my guess. The white students were probably operating at something of an information disadvantage here because we had more to go on than they did. The local media, which was largely controlled by whites, made plain the white students' general dislike of blacks. I don't think the white students could have known whether we really wanted to be with them or not. Nobody had asked us that question, not even the writer Ted Beaseley over at the *Richmond Afro-American*.

By 1960, the Supreme Court's edict seemed, at least in

Richmond, to have been rendered for naught. The decision had had little effect on our lives. The public schools and the city in general had remained as segregated as ever.

But the action that the four college freshmen took was different—readily transferable, contagious. Every Southern city had lunch counters. In Richmond, there were twenty-seven of them on Broad Street alone. Someone had counted them. Twenty-seven lunch counters with over 300 stainless steel pedestals under 300 round faux leather–covered seats that swiveled thousands—no, tens of thousands, maybe even hundreds of thousands—around to Formica-top counters upon which zillions of burgers and fries and shakes and pies were served up lickety-split to any white person with a quarter or two. No references required. No questions asked.

For years, we blacks had looked with Pavlovian suspicion at the stools—saw them spinning languidly behind a ruddy diner's retreat, saw them bracing up ravenous white patrons leaning into steaming plates, saw them standing straight and empty, waiting, watching, eyeing us passing near to them like hostile sentinels.

The four freshmen, scarcely six months in college, just upped and left campus, went to downtown Greensboro, found four empty stools, and sat down on them, just like that. I'm ashamed to admit that I could never have done that, been that brave. Amidst the lynchings still very much going on across the South. With storied old lawyers jousting still in the highest courts. No mass meetings. No Kings. No Shuttlesworths. No C.T. Vivians. Just four college freshmen who looked like me and had scarcely even begun to shave.

Four young men, boys really, walked to downtown Greensboro with only each other for comfort, for reassurance, and covered a wretched symbol of the old South with their bottoms. Turned the place on its head. Four boys. Hell, man, that was really something. Bad-ass something.

After that, I had to do something. I thought then that we all had to. And Gordon and I *did*. Lots of us did. We knew Mama and Daddy wanted us to be safe. They would be against us getting involved like this, but we did it anyway. Though we were still mere boys, we wanted—needed—very much to be men, not grown-ups of course, but *men* in the spinal sense.

Ironically, the whole thing was Gordon's idea. It happened only days after the news flashed around the country about what had happened in Greensboro. Gordon and I went downtown after school on Friday to buy a stylus for the Philco phonograph machine in the living room. The specialty shop that sold it was located on Broad Street between 5th and 6th next to the big new G.C. Murphy store with the running plate-glass window that gave onto Broad Street. I was walking ahead of Gordon when he stopped to look through the big window. I walked back to find him peering through the glass at the store's long L-shaped confectionery counter and the fifteen gleaming pedestal stools standing empty around it, watching us, daring us.

"Let's do it," Gordon said.

"Let's do what?" I asked.

"Let's go in and sit down—and order something."

"Mama and Daddy will kill us."

"They don't have to know about it."

"But what if we get arrested?"

"We'll deal with that when it happens."

"Jesus, Gordon. Do you know what you're doing? You of all people. What about your scholarships? You know what could happen to you?"

He did not seem himself, or at least not the deliberate mulling, measuring *himself* that I had always counted upon as a firebreak to my own natural heedlessness. Only then did I realize how opaque to me he had always been. How veneered was his self-discipline. Looking in the window, he gave every appearance of someone who'd tipped over and given in to some urgent irresistible exigency that required him to address smack-dab, with this one rashly considered act, a short shame-soaked lifetime of tacit accommodation and quiet cowardliness.

"I have to do this. I have to do it. If I don't do it now, I never will." If he had deliberated upon his decision, I did not know of it. He had always been serious about everything. In that respect, at least, he had remained consistent.

"Okay, man, I'm with you. Let's go."

With that, the March brothers walked into the G.C. Murphy store and took two center seats on the long side of the L-shaped confectionery counter.

The store was virtually empty. The waitress, a plump fair-skinned white girl whose face was framed by parentheses of blond Shirley Temple curls, refused to serve us or even acknowledge our presence. Without uttering so much as a word, she walked off, leaving us alone at the counter. No doubt surveilled by watching eyes somewhere, we sat there facing a wall-mounted menu for fifteen minutes. Having no thought-out idea of what to do next, Gordon and I eventually got up and went home.

CHAPTER SEVEN

S unday week, Mama and Daddy invited the Reverend
C.C. Boynton and Grandma to the house for dinner.
Mama fussed over the table a good part of the day,
sending Daddy just after breakfast to fetch the folding table pad from its box in the hot airless little storage attic
that was reached with a pull-down retractable ladder in
the upstairs ceiling.

Gordon and I had been assigned by Mama the task of
"thoroughly cleaning" the house on Saturday.

Mama kept the kitchen door shut all Sunday so as to
keep "the whole house from smelling like pot roast."

Dinner was set for two o'clock. Grandma rode home
from church in the backseat of the car between Gordon
and me. She had changed in the church cloaking room out
of her white deaconess dress and into an elaborately embroidered orange African gown that a taken-aback Reverend C.C. Boynton would affect to like, but would, in fact,
distinctly detest. It was the first time Reverend Boynton
had seen my grandmother outside of church.

Just as Daddy pulled to the curb in front of our house,
a neighbor's collie ran at the car and leapt about it barking
playfully. This terrified my grandmother, who'd professed
a fear of dogs for as long as anyone could remember.

She pressed her Braille leather-bound gold-embossed
Bible fast to her chest, interposing it like a shield between
her and the loud baying voice of the dog. My father got
out of the car and shooed the animal in the direction of its

owner's house. My grandmother sat straight-backed between Gordon and me on the car's rear seat until she was
well enough composed and confident that the dog would
not return. This would be the only time that I would ever
see her appear frightened.

While Mama and Daddy and Gordon and I busied ourselves with last-minute preparations, Grandma sat quietly
in the living room in a leather armchair awaiting dinner
which would not begin until Reverend Boynton arrived.
Sitting alone with her thoughts for periods of time never
seemed to bother my grandmother. She appeared to live
more from within than from without, as if she were of an
unknowable place, to which no one of us could be made
privy, even were such a view into her deepest cerebrations
hers to grant.

At ten minutes after two o'clock, Mama, peering
through the venetian slats at the dining room window,
called out to Daddy, "David, Reverend Boynton is here,"
speaking with the slightly elevated pace of one expecting
the arrival of a special personage, a measure that squared
entirely with the Reverend Boynton's view of himself as he
hoisted his considerable bulk from the driver's-side seat of
the big black four-door Lincoln sedan the church had given
him on the silver anniversary of his pastorate.

My recollection is that Reverend Boynton never spoke
in conversational English, but rather in a relentless *pulpi-
tese* spoken loudly (even when mouth-to-ear) and with an
overlaid relish for pontifical enunciation. Indeed, he must
have been well-educated in the formal sense of it, at least.
His doctorate, real, not honorary, had been conferred by
the Yale Divinity School. Still, his booming sermons, for
me, were tedious affairs, filling the hall but not the heart.

Daddy's hand disappeared into the Reverend's paw.

"So good of you to have me, David. So good of you

to have me." Pulling off his knee-length gray camel-hair chesterfield and turning toward my mother: "Aah, Alma, my dear, so good of you to have me, so good of you to have me."

My mother steered Reverend Boynton from the vestibule into the living room where my grandmother sat composed with her fingers laced over the Bible which lay closed on her lap. Upon noticing her sitting quietly with her gown of brilliant orange spread over the arms of the chair, Reverend Boynton spoke more moderately, "Sister Mattie, what a nice surprise. And don't you look pretty." Reverend Boynton then seemed to sustain a temporary loss of confidence. Blind people had always affected him in this way. He likely sensed that they could *see* him better than sighted people could, and thus he lost with them the considerable advantage of his imposing physical presence. Had my grandmother been sighted, she would have noticed on Reverend Boynton's face features that confessed an enfeebled soul.

I can't recall what my grandmother said in response. I only remember that whatever it was amounted to little more than a word or two. I can still visualize the subtle tilt and nod of her elegant head which gave the impression of a royal receiving a subject.

Recovering with relief his bonhomous bearing, Reverend Boynton elevated his voice and said, "Gordon, Gordon. Aren't you something, young man. Which is it going to be, Harvard or Stanford?" Not waiting for an answer, the reverend bore forward: "And why didn't you apply to Yale, young man? Better than Harvard, really."

Reverend Boynton was not an unkind man. He was simply one of those people who'd been born uncomfortably without a talent for gauging their effect on the people they encountered.

As the group moved through the vestibule en route to the dining room, Reverend Boynton rested his hand on my shoulder and said disinterestedly, "Graylon, you're looking more like your mother every day."

Years later, my mother would confess to me that she had worried a great deal days before that Sunday that the dinner conversation would founder in controversy and tension. In the weeks after she had extended the invitation to Reverend Boynton, the country had been roiled by an incipient, but startlingly fast-growing civil disobedience movement ignited by the bold act of the four young men in Greensboro.

I was ten years old when our new seventeen-inch Dumont television set had arrived in the back of our neighbor Mr. Yelverton's panel truck. Before then, I had not yet gotten the full sharp point of segregation. I knew of course that, pretty much, all Southern white people did not like Negroes, and because of that kept us from going to various places they went to. But this did not affect me at the time in any conscious way. In fact, I would go for weeks, and often months, without seeing a white person, and even then it would happen only when my mother took Gordon and me along when she went shopping downtown. Later, of course, I would see white people on the television. But before this, when I was small, I never doubted that all the Negro grown-ups who wore suits and dresses with big elaborate hats to our church on Sundays were estimable people, and not just to me who addressed them deferentially as Mister This and Mrs. That, but to the wider world as well. It was not until later that I learned full on the heart how white folks really saw us—Grandma, Mama, Daddy, Reverend Boynton, the lot of us—and that was as a faceless gob of menial service providers.

My mother and father contorted all reason to shield

Gordon and me from the truth, but in the end they failed as they had to. What really frightened us, however, was seeing them have no choice but to accept their complete inability to protect us.

Reverend Boynton, for many years, had been a member of the National Baptist Convention, a powerful black church organization whose president, Reverend Joseph H. Jackson, had supported Reverend King's Montgomery bus boycott, but strongly opposed the burgeoning nonviolent civil disobedience campaign that was igniting the country's black youth.

Through most of the Saturday before Reverend Boynton's visit, my mother had washed, stripped, and boiled the collards, grated the cheese, and baked the macaroni. By nine o'clock Sunday morning, she had roasted the meat, made and rolled the dough, remembered to add the yeast, shaped the dollops, and spaced them on a pan to grow as we all went off to church to hear Reverend Boynton hold sumptuously forth on the jailing of Saint Paul in Ephesus.

Incongruously, like his spiritual leader Reverend Jackson, Reverend Boynton strongly opposed the students who were offering themselves for arrest at lunch counters across America. For all of Saturday and most of Sunday, my mother seasoned and sautéed and kneaded and baked, all the while worrying that Reverend Boynton's first visit to our home would collapse in a ruin of sharply differing opinions.

Mama and Daddy knew that Gordon and I supported the new civil rights movement. It was pretty plain that they did as well, although they did not want their sons to get themselves arrested. We had not told them about the episode at G.C. Murphy.

No one in the family could predict what my grandmother would say should the dinner discussion drift into politics. Although they knew nothing of my grandmother's strange dream experience, they did know well by then that Makeda Gee Florida Harris March was possessed of a spirit that was different from that of anybody they had ever known.

Mama and Daddy sat at the ends of the table while Gordon and I sat side-by-side across from my grandmother and Reverend Boynton. I suspect it may have been Reverend Boynton's bottom choice of a place to sit, with him pinioned between Daddy, the doubter, and my grandmother, the mystic, while looking across the table at two strapping young men who were on the other side of six feet and taller than he.

The only time that I had been this close to Reverend Boynton for anything more than a handshake was three years ago on the Sunday I was baptized by him in the new baptismal pool beneath the floor of the old church's pulpit. He was a strong man with thick spatulate fingers that he placed behind my neck and waist to take me down into and up from the water in less time than it took to wake the nerves the cold water had shocked numb.

Mama and Daddy had not reared Gordon and me to speak to adults as equals, thus it would have upset them had we joined in the dinner discussion as such. We were taught a *manner*, befitting our years, of polite observation, and the importance of responding intelligently to adults' questions with complete grammatical, well-enunciated sentences ending with the word *sir* or *ma'am*. The attitude of our speech, however, had been cultivated to bear no color of shyness or fear or servility. My grandmother and my parents had been of one mind on this point, although my grandmother seemed to have thought the purpose of this through rather more tactically.

"These are your best years for learnin'," she had said

to me once, "and you can't learn when you're talkin'." She had chuckled before going on, "You'll learn when you grow up that most everybody is a stranger, even folks you know well, or think you know well, and when strangers talk too much, it's because somethin' is wrong inside them. The more they talk, the more you learn about them, the less they learn about you. It's a good thing to learn to talk only when somethin' needs to be said, when you're addin', not subtractin'." On another occasion she had said to me, "Never rate people by the jobs they hold or the money they have. That stuff comes and goes like a suit of clothes. Look deeper. Find the soul of a person. See how decent it is. Then make a judgment."

I looked across at Reverend Boynton through the lens of my grandmother's advice.

". . . We're planning a glorious twenty-fifth revival week for next summer, Sister Alma. We've got preachers coming from as far away as Atlanta, Georgia. Pastor B. David Riddick told me that he's gonna try to make it in from Chicago if he can get a break in his schedule. You know, everybody's trying to get the man. Lord, can he preach. It's gonna be a great time . . ."

I looked at Daddy looking at Mama looking at him, and knew well the measure of his love for Mama which could be calculated in the units of his sufferance of Reverend Boynton who bore on. Oblivious.

". . . We should be able to complete the air-conditioning project before next summer hits . . . Sister Mattie, we got to put a stop to Sister Ann and Deacon Short's campaign to pull away from the church and buy Big Bethel's building in Northside . . . This morning, the youth ushers turned the wrong way with the offering . . . So what do you young men think about all of this civil disobedience?"

Mama gave Daddy a covert look of dread. Then Daddy,

in a single cleanly said word, interposed a choice: "Gordon."

I glanced at Grandma and saw her handsome features form into a betrayal of sympathy and understanding that fought the old hurt which raked over me once again.

CHAPTER EIGHT

My feelings had been crushed when my father called upon Gordon, and not me, to speak at Sunday dinner in the pontifical Reverend Boynton's presence. The blood had rushed into my defenseless fifteen-year-old face for all except, of course, my grandmother to see. Yet only she seemed to register my adolescent humiliation.

Monday, the next day, was unseasonably warm for April. Wanting my grandmother's company, perspiring heavily, I reached the walk-up on Duvall Street after school shortly before four.

I could see when she opened the door that she was tired. Turning to leave, "You get some rest, Grandma. I'll come back tomorrow."

"I'll not hear of it, son. Get yourself in here." Revivified.

We sat in the magical little parlor and were silent for a time. As always, I waited for her to speak first. As always, she would somehow *know*.

Suddenly and without preface, she said, "He didn't mean anything, Gray. He doesn't mean to hurt you. His soul is not the giver of yours. Your spirit knows not from seeing, but from feeling. He is not like that. We won't be. He can't be."

"Why am I always getting my feelings hurt?"

"See it as the price of your gift."

"What gift?"

"To understand with the heart what cannot be seen

with the eyes. To know what pictures to show and value in your head, and what pictures not to keep there."

She sensed that I did not understand her. Then, out of the blue, she said, "You know that fellow Einstein, he never learned how to drive a car. Said a car was too complicated. What do you think that means?"

I was surprised by what she said, and did not know how to answer her.

"Most people live enclosed in small yards behind tall fences, son. They don't look out. They don't *try* to look out . . . They spend their lives looking at—even worshipping—the fence."

"Is that why you won't let Daddy get you a telephone?"

"Could be. I have lived across the ages. Why would I choose to stare at the fence? Hear that Boynton going on and on about buildings and air conditioners? Sittin' on the ground. Playin' with toys. Starin' at the fence. Not so good in a man of God, eh?"

I was beginning to feel better. She was for me, I guess you'd say, affirming. It may have been then that I first began to understand the distinction between education and wisdom. I smiled and asked in jest, "How did you get so smart, Grandma?"

Smiling back at me, "It helps that I'm blind, I think."

We were quiet for a while again, both looking, I imagined, at pictures in our heads—pictures on the other side of the fence.

"Grandma?"

"Yes, son."

"You know what I've been wondering since you told me about the dream?"

"Tell me, son."

"There have been other dreams—haven't there?"

"Yes."

"When did they start?"

"When I was just a little girl. I didn't understand them at first, but I knew they were about things that had happened to me long, long ago. I never told anyone before you. I told you because I somehow always knew that you would understand and believe me."

"You believe, Grandma, that the soul does not die?"

"I don't know. I've had these dreams. They are real and not like dreams." She sensed a puzzlement in me. "What, son?"

"One of my teachers said that half the people who've ever lived on Earth are alive today. That means that if old souls don't die, there must still be a lot of new ones."

My grandmother just smiled.

CHAPTER NINE

During my high school years, I visited my grandmother less frequently than I had before. In 1960, just before I turned fifteen, my family moved to Church Hill which was halfway across the city from Grandma's house on Duvall Street. For a time following the move, I visited with her several times a week just as I had when we were living close by in Jackson Ward. It had been during one of these visits that Grandma told me about the dream of her life as a Dogon girl. Shortly after this, she suggested that we adjust our schedule a bit.

"Gray, you mustn't worry so much about me. I'm fine. Better than ever."

"I know, Grandma, but—"

"No. I won't hear of you coming all this way on the bus to see me after school two, three times a week. You got to study, boy. You still want to be a writer, don't ya?"

"Yes, Grandma."

"Then you got to work. You got to put the time in."

She suggested that I come just once a week—on Thursdays—her "day of rest," since my Saturdays and Sundays by then were being taken up with Kensington Hospital, a segregated white hospital up on Kensington Avenue in the West End, where I washed dishes in a big, deafening industrial machine on weekends with three older black guys who'd worked there for years.

From 1960 until I finished Armstrong in June 1963, I would arrive at my grandmother's door virtually every

Thursday just a little before four, and punch the dimpled brass button that activated the rusty old clapper in the tarnished round bell that encompassed it.

During my three years of high school, my grandmother made a studied effort to settle my spirits. Though my parents were obsessively decent people and reasonably solicitous of my contentment, they only on rare occasions—one being a disturbing and peculiar unburdening to me by my father—talked at length to Gordon and me about anything requiring a significant emotional investment. They hadn't, I think, the expendable resources to allocate to such. They were tired, I believe, dog-tired, and their psychic stores had scarcely enough fuel to cover the day-to-day logistics of living under segregation while managing the imminently realistic prospect of sudden family poverty.

My father, deciding, I suspect unilaterally, had taken it upon himself to be the family's sole breadwinner. He had done this, no doubt, for what he believed were noble reasons. Nonetheless, everything the five of us required (including a monthly subsidy to my grandmother's meager pension package)—food, shelter, electricity, heat, transportation, school fees, alms to those poorer than we—everything, every big and little thing, including the scratch fee of nine cents to enter the Hippodrome movie theater at 2nd and Leigh on Saturdays, depended upon him and him alone. He bore the strain of this burden much, I suppose, as Sisyphus had borne his under the crushing weight of his rock.

My father's face was a veritable map of exhaustion. Although I knew next to nothing about the details of the family's finances, it was clear enough that a subpar month of policy sales and/or premium receipts was virtually all there was standing between us and disaster.

I couldn't bear to load my troubles onto his troubles.

Thus, it should surprise no one that I am unable to recall, before leaving home forever at eighteen, ever talking to my father about who I really was or the life matters that concerned me most. Not once, neither before nor after the tragedy.

My grandmother, of course, knew about all of this and literally talked me through high school, seldom speaking during this period of the dreams.

"Look, son. My dreams will wait. We've got to get you ready to go to college, a good college, so you can prepare to be the writer you want to be, you hear? You got to work. You got to push everything else out of your mind."

I tried my best to do what she told me to do. My grades rose, much to my parents' surprise. On weekends, I continued to work at Kensington Hospital. Though never once asked to do so, I gave a portion of my salary to my mother to help with family expenses on the condition that she would not tell my father. I saw my grandmother every Thursday except when my presence was required elsewhere, like the after-school appointment I had with the yearbook photographer in the fall of my senior year.

On August 17, 1963, I paid my last visit to my grandmother before leaving the following week for college.

"Get on in here, boy. I'm so happy to see you." She hugged me with heartening strength and led me into the parlor. She took her seat in the rocker and patted the chair that had been placed where I customarily sat.

She wore a long, flowing forest-green gown that was festively filigreed with yellow silk along the neckline, sleeve, and hemline. Her hair was dressed in thick salt-and-pepper braids that draped over her shoulders.

"Sit, sit, boy—tell me everything—school, college, writing." No one in the world gave me the time and attention that my grandmother gave me.

We talked for the better part of three hours—voices

climbing, challenging, overlapping, laughing, a time or two uproariously. Eventually, the pace of our talk would slow with the dying light of the day. We went for long, easy moments without speaking. I looked up at the symbol on the wall hanging which had been there on the wall in the same spot, by then, for years.

Looking at the symbol, I asked her, almost languidly, "Grandma, how many of those dreams have you had?"

"You mean about the Dogon people and the stars?"

"Yes."

"Only the one I told you about."

"You told me there had been others."

"Yes."

"How many?"

"One before the Dogon dream and two since."

"Do the dreams scare you?"

"No, son."

"I think they would scare *me*."

"Why would you think that?"

"Well, if they are as real and lifelike as you say they are, I would think I'd get confused."

With that, she gave a short self-deprecating chuckle. Then she smiled and said, "I think I see what you mean."

She turned her face to the setting sun. The umber-warm color of the late-afternoon light gave the profile of her features a wistful cast. She sighed. When she spoke again, her voice seemed to start from far away. From some painful place in a bygone girlhood.

"When I was little, I hated this darkness. I wanted to do away with myself. I cursed God." She spoke with a sharpness that unsettled me. Then she exhaled audibly. "I was poor and blind and fatherless. In desperation, I made some bad decisions. It didn't seem like I had much choice at the time."

I knew that she was talking about her brief, failed marriage.

"I had no idea how to take care of myself. It was like I was all alone in the world. I was bitter. I was very bitter." Her blank eyes moistened. The sight of this caused me to shiver slightly. "Then I found Christ, and I think the church saved me—gave me a place to be, a world to be safe in before I had your father. But, you know, even then I think I knew or at least I sensed, that I was not just blind, but I was different from other folks in some other ways as well."

"What do you mean?"

"I don't think I knew it for sure before the second dream—the Dogon dream."

"Knew what, Grandma?"

"You asked if the dreams frightened me—because they were so real."

"Yes."

"That's why I told you how unhappy I was when I was young. I hated being blind, but not anymore. The dreams have changed that. They have allowed me to see things I could never have seen if my eyes worked. Regular folks see only the physical things that are right in front of them, Gray. I can't see the physical things that are right in front of me, but I can see beyond those things. Worlds beyond. I have seen my soul when it was young. For old souls who are blind, the worlds of the living and the dead are not so far apart."

She paused and then said, with heightened intensity, "I was an African, Gray. In every life, I was an African. For an African, the worlds of the living and the dead are one."

I was silent.

"Am I scaring you, son?"

"No, Grandma. I'm just trying to think hard about what you're saying."

"I believe now that this is why I was born blind. I have been blessed, because of it, to know my soul before it was forced to borrow a faith that was not originally mine."

I did not know what to say. I felt rudderless, queasy.

The specter and prospect of death had always provoked in me considerable discomfiture. I simply could not comprehend the bat-of-an-eye transition from a state of riotously bubbling organic *life* to the plasticized facsimiles of it that reposed like boards in coffins.

When I was eleven, my mother and father had required Gordon and me to go with them to attend the funeral in North Carolina of a distant cousin on my mother's side named Bill, who'd died of a sudden illness in New York City when he was nineteen. Bill hadn't visited his home in rural North Carolina for years before his death and the local folk wanted to see him one last time for as long as they could. So Bill's coffin remained open during the funeral. Because I was a member of Bill's family, I sat in the center of the church, second row, with my face level with Bill's.

I was eleven and couldn't understand why we were being made, for the duration of the service, to look at Bill in his coffin. In any case, I didn't believe that it was really Bill in the coffin. The pastor said that Bill had gone home to be with Jesus. I didn't know where he'd gone. But I did not believe he had gone home to be with Jesus. I did not believe that the pastor or anyone else in the church who was gawking at Bill in the coffin actually believed that or else they would not, themselves, have been so afraid of dying. They all seemed to prove this by holding death at bay for as long as they possibly could.

It was through my grandmother that I learned, over time, not to fear death so much, but to see it as a portal to a spirit world of old ancestors and new lives.

Toward the end of that last visit I had with her before

leaving for college, she told me about the two dreams that had followed the Dogon dream.

One of the lives she had lived, apparently, had been as an Akân woman during the 1600s in what is now called Ghana. The other life had been lived in the eighteenth century as a Benin girl of twelve, living in what is now the modern country of Nigeria.

Grandma said that her people, the Benin people, or Binis, believed that God, whom they called Osanobua, granted each person fourteen journeys through life from birth to death, leaving each person's status in the ultimate afterlife to be determined by the moral plane taken over the course of the fourteen journeys which were trials of a sort. Binis' dead were not made inaccessible to the living who were, as was the case with my grandmother, visited by the dead, revealing themselves to the living in dreams. For Africans, my grandmother told me, death does not separate the dead from the living.

Two years before Grandma had the first of these two dreams, the dream about her life as an Akân girl living in the seventeenth century, I accompanied her on a Saturday morning to the 6th Street market to buy vegetables. The market counted seventy or more refrigerated meat display cases and produce stalls that filled the cavernous main floor of the redbrick building that had originally served as an armory.

I remember what happened that morning as if it were yesterday. Grandma wore one of her bright African gowns and carried a carved ebony-wood walking stick. She was well known at the market, and many of the stall operators called out greetings to her. During our tour of the stalls, an elderly black man in a dashiki, speaking elegantly accented English, greeted her from behind a small table. His syntax was formal and out of place in the bustling, working-class crowd of shoppers and vendors. On his table were not vegetables, but bolts of exotically printed fabrics, a set of hand-carved reliquaries, and four or five softcover books.

"Madame," the man said softly.

Grandma turned in the direction of the man's voice, as if she had been listening for it.

Without preamble, the man asked, "Are you Akân, madame?"

Grandma did not give the answer that I expected her to give to the strange question. "I don't know, sir," she said as she stopped and turned to him.

"I believe that you are Akân, madame."

The man did not give his name and did not inquire after hers.

"How can you know that, sir?"

"Do you know of the Akân people, madame?"

My grandmother hesitated and for moments remained silent.

The cultured old gentleman then smiled, but only with his eyes. It was as if he had come to the market expecting to see my grandmother. "I have some things for you that you may find helpful."

He presented her with the reliquary objects and explained their significance. My grandmother slowly rolled them about her fingers, feeling every bend and curve, appreciating the textures and liking the way they felt in her hands.

"These are from the Kota people of Gabon. They are guardian figures to be placed near the remains of ancestors to protect them from evil forces. They also bring to their living families health and prosperity."

The reliquary guardian figures were small, very old sculptures of human forms that had been fashioned from copper, brass, and wood.

The old man then handed her the rolled wall hanging with the large symbol on it. "This is from the Akân. The Akân are my people and your people." He picked up a book of yellowed dog-eared pages and handed it to me. "You will read from this to your grandmother." He patted my shoulder to soften the words that he had spoken as a command.

Without saying another word, the man turned, left the table, and quickly lost himself in the eddy of shoppers.

In the years that ensued before I left Richmond for Morgan State College in Baltimore, Maryland, I read passages to my grandmother from the little book given to her by the mysterious Akân man at the market.

The title of the book was *West African Traditional Religion*. The author's name was Kofi Asare Opoku, a professor at the University of Ghana in Legon.

One passage in the scholarly book that my grandmother asked me to read to her over and again was this:

> It is also believed that the ancestors enter a spiritual state of existence after death. They have their feet planted in both the world of the living and the world of spirits. Therefore they know more than the living and are consequently accorded great respect.

The day of my last visit before leaving for college was gone and Grandma had grown tired. She heard me rise from my chair and her voice mixed regret with affection.

"Tomorrow, son, you begin your great adventure. I can't tell you how proud I am of the man you have already become."

"I will miss you, Grandma."

We embraced for a long time. Then she said, patting my back, "Okay, son, okay."

"Grandma, I don't have a picture of you to take with me. Come, stand here."

I posed her against the long wall with the Akân wall hanging showing over her right shoulder. I picked up the Kodak Brownie Hawkeye that my parents had given me for my tenth birthday. She stood still until the small clap of the camera's shutter released her.

"Let me get one more, Grandma."

"Here. Take this with you." She held out the little book that the Akân man at the market had given her years before. Placing it in my hands, she said, "Don't forget to take with you the Dogon notes."

"I won't forget, Grandma. I won't forget."

"Guard them, Gray."

"I will," I said and hugged her one final time.

PART TWO

PART TWO

CHAPTER TEN

I t was at college that I was first introduced to a notion that one of my more thoughtful professors called "the intellectual ideal."

As Negro students, we did not know how the politics of the country's white society functioned internally, how its edicts were formulated and lowered down for our consumption and compliance. It had never before occurred to me that we might try and puzzle out its functions with an eye toward influencing them. White America was opaque, indecipherable, and entirely separate from our America. We were bottled up and over by its stolid mass camped on our borders. If the circumstances of our poverty seemed to me irrefragable, so did their power. It had seemed best not to think about it, which was what the freshmen class did, *en masse*. We were powerless, a conclusion most of us reached without deliberation.

Early in my second year, I began doing extra reading in an effort to understand the various and confusing political chemistries of Washington. This business of *left* and *right* was a new and disturbing discovery that was starkly antithetical to how I had been taught for the short nineteen years of my life to view the world. The Negroes I knew measured the arrangements and equities of society in vertical terms: right over wrong; justice over injustice; freedom over oppression; fairness over unfairness; comfort over pain. For Negroes, life and politics were not board games that could be played laterally—for the sheer fun of playing them, or for simple ambition's sake, without risk of mortal consequence. As I read on, it increasingly seemed to me that white people played their game—the left-right sport—with other people's lives and other people's fundamental rights. Thus, with an air of *noblesse oblige*, they could ply their rulership craft in a mannerly fashion, without risk or emotion or fear of personal injury. Yet our game was not a game at all, but rather a social struggle that was very much up-down, vertical, dangerous, and gravely unfunny.

By the age of nineteen, college had already changed me dramatically. There was a new me, and every night before falling asleep, I thanked not the college but my grandmother for getting me there.

Dr. Benjamin Quarles, the professor from whom I first heard the term "intellectual ideal," was already an old man when I met him, his seminal study on the life and times of Frederick Douglass long behind him. But preeminent historian though he indisputably may have been, his was anything but a household name in the country's black community. Yet he remained easily the most brilliant teacher I'd ever had. Indeed, he was recognized by his peers, black and white alike, as one of America's most important historians. I'd never once seen him, however, on television, or read mention of him in any magazine or newspaper, not even in *Jet*. With a minimum of noise, he taught his classes at Morgan and wrote his splendid books that, I thought, scarcely disturbed the cultivated inattention of what ought to have been his natural audience. I ascribed this troubling condition to Dr. Quarles's apparent disinterest in public notice. But Dr. Abana, a visiting professor from the University of Ghana, thought otherwise. Although he didn't mention Dr. Quarles directly in his somewhat shocking remarks, what he said to a senior seminar class in the first few weeks of term would appear to have explained why the black community was not more broadly interested in the man. What Dr. Abana said that roiled the campus was, "The trouble with black people is that we have no insides." This, of course, was reported in the campus newspaper out of context and made everybody mad as hell. This, before anybody even bothered to learn what Dr. Abana was talking about.

The tempest immediately served to lengthen the already yawning social distance between the school's African and African-American students. The African students worried that Dr. Abana had offended their "hosts," and the African-American students, who'd never taken much pain to host anyone, not to speak of the African students trying to navigate a new and indifferent culture, thought that Dr. Abana was attacking *them* in much the same way that all stripes of folks always had. What everyone seemed to overlook in the single sentence that Dr. Abana was reported to have uttered was the word *we*. Dr. Abana thought that this proved his point—a point he'd still yet to explain. "They've all forgotten that I said *we* have no insides. They've forgotten it precisely *because* we have no insides."

Within days, Dr. Abana received a letter of support from a wealthy black alumnus and member of the school's board of trustees who'd presented to the school a gift of a million dollars during the spring term a year before. At the commencement exercises that followed the gift by twenty-six days, the school's president had lavished what appeared to be fawning praise upon a white *Wall Street Journal* editor who was there for unspecified reasons to accept an honorary degree, but said nothing that anyone could remember about the black alumnus sitting beside the editor, who had just given the president a check for a million dollars. No doubt influenced by this experience, the black alumnus/trustee/philanthropist wrote to Dr. Abana: *If you meant what I think you meant, I support you one hundred percent. Black people* don't *have any insides*.

In the ensuing issue of the school paper, it was reported that Dr. Abana had also said during the same lecture to the same seminar class that "black people are, by and large, highly suggestible. This condition results from our having no insides."

The following day, the Black Student Union, a "union" made up solely of African-American students, picketed Dr. Abana's ten o'clock class. No students enrolled in any of the three courses he taught, however, were among those doing the picketing.

It was clear enough that Dr. Abana had not gone out of his way to cultivate alliances during the year he spent at Morgan, having once described much of the faculty (and, pointedly, the president) as the "all too practical intellectual heirs to the lost (as in mindless) tribe of personal convenience seekers," a view to which Dr. Quarles subscribed, albeit not publicly.

In the African scholarly world, Dr. Abana had been thought of by several well-known authorities as something of an intellectual misanthrope among a handful of black writers who wandered large and lonely in the wide, unpopulated space between the current conformist practitioners of convenience and the pioneers of the angry new rhetorical coarseness, who Dr. Abana thought informed more by emotion than information. "Good-hearted, well-intended desperados," he called them in one particularly powerful lecture that was recorded and transcribed by one of his students.

"Self-rescue squads in loud speeding vehicles. The information—the books, the ledgers, cultures, customs, languages, religious rituals in which black people's *memories* were stored—all systematically incinerated by the white world over the 246-year course of slavery in the Americas. Virtually the entire recorded story of who they were. Gone! Our *insides*. The insides that the people around here do not even know have gone missing long long since. *Tabula rasa* in academic regalia. Idiots. Though many are very nice, which makes it all the worse. More depressing to regard than the lot of the unlettered black underclass. At least they are more nearly aware of what slavery has cost them.

"In many ways figurative, the black race now breathes and functions worldwide in a dire postapocalyptic psychosocial condition. We are joined only by our common pathology. The damage is more spiritual than physical. More interior than exterior. Centuries of enslavement, segregation, discrimination, family deconstruction, rape, and slaughter—all tools of extreme social coercion—have taken an incalculable toll on us. The word *coercion*, you know, is from the Latin, meaning to shut in—to close off—in much the way that we all have been closed off, closed off from each other and closed off from ourselves. Closed off in the ageless night of our stolen memories—memories that once served as our spiritual insides.

"We simply cannot remember what we need to remember, what we need to remember to sustain us in self-appreciation, what we need to remember not only with our finite living minds, but in the social glands of our habits and cultures."

Then Dr. Abana slowly raised the large prow of a brow creased with thought and looked directly at each of the nine students in the small seminar. They seemed to have been listening on a rope.

"No people can flourish without a recalled past." He paused and made a gesture that suggested the realization that his life and lectures were exercises in futility. He drew a long breath and continued tiredly, "I don't care about what you become. I care about what you *do*. Not with your bodies to be insinuated upwardly and uselessly into ever more expensive manufactures. I care about what you do with your minds." Then he shouted. "Think! Think! Think us out of our small imaginations! Think us out of the darkness of our estrangement from ourselves and each other! Think us above the moment and its frivolous nonsustaining sweets! Think us above the small circumscribed plane of our short mortal lives to a place from which to see once again the black ancients who've something important to tell us still! Think us out of time's injustice! Think us home to our immortal selves!" The students heard him, if for no other reason than he was speaking very loudly.

It wasn't that Dr. Abana wished his students to agree with him. He simply wanted them to learn to *think*, to reason their way either toward his views or away from them. The direction of reason mattered less to him than the value he placed on the discipline of reason itself. Personal freedom was not to be discovered in any particular conclusion, but rather in the ordered cognitive process of reaching one. Ideology for him marked the cessation of thought.

In his book *The Ideal African*, he'd revealed what many found to be an off-putting cynicism by arguing that decent modern African political leaders were all but impossible to sustain given what the West had done historically to Africa, and did, even still, to compromise away the smallest loyalties that prospective African leaders might incline themselves to hold for their own people. *America prefers kleptocrats for Africa. They are more manageable.*

Privately, he held the unpublished belief that virtually *all* leaders—the rich, the poor, the black, the white, the Christian, the Muslim, the Jew, the Hindu—were self-interested and self-absorbed, and for that reason he felt that democracy led to the near same result, albeit more slowly, as dictatorship. In either case corruption of purpose was inevitable.

But his main purpose was provoking black people, disgorged from whatever jerry-built cultural lifeboat they braved the tall night swells in, to search with the tools of reason for the origins and causes of their common psychological dilemma. Getting them to eschew their *outsides* in search of their missing and vastly more valuable *insides*.

Dr. Quarles, not at all flamboyant or colorful, wasn't much for *outsides* either, and given that blacks generally hadn't valued their *own* missing *insides*, they hadn't bothered in critical mass numbers to value Dr. Quarles's intellectually serious *insides* either. Dr. Abana believed that this, worldwide, was pretty much the main thing wrong with black people. After centuries of unrelenting havoc wreaked against them, he had come to believe, a large part of the problem was now *us*.

Early in Dr. Abana's one full year spent at Morgan, Dr. Quarles, his faculty sponsor, arranged to have him address a school-wide special convocation. Students were encouraged (but not required) by the school's administration to attend. Dr. Abana was not a famous man. Indeed, he was little known even within African-American academic circles. That he had been invited to visit at Morgan at all was more a testament to Dr. Quarles's stature at the school than to anything the school's leaders knew firsthand about the Ghanaian scholar whose canon of critically acclaimed writings was largely unknown to American readers.

The convocation was held in a large assembly hall on a late Monday morning so as not to conflict with scheduled classes. Twenty minutes after the program was to have begun, Dr. Quarles introduced Dr. Abana to 151 people scattered dishearteningly across the cavernous assembly hall.

There were 137 students, nine faculty members and five Ghanaians living in the Baltimore area who had heard on the radio that Dr. Abana would be speaking that day. I had not planned to attend and only changed my mind after Dr. Quarles told the students in his Negro history class that we "would be well-advised to be there."

I was a sophomore then, as were all but five of the thirty-three students taking Dr. Quarles's course that year. The people and events that he spoke about in his lectures were those that figured large in the story of Africans in America dating from the arrival of the first enslaved man in Jamestown in August of 1619.

He was a fascinating teacher who gave a credible impression of having known his long-dead subjects personally. While I had learned the material well, I was never quite able to fully humanize (*engage* might be a better way to put it) the great American drama's principal actors. "We're not talking about ancient history. We're talking about very knowable human beings and what they strove for and were caused to endure." While the suffering was not academic, the people who bore it were, for me, sepia abstractions.

Experienced in reading the shallow maps of nineteen-year-old faces, Dr. Quarles pressed forward to link us to what was for him the very recent past: "How many of you know of Frank Lloyd Wright?" Of course we all knew that Wright, a contemporary, was the grand old man of American architecture. "Well, the Wright who lived during your very lifetimes was born just forty-two years after Thomas Jefferson died, so the period in history we are studying was not really very long ago, was it?"

I thought of the *Life Magazine* pictures taken in 1905 of the exhumed corpse of Abraham Lincoln and a boy standing graveside. The accompanying story was about the boy, now eighty, and what he remembered of the experience, seeing Lincoln there in the coffin, looking, face-mole intact, very much as he had in life.

It was at this juncture that Dr. Quarles impressed upon the class the importance of attending Dr. Abana's lecture. "He will help you know how old you are." He then smiled, knowing that we were not following him. "Just go, you'll see."

CHAPTER ELEVEN

D r. Abana was a short man, short enough to rest his folded arms flat on the surface of the lectern that hid three-quarters of his body. His uninflected voice was high-pitched, small, and raspy. It was his habit to speak with no attempt to entertain or provoke. He wore a long elaborately woven white robe and a brimless white cap that listed forward on his head halfway between the hairline and the gray-flecked mop of the brow.

He was an attractive man of fifty-four years who had been told repeatedly as a teenager that he was black and ugly by the younger daughter of his British colonial missionary school teacher, a certain Mr. Horsford.

He looked overlong down at his notes. Because he was short, his face fell close to the white paper on which his notes were scrawled in an indecipherable hand. The thick eyeglasses he wore gleamed opaque and white in the bright reflected light of the lectern lamp.

Dr. Quarles had been uneasy before the program. He worried that his friend detested public speaking and was purposely not good at it, holding that ideas spoiled when bellowed and that the public speech was necessarily the tool of one form of demagoguery or another. This was a relatively new view that Dr. Abana had developed in reaction to a mistaken impression that public speaking in America was characteristically sermonic. Making his acknowledgments, Dr. Abana turned and looked at the empty chair on the stage in which the school's president had been expected to sit.

He began to speak in a quiet voice as if he were alone in the room. Were not the microphone, owing to his lack of height, so close to his mouth, no one would likely have heard him begin with little preamble from what seemed the middle of a foreign and strange tale.

"How do you see me?"

Pausing, he looked about the vast, scantly populated hall into puzzled faces. Students were not accustomed to convocation speakers beginning their remarks with a question.

"What joins us, if anything more than your discomfort over what we should mean to each other and our mutual ignorance of each other's circumstance?"

A rustle of disquiet could be heard over Dr. Abana's long pause.

"The differences that are obvious set me apart from you, no? How I appear to you. How I dress. How I speak English.

"You may even see me as a complete stranger, a stranger to be shunned, a stranger with embarrassing custody of your past, a past you remain ambivalent about, a past you have been caused long since to involuntarily discard. You have new names and manners and ways now. I am the leper obstructing your flight from yourselves. Or for those of you who are rather more psychologically advanced, at best you see me as the inconvenient cousin who, during your long centuries of bondage, disappeared from the family portrait. Cropped from memory by a grand interloper."

He sensed that he sounded cantankerous, unpleasant, and that the few who were listening had shrunken from him.

"Other than our separate experiences of shame and degradation, we have no common memory. Thus, absent memory, there can be no proud, joyous, painless *we* that joins us, you and me. For the only memory that survives reposes in the photographs that others have taken for their own purposes, where the camera of our common experience was never moved far enough back in time to frame us all—one whole family in one common, unbroken belonging."

He noticed that some students sitting about in pairs had begun to talk to each other. He then swung around to glance at Dr. Quarles who was sitting forward in his seat on the stage. Dr. Quarles smiled inscrutably. Turning back to the audience, Dr. Abana sighed and changed the meter of his speech.

"How many of you have any idea of what I'm talking about?"

Three hands rose. One of the three but halfway.

Dr. Abana had not wanted to strengthen any well-developed social complexes he strongly suspected many of the students were afflicted by. This concern caused him to speak next in a more sympathetic tone.

"Make no mistake. We are not alone in our long, costly experience with powerful forces in the world. The truth often has ruthless enemies—enemies so powerful they can all but make the truth disappear, go away—our truth, and the painful truth of other peoples you probably don't know much about."

He paused to decide how best to explain himself.

"One of your presidents, Theodore Roosevelt, is believed by most in your country to have been a great president. While this may have been true on American terms, Theodore Roosevelt was not just the person many of you have heard about. For instance, he believed that the most desirable lands in the world should by natural right belong to the white race, the race he very wrongly believed solely responsible for world civilization. He expressed this view in 1897 before becoming president. These are his words: *Nineteenth-century democracy needs no more complete vindication for*

its existence than the fact that it has kept for the white race the best por-
tions of the new world's surface. In 1906, after becoming president, Roosevelt wrote, *The world would have halted had it not*
been for the Teutonic conquests in alien lands.

"In much the same conquering American spirit," Dr.
Abana continued, "Mexicans lost most—and American
Indians all—of the lands they had once owned in North
America. Calling Filipinos *Pacific Negroes*, Roosevelt, wield-
ing brute American military force, simply took the Philip-
pine islands from that country's people. So you see, we are
not alone. A great many others in the world, including myself, have suffered in ways that no one has told you about."

Dr. Abana had only arrived in the United States three
weeks before the convocation, and it was his first visit to
the country. He had read much about American Negroes
and had spoken at length about them to Dr. Quarles during the historian's several visits to Ghana. But not until
that precise moment in his talk did it appear an absolute
certainty to him that the American Negro had no insides
left to speak of. All that seemed to remain was the will
to fight against an immediate or proximate nemesis like
the white Southern segregationists. This seemed the only
facet of their problem left visible to them. The far past and
future, *they* seemed to have lost the ability to see and find
sustenance in. The years of slavery and the cultural isolation it imposed had produced in the American Negro an
apparent partial loss of *self*. *They* were no longer their own
they but someone else's, a *they* born of the afflictions of a
terrible and sustained oppression, a group dismembered
and rebuilt by its "dismemberers" in the form of the missing self the "dismemberers" had removed and hidden.

"Let me then tell you a story to illustrate my point, a
story that, though you may not have heard it, belongs as
much to you as it does to me. Remembering the story, tell-

ing it, moves the camera far back in time. Far enough back so that it pictures not only the people named in the story, but by inference, all of their direct and indirect cultural and racial descendants who have fanned out all across the world in the centuries since the events took place nearly 1,000 years before the birth of Christ. Like all accounts of religious history, the story is part fact, part legend, part verifiable, part thesis of faith."

The auditorium was funereal with a kind of embarrassed disturbed quiet. I sensed a thin sweeping dislike for Dr. Abana in the room. I did not share this antipathy, however, and oddly wanted to interpose myself between the unwitting professor and the students who, I suspected, had mistaken intellectual candor for rebuke.

"Before coming to the United States, I read that there was a great church in Harlem, New York, called Abyssinian Baptist Church, once pastored by the Negro congressman Adam Clayton Powell, Jr. The name of the church comes from a place in ancient Africa called Abyssinia. Abyssinia is today known as Ethiopia. At the time of the story I am going to tell you, Ethiopia was a land called Axum and Sabaea, or Axum and Sheba. The Queen of Axum and Sabaea from the year 1005 B.C. is referred to in the Old Testament of the Bible in Kings, Chronicles, Psalms, Matthew, and Luke. The queen lived in the capital of Axum, which was in the south of her vast lands. Ethiopia was a much bigger country then than it is today. Then as now, however, Axum was, and remains, in Ethiopia. The lands of Sheba, once northern Ethiopia, are now a country called Yemen. The Queen of Axum and Sheba ruled over her sprawling empire more than 1,500 years before the Arabs arrived in the region. The people of Axum and Sheba are said to have been tall, attractive people with woolly hair. *Ye are black of face*, wrote the ancient priest Azariah of the queen and her subjects in Ethiopia's most sacred book, the *Kebra Nagast* (*The Glory of Kings*)."

Dr. Abana stopped to study the students' faces for an index of interest and detected a spark, caused, he guessed, by his mention of a name and word familiar to them, *Powell* and *Abyssinian* (known only to us in reference to the church, just as *Rabza*, a desert in North Africa, had been known only to me as the name of my high school yearbook).

Dr. Abana then began to speak extemporaneously. In the back of his mind, he knew that this was ill-advised. It was a mistake he had made before when falling prey to feelings of angry futility.

"How many of you have heard of the Queen of Axum and Sheba?"

This time, no hands were raised, not even mine.

"Now, how many of you have heard of the Queen of Sheba?"

As far as I could tell, every hand in the auditorium went up.

"Well, her formal title was Queen of Axum and Sheba. She lived all of her life in Axum, the part of her kingdom that roughly corresponds to modern Ethiopia. During her life, she only saw Sheba once while passing through its lands en route north with her royal caravan to visit King Solomon in Israel.

"Do you find nothing suspicious here, dear young people?"

If anyone did, no one seemed to know specifically what it was.

"After 3,000 years, 'history'—not the history of the *Kebra Nagast*, not the Ethiopians' version of history, their own history, but history written by outsiders—has altered the queen's title. Why? Why was this? Why has history misidentified her as the Queen of Sheba? And why did it not choose, if it felt compelled for some unscholarly reason to shorten her title, to misidentify her as the Queen of Axum, which lay fully on the African continent where she was born, where she reigned, where she spent the entirety of her life? Perhaps it was the arrival of the Arabs in the region, 1,500 years after the queen's death, that gave foreign historians the idea that this beautiful dark queen with woolly hair from the heart of Ethiopia—this impressive monarch that Jesus Christ 1,000 years later would call, while citing her virtues, *the Queen of the South*—could be passed off as something other than the black woman that she was. This is but one of the many outrageous distortions written cunningly by others that fog our view of ourselves—this one, this lie, so large, so pervasive, so invidious, that an Italian actress named Gina Lollobrigida got to play the queen in the American movie about her relationship with King Solomon. And few in this country—and I daresay none of you here—found anything strange about a white woman playing a black queen of ancient Ethiopia."

Dr. Abana sighed, shook his head slightly, and collected himself. The room was silent. He then studied his notes and bore doggedly on with his prepared lecture.

"Axum and Sheba was a wealthy and highly developed country with advanced systems of irrigation and hydraulic energy production. Its people built massive wells and dams reaching heights of sixty feet to produce an abundance of food. The country was also rich in gold and spices which it traded along hundreds of miles of road and sea as far away as Israel. Saffron, cumin, aloes, and galbanum were to be had by broad numbers of the country's people. Myrrh both healed and perfumed. Frankincense eased a body's pain and appeased the gods.

"The queen was said by the ancient scribes to have been a beautiful woman. She was born to great wealth in

1020 B.C. and took the throne at the age of fifteen upon her father's death. She ruled Axum and Sheba, the ancient texts tell us, for forty years with wisdom and skill. The historian Josephus wrote that *she was inquisitive into philosophy, and one that on other accounts also was to be admired.* The queen herself wrote in her memoirs, *Perhaps many people will say that I am inquisitive, but that is simply because they do not understand me. I am always anxious to learn and serious minded."*

Dr. Abana, by then, had won a small listenership, even though we had little to no idea where his story was leading us. Already I felt from his telling of it both familiarity and surprise. For years, I had heard unexplained references to "the Queen of Sheba," a common first cousin to phrases and words like the "Wreck of the Hesperus" and the "Midas touch." But I had known nothing further, neither that "Sheba" was a misnamed country of the ancient world, nor that the country was the modern Ethiopia of East Africa.

I sat alone midway back in the graduated seating of the vast hall that had been built two years before as a multipurpose facility for large lectures, major theatrical productions, and the commencement exercises that drew thousands in the spring. The high ceiling and walls were clad with an acoustical material of a cut and quality common to state-funded middle–twentieth century architectural expediencies.

"Early in the queen's reign, while beset with doubt owing to her inexperience in the art of statecraft, she decided to travel to observe and learn from the legendary King Solomon of Israel. One night, after plying the young queen at dinner with a variety of royal wines, King Solomon was to slake his lust upon the defenseless body of his comely guest.

"That night, God revealed to King Solomon in a dream that the line of religious succession and responsibility would be transferred to a new order that was to be realized upon the birth of the king's son now growing in the queen's womb.

"Born in Axum, the capital, after the queen's return from Jerusalem, Menelik traveled to Jerusalem at the age of thirteen, whereupon later wishing to return to Ethiopia, he refused his father's offer to make him the crown prince of Israel. Upon leaving Jerusalem, Menelik is said to have taken with him the Ark of the Covenant which he stole from King Solomon, his father, with the approval of God, who levitated Menelik and his cargo across the Red Sea before the king's men could give chase.

"It is written in the *Kebra Nagast* that Menelik defeated his father and avenged his mother's humiliation with the consignment by God of his covenant with man to Ethiopia. Thus, according to the writers of Ethiopia's holiest book, the *Kebra Nagast*, Ethiopians became God's chosen people and Ethiopia Israel's successor."

During the question-and-answer period that followed Dr. Abana's remarks, a student named Herbert Brody walked to one of the two standing microphones that had been placed in the hall's two aisles. The room fell quiet in anticipation. Even in the semidark, we knew it was Herbert from the shape of the large head which rested on his body like a macrocephalic boulder. His nickname was *Brain* and he was a 4.0 student headed the following year to Harvard Divinity School.

"Do you believe that Menelik *really* took the Ark of the Covenant to Ethiopia, Dr. Abana? And where is it now?"

Dr. Abana peered through his thick eyeglasses into the gloom at the well-confident Herbert Brody and paused for what seemed an age. Sensing what was to come, Dr. Quarles's face wore an expression of restrained amusement.

"The Ark of the Covenant, containing God's decalogue of law, is believed to have been made by Moses. The Ark is said by the historians to be a gold-plated hardwood box measuring four feet long, two and a half feet wide, and two and a half feet deep.

"The Ethiopians believe that the Ark of the Covenant remains to this day in Ethiopia. There is a fair body of evidence that at least until recent times it was preserved at Axum, the ancient capital. Axum is a place in Ethiopia that you should visit. I should add that Menelik's return to Ethiopia with the Ark was assisted by a group of Jews who left Israel to come with him. The modern Falashas of Ethiopia are Jews who trace their descent from these ancient people."

Herbert Brody looked as though he thought Dr. Abana might be trying to make fun of him by suggesting that he visit Axum, which was not the case.

"May I ask your name, young man?"

"Herbert Brody. My name is Herbert Brody."

"Mr. Brody, do you believe in the divinity of Jesus Christ?"

The question was unexpected and it momentarily startled Brody. "Yes, I do believe in the divinity of Christ, but what does that have—"

"Do you know, Mr. Brody, that Jesus, who had been considered an influential but mortal prophet, was not given divine status until nearly four centuries after his death?"

"With all due respect sir, I don't see what your question has to do with mine."

Dr. Quarles sat back in his chair and folded his arms, looking pleased.

Dr. Abana's demeanor did not change from its initial fix. "Have you ever heard of the Council of Nicaea, Mr. Brody?" This was asked quietly after another of his long pauses.

"No, I have not."

"The Council was convened by the emperor of the Eastern Roman Empire," pausing, "a pagan who worshipped the sun just as the Queen of Axum and Sheba had 1,400 years before him. She converted to Judaism before her son brought the Ark of the Covenant to Ethiopia. Emperor Constantine was baptized as a Christian only on his deathbed—unwillingly, it is believed. It was Constantine, a pagan Roman politician, who organized the ecumenical meeting known as the Council of Nicaea to vote on the matter of making Jesus Christ divine. That which you believe, Mr. Brody, was accomplished for you by a pagan Roman emperor who did not believe in Christ's divinity himself. He did what he did for political and business reasons. The Roman Empire was divided by the growing Christian movement. In one stroke, the clever, cynical Constantine co-opted the Christian movement and consolidated political and economic power for the Roman Empire and, not unimportantly, for the Roman Catholic Church."

Dr. Abana stopped and looked at Brody who found himself suddenly unnerved and without a riposte.

More kindly, almost sweetly then, Dr. Abana continued, "You asked if I believed that Menelik took the Ark of the Covenant to Ethiopia. The historical evidence would suggest that he did. The queen had been both a good mother to him and an important coming figure in the history of two of the three great Abrahamic religions, Judaism and, through her line, early Coptic Christianity. Menelik loved his mother and he was very much Ethiopian. He, on the other hand, had little reason to love his father, King Solomon. Thus, it is reasonable to assume that he did return to Ethiopia, and with the Ark of the Covenant. I do not believe, however, Mr. Brody, that he did so by levitating over the Red Sea, but then I do not believe that Christ walked on water either. The mortals who wrote the *Kebra*

Nagast and the Bible were indeed fanciful and poetic. It was the literary fashion in those days. But all that they wrote was not meant to be taken literally."

Brody stood at the microphone alone, with no one in line behind him to speak. He very much wanted to get back to his seat.

Dr. Abana began again, but more solicitously this time. "We have all been taught that Christ died on a cross. The Dogon people of Mali, however, believe that their Creator God, Amma, sent Nommo to Earth to sacrifice himself to cleanse the Earth. They believe that Nommo was crucified on a tree."

I listened with fascination to Dr. Abana's affirmation of the story my grandmother had told me when I was fifteen.

"Would it surprise you to learn, Mr. Brody, that the New Testament of the Bible, in Acts 5:30 and I Peter 2:24, describes Christ not to have been crucified on a cross, but to have been hanged on a tree, not unlike, in addition to Nommo, the tree-slain savior figures of Krishna, Maryas, Odin, and Dodonian Zeus?

"Things may not always be as told to us. It is particularly important that we understand that, you see, Mr. Brody?"

Brody, feeling bested, did not know what to say. He felt somewhat foolish and was glad that the hall was dark.

"Mr. Brody," Dr. Abana said as the young man turned to walk back to his seat, "I believe in the divinity of Christ. I have reached that view without fear of discovering the full glorious story of civilization. Read all that you can, curious and unafraid. Education requires that we open books, not close them. I doubt that what you find will weaken your faith. It, more likely, will strengthen it."

The program ended there. Dr. Quarles, a full head taller than his friend, shook Dr. Abana's hand and said the words, "Splendid, simply splendid."

I sat awhile in my seat as one often does after watching an especially thought-provoking movie and gave fresh thought to what Dr. Quarles had said to our class about discovering how old we were.

The next morning, Dr. Quarles, appearing unusually cheerful, called our class to order. He was dressed in a carelessly cut single-breasted suit of sober tweed. He held in his hand a pair of thick rimless bifocals with which he gestured toward a student seated in the rear of the room.

"What did you take away from Dr. Abana's lecture, Mr. Daughtry?"

Daughtry, distracted, had heard the sound of his name and nothing more. "Sir?"

"Anybody?"

A small, dark-skinned, pretty young woman, seated in the second row on Dr. Quarles's left, raised her hand.

"Yes, Miss Branch."

"Well, the truth is, Dr. Quarles, that most of what Dr. Abana said was new to me and I don't really know yet how to think about it. Something that doesn't feel so good in me doesn't want to believe it. I don't know why that is. Could be that, you know, all these years no one has ever said anything close to what he was talking about." She paused, knitted her brows together, opened her mouth to continue, and then stopped. Claudia Branch was an earnest young woman of better than average aptitude.

"What, as you see it, Miss Branch, is the purpose of education?"

"To prepare us for the world."

"What does that mean, Miss Branch?"

"To qualify us for good jobs."

"Is that all, Miss Branch?"

"Well, I guess, maybe, also to broaden us as human beings." She fought off a shrug as she said this.

Dr. Quarles, not wishing to press Claudia Branch further, wasn't sure whether she really believed this last thing, or was merely regurgitating a commonplace from school officialdom.

"What do you think, Mr. March?" Dr. Quarles had a habit of asking the question before choosing a respondent. The method allowed his students to hear the question without pressure, although it hadn't worked quite that way with Daughtry.

"Well, a lot of what he said was familiar to me."

"The context, Mr. March, please give us the context."

"Well, I can tell you, Dr. Quarles, that like Claudia, I never heard in a classroom anything vaguely related to what he said yesterday."

"Please go on, Mr. March." Dr. Quarles's patience exceeded my confidence which was embarrassingly small, particularly in this matter.

"My grandmother is blind," I said. "She reads her Braille Bible and talks to me about it. She knows about the Queen of Axum and Sheba and King Solomon from the Bible. When I was a little boy, she told me about Menelik and how he brought the Ark of the Covenant to Ethiopia."

"Did your grandmother also read the *Kebra Nagast*?"

"No, I doubt that she's ever heard of that book."

"Then how could she know about Menelik carrying the Ark of the Covenant back to Ethiopia?"

"From reading the Bible."

"The story of Menelik's flight with the Ark of the Covenant is not told in the Bible."

"Then I don't know, sir."

That evening I called my grandmother at her neighbor's house on Duvall Street.

"Grandma, have you ever heard of a book called the *Kebra Nagast*?"

"Say that again."

"*Kebra Nagast*."

"No, son. I'm sure I've never heard of that. Why do you ask?"

"You told me once that King Menelik brought the Ark of the Covenant home from Jerusalem to Ethiopia. I thought you read this in the Bible but Dr.Quarles said the story wasn't in the Bible. How did you know about it, Grandma?"

"My mother . . ."

"Your mother? Your mother told you. How could that be, Grandma?"

There was silence on the line. Then my grandmother seemed to begin in the middle of some long past experience. "I was watching the Fasika procession with my best friend Meron." She trilled the *r* when she pronounced her friend's name. "It was the Sabbath and we were consecrating one of our new churches. My mother told me the story of King Menelik and the Ark. That's how I knew."

"You learned this in a dream, Grandma?"

"Yes, son."

"When did this happen? How old was I?"

"I was asleep dreaming in my rocking chair. You were seven. You woke me up when I was talking in the dream to my friend Meron."

"Where was this? Ethiopia?"

"It was called Abysinnia then."

"When was this, Grandma?"

"The year was 1186. I don't know the date."

Later, I took from the tin box the plastic sleeve from which I retrieved my notes and the Dogon map my grandmother had guided me in drawing when I was fifteen. I pored over the materials for the better part of an hour. It was then that I began, at least in my head, planning the writing of my first book.

Chapter Twelve

March 1970
Morgan State University, Baltimore, Maryland

I was reading James Baldwin's *Go Tell It on the Mountain*. Sounds from the television in the bedroom played through the door into the small apartment's living room where I'd sat making small headway.

. . . Swedish scientists today in Uppsala, Sweden, released the first known computer-enhanced photograph and orbit simulation of a tiny, little-known star which moves in an elliptical fifty-year orbit path around the larger star, Sirius. Doctor . . .

Baldwin's book fell from my hands onto the floor. I ran from the living room into the bedroom. With my eyes fixed upon the small black-and-white screen, I inched laterally toward the foot of the bed and dropped awkwardly into a sitting position. Finding something in the moment mildly frightening, it was difficult for me to focus on the image that filled the screen. The lines in the image appeared to swim and undulate. I felt a gallop in my chest and my temples. My cheeks began to bake and itch beneath the skin. My eyes started to water as if I were about to cry. I took a succession of small breaths in an effort to gain a measure of control over my faculties.

I blinked hard and stared at the high-resolution photograph on the screen. The image had been caught through a high-powered telescope by a Dr. Jan Bergman, a member of the Swedish Royal Academy of Astronomy and a Nobel Prize–winning astrophysicist. The NBC announcer described the image as the first picture ever taken of the small star, shown moving along an elliptical fifty-year path around the big star Sirius, the blue queen of the north sky. The announcer called the little star not Po Tolo, but a name that meant nothing to me. There had been no doubt, however, no doubt at all. The picture on the screen was virtually a perfect copy of the sketch my grandmother had made from her dream about a previous life with her Dogon father. The drawing was in my closet, still stored in the ten-year-old plastic sleeve. I would get it down later and review it, though I would have no real need to do so. My grandmother's recreation of her father's diagram had been burned long since into my memory.

The photograph remained on the screen while the announcer interviewed an American astronomer from Princeton about the little star's significance. I couldn't pull my eyes away.

It was Po Tolo. It was some sort of miracle. Some gift from the spirit world. "My God! My God! My God!" I shouted at the walls of my apartment.

I squeezed my eyes and lay back on the bed with my arms stretched hard behind me in joyful catharsis. Then, for the first time in nearly ten years, I cried.

MORGAN STATE UNIVERSITY
BALTIMORE, MARYLAND

March 26, 1970

Mrs. Makeda Gee Florida Harris March
521A Duvall St.
Richmond, Virginia 23232

Dear Grandma,

How are you?

Much of this letter is about your "travels." Stop Mrs. Grier now if you don't want her to read it to you.

I am sorry that I will not be able to be there on your birthday. I am literally tied to the library here trying to complete the requirements for my master's degree so that I can participate in the commencement exercises in May.

Mama tells me that you are well. That is wonderful news. I still, however, miss very much hearing the sound of your voice. I miss having our talks. I am planning to drive down in the first week of May to spend a day with you so that we can catch up.

I have been accepted into the English literature PhD program at the University of Pennsylvania. Mama seemed very pleased by this news but I can never really tell for sure, things being what they are. In any case, it is more important to me that you are proud of what I have been able to accomplish academically. I have worked very hard, but, I am beginning to think, for many of the wrong reasons. I am not happy, and have not been for a long time. The grind, rigor, and regimen of academic life serves only to distract me. The harder I work, the less I think about what happened. This and, I am afraid, only this, explains the high honors I have won. But more on this later.

First, the good news, and it is, I believe, fascinating. I have kept the notes I took on what you told me in high school about your Dogon dream, your father, the holy man, the big star that the Western scientists call Sirius and the little star that your father said orbited around the big star. Your father in the dream called it Po Tolo and said it was made of a heavy material called sagala that did not exist on Earth. I also kept the sketch you made of the ancient Dogon drawing showing *the elliptical path of the little star around the big star. Well, Western scientists did not know until recently that the little star existed. They had seen its companion, a star they called Sirius A, through a telescope in 1862. But a Dogon drawing, made hundreds of years ago before the telescope was invented, has recently come to light. It shows that the little star, Po Tolo (whose orbit around Sirius, the Dogon have celebrated in their ceremonies since, at least, the thirteenth century), moves around the big star in an elliptical orbit. What is more fascinating is this. The ancient Dogon drawing that was recently discovered looks exactly like the drawing you made of the one your father, the priest, showed you in your dream. What's more, Western scientists now say that Po Tolo, which they call Sirius B, is made of a substance so dense that a teaspoonful of it weighs ten thousand pounds.*

This whole thing has stumped Western scientists, and perhaps me as well. How could the Dogon people have known, maybe for thousands of years, about a star that cannot be seen without the aid of a telescope? How could they have known about the path of its orbit and the substance it is made of? That it spins on its axis and makes the big star wobble because of the heavy material Po Tolo is made of. That the little star's orbit around the big star requires fifty years. No one any longer questions that the Dogon knew these things, but how is this possible?

What is even more fascinating, Grandma, at least to me, is how you could have known all of this. Everything told to you by your father, the old Dogon priest, in the dream you described to me ten years ago when I was fifteen, has recently been established by Western scientists as scientific fact. Every detail.

I never doubted that you dreamed what you dreamed. I even began to believe much of it after I found out about the Dogon at the high school library, but tonight on the network news, they showed the first photograph of Po Tolo with its or-

bit path drawn in. I don't know why I was stunned but I was. I don't understand. But maybe there are things that are not to be understood.

The rest of what I need to talk to you about I shouldn't put in a letter and I think you know what I am referring to.

I've met a girl that I care for very much, but I'm a mess, you know, and no good for her or anyone else.

I'll be home soon.

Your loving grandson,
Gray

Three days after I posted the letter, my grandmother telephoned me from Mrs. Grier's house. She sounded guarded.

"Gray?"

"Grandma?"

"Yes."

"You got my letter. You let Mrs. Grier read it? All of it?"

"Yes. Well, when you write me a letter, I know it must be very important."

"I'm sorry, Grandma. I knew I shouldn't have put the dream business in a letter, but what I found out was so unbelievable that I guess I didn't use the best judgment."

"Oh, don't worry about that, son. Mrs. Grier couldn't make any sense of it. If anything, it's you she thinks might be a little bit fruity, not me."

"I still have the drawing and my notes stashed away in that plastic sleeve. The rest of the information I've gathered fills up two drawers in my file cabinet."

"I trust you'll know what to do with it. You're a grown man now and out in the big world, a bigger world than I ever had a chance to learn much of anything about."

I thought about what she said and how cosmically far it was from the truth. "Grandma?"

"Yes, Gray."

"Remember when I told you I wanted to be a writer?"

"I remember very clearly."

"I was just saying words then."

"Oh, I knew that, but even then you said those words for a reason, Gray. Some people's puzzles have more pieces than other people's puzzles. The people with a lot of pieces have to worker harder and longer to put the picture together than ordinary people with a piece or two, but in the long run, when they stick it out, they make the best pictures. You're one of those people, Gray."

"You really think so, Grandma?"

"I know so, son."

"That's part of what I need to talk to you about when I come down. Something I want to write about."

"Something's wrong, son . . . ?"

"Well, I think you know . . . ?"

"Your letter worried me."

"I worry about myself." I pulled myself erect in the chair in which I had slouched. "I'm sorry I missed your birthday party. How was it?"

"Oh, everybody came. Alma baked a cake. Mrs. Grier helped out. She's got a good heart, you know. I think everyone had a good time."

"D-does Daddy still come by every day?"

"Yes, son."

"Does he know we talk?"

"Yes."

I hadn't the courage to inquire further and we fell silent for a while. Then she said, "I've had another dream."

"About the Dogon?"

"No, somethin' different."

"Tell me."

"Let it sit until you come."

PART THREE

CHAPTER THIRTEEN

The month of March seems invariably to promise more than it delivers, teasing spring, frustrating hope's impatience.

An unseasonal light snow was in the morning forecast for Baltimore. The low skull-gray sky choked on angry dark clouds that scudded before swirling winds beneath a thick overcast ceiling.

I did not look forward to the day, much of which I would spend in the library polishing the thesis draft I had entitled "A Critical Appraisal of the Harlem Renaissance Poets." At three o'clock I was scheduled to meet with my thesis advisor, Dr. Harold Waters, who was chairman of the English department and a black conservative of the bow tie genus whom I had taken unkindly to calling in my angered head a *chestycrat*, my name for the self-important vainglorious sorts. Dr. Waters, I suppose, was not a bad sort really. It was just that I had corrupting my personal assessments a sharp and indigestible shard of glass in my craw that I could neither expel nor frontally acknowledge. The disability did not affect the social manners that were well-taught to me early on. Nor was I outwardly unpleasant to acquaintances that inconsequentially slid past as I moved, day in and day out, from where I was coming to where I was going. People were seen by me, firstly and safely, as solid obstacles not to be collided with. Quite literally so, and however sadly, little more.

No girl had ever seized my attention like Jeanne Burgess.

Notwithstanding my low emotional state, I have to confess that the mere nearness of her exhilarated me beyond reason. To leave it said only that she was beautiful would be, I think, unforgivably banal. Indeed she *was* beautiful, but I only use, first, this term to explain my attraction to her because it was the easiest and simplest, though most inadequate, thing to say about her. The problem here is that I find the whole business of diagnosing romantic appeal to be witheringly abstract and undoable. The truth is that the entire matter of physical appeal is so inherently subjective that to describe what I really found irresistibly compelling about Jeanne would sound silly when said aloud. The small Haitian accent, for instance, and the colorful way it inflected her near visual use of language. The soft susurrus melody of her name when rightly pronounced—*Sh-jen*—educed the tender sensation of art wedded by mystery. The long, sweet flowing line of her neck and spine. The deep, low glow of her dark brown skin. And something more that may have been appreciated only by me. Something subtle and indescribable that she did with her head when she smiled. This little otherwise insignificantly shy something, whatever it was, would cause me to vibrate slightly. Before I even *knew*. Such, I suppose, is the power and insanity of romantic attraction. Whenever I could look at her, I quite helplessly could not *not* look at her. And indeed, I may have been the only man to have seen her who'd been so completely smitten by her—or at least superficially so. I realize (merely intellectually, of course) that these powerful surface charms of hers—the language, the liquid line of her form, the flawless skin, that head thing—were but elements of her own particular opposite-sex ignition system, much like the small delicate pieces of kindling that burn easy, fast, and hot to light the real blaze that burns for the long haul.

But as I was saying, she was, all the while, pretty, much as my mother had once been. However, I did not know enough further about her or my mother, for that matter, to compare the two of them very much beyond that. This sounds, I know, a terrible thing to confess. Nonetheless, my guess is that it is not, in the least, unusual. Parents of my mother's generation hid themselves from their children behind walls of parental propriety that had been taught to them just as, I suppose, it has been taught to me.

As such, I didn't know who my parents really were, and likely less still about the geography of their relationship, which appeared on the surface more decorous and habitual than anything that could possibly be identified as passionate. For instance, I never saw them playing, which, I suspect, means something.

I did want to *know* Jeanne, perhaps even to love her, but I was reflexively cautious. I would, in any case, have to *know* her first, and one cannot decide at the outset whether such is even possible. At best, *knowing* travels a long twisting road with ruts and bumps whose end cannot be seen from the dull safe start. But had I not endured enough? Why go to all the trouble to expose nerves believed cauterized?

Yet the urges that I felt were likely lymphatic by nature and did not fall, so much as one might have thought, within the discretions of a rational mind to control or direct.

She was such an exquisite vision, both of flesh and of spirit, which I must have known myself, by then, lost to investigate, shoals be damned. Already she had taken over a large space in my consciousness. Though hardly perceptible, I thought I may have started, even, walking differently.

My upbringing had been passably pleasant, or at least sufficiently so for me to have seen all of those associated with it as *standard* people, their attitudes, values, beliefs, social practices, and even their fatuities as *majority normal*.

Gordon and I never slept over at friends' houses or ate at their tables. The March family was a self-contained and socially insular idea. Should I have thought about it at all, I'd have thought that we were like everybody else, or, upon reflection, that everybody else was like we were. My mother and father never went anywhere together, except to church or to errand-run.

There were no dances, restaurants (most of which were, in any case, for whites only), movies, vacations, or family excursions of any kind that I can remember. My mother and father just worked, she in our tidy house and he at his machine-gray metal desk borne under by tables and policies, tables for death and policies for life: term life, whole life, his life, Mama's life, Grandma's life, and anybody else's life that his company, Bradford Life Insurance, was willing to place a bet on.

Their tedious daily routines passed unexamined, even by them. Never once had I heard them speak in a language of abstraction, in that upper breathing space, material and metaphysical, afforded by higher education itself and the creature comforts that it buys. (This was so, even though my mother had finished college). They talked about the state of our health. Never about the tone of our lives and the race-nasty boxed-over society that had foreordained it. This was all *normal* to me, even satisfactory in a numbing sort of way.

I had found sex when I was sixteen with a girl whose mother worked afternoons typing until six. Her name was Geraldine Trice. She introduced me in the soft comfort of her mother's detached white clapboard house to Dakota Staton, Duke Ellington, and premature ejaculation. Started her *life* at thirteen. Guys, been there, loved it, labeled her *loose*. Taught me. "How long have you had this thing in your wallet, Gray? No. No. Not like that, Gray. You roll it on like this. Slow now. Slow, Gray. You like that? Does it feel good? Oh, boy. Don't worry. That always happens the first time."

I liked Geraldine Trice. Never called her *loose* to anyone. Never bragged about *it* to the guys. Never told a soul. She was my friend. But, in sated retrospect, she was not someone I would ever have considered suitable for marrying. No, never to marry. Not *that* kind. *Nice* girls were for marrying. Geraldine was nice but not *nice*, although, I thought even then, she was only looking for love like the rest of us, love that just happened not to live in her house. Father gone. Mother busy. But that was something I couldn't help her with. My life stretched out ahead of me. I had to move on. Back then, I could, she couldn't—even though my secretions had mixed luxuriously on even and democratic terms with hers.

I was attracted to Jeanne Burgess in a completely different way, or to put it more accurately, in a much broader, more complicated way. For this, I had only my mother to use as a model. My mother was my *normal*. But Jeanne Burgess was nothing at all like my mother.

At times like that I wished that I'd had a sister, for I knew next to nothing about the female temperament and I had been told that boys growing up learned a lot about the thinking of girls by listening to their sisters talk to their mothers about boys. In thin rationalization, I reasoned that Geraldine Trice might have benefited from a brother figure that my very nonbrother new male animal chemistry had not allowed me to serve as. In any case, the small guilt that I felt was softened by the mitigating relief of knowing that it was she who had taken my virginity, not I hers. With a mostly clear conscience, it was that for which I have always been deeply grateful to Geraldine Trice.

While I was physically attracted to Jeanne Burgess, her

beauty may have been the least of why she took such stubborn root in my thoughts, crowding against the demons that had been in residence there since high school.

I said earlier that she was nothing like my mother. That may have been too strong. I did not really know my mother, a formerly smart woman out of whom male society had domesticated any instinct she must have had to hold forth helpfully on the larger public issues of her time. Over the dreary downward pull of time, she had been reduced to coupon clipping, housekeeping, and vicarious ambition for her sons. Loving her all the while, my father, devolving all of his hope upon Gordon and, less so, upon me, never understood the drab common fate (which I suspected took the place of "love" in their marriage) to which they had been consigned by the era's circumstance.

While I wanted to believe that I was very much unlike my parents, I was constrained to concede that I was more than biologically *of* them as well. This, added to the baggage I bore like a broken porter, caused me to question the wisdom of *knowing* a woman as forthrightly brilliant and self-possessed as Jeanne Burgess.

Jeanne, younger than I by two years, had earned her PhD in economics the year before from Oxford University with highest honors, the first black to do so. Her father, Dennis Burgess, was a Chicago neurosurgeon and her mother, Marie Cesaire-Burgess, a celebrated playwright and daughter of the great Haitian painter Montas Cesaire. Jeanne was confident and pleasantly self-assured in the congenitally unaffected way of the privileged that attracted and unnerved me at the same time. She was doing a year of postdoctoral research at Johns Hopkins University downtown. I had been introduced to her three weeks before at a Haitian art show running at a gallery near the Inner Harbor that had featured three of her grandfather's paintings.

RANDALL ROBINSON ❦ 123

We had found ourselves standing alone before a painting entitled *Eve au Paradis* by Salnave Philippe-Auguste. At the center of the painting was a black Eve reaching for an apple amidst the luxuriant green lushness of Eden. Depicted in bold primary colors were two giraffes, a lion, a tiger, a zebra, an elephant, exotic birds, and a watching venomous tree serpent coiled inches from the apple that was all but within Eve's grasp.

Looking at the painting I said, "Ethiopia."

"Of course," she replied with a look of surprise, and favored me with an intoxicating smile.

Emboldened, I said, "Genesis, chapter 2."

She gave me a quizzical look.

I said, "Eden, cradle of creation. Bordered by the Gihon River of Ethiopia. Genesis 2:13." Showing off. Shamelessly.

"I'm impressed." She continued to smile and look directly at me, nearly causing me to sway.

"Well, the truth is, my grandmother told me."

"Your grandmother knows a lot about Ethiopia?"

"Seems to."

She saw that I was trying to appear mysterious, clever. It amused her. She looked back at the painting.

"In any case, she knows a lot about the Bible," I said softly.

We stood there for a while in silence enjoying the presence of each other.

"Your grandfather's paintings are beautiful."

"Thank you." She smiled again.

"Is he still alive?" Clumsy.

"No . . ."

"I'm sorry. I—"

"Don't be. He died when I was five. I remember visiting Haiti in the summers and sitting in his atelier, watching him paint."

She pronounced the word *atelier* with a French accent. I did not know what it meant. I did not ask.

I said, "I don't know much about art."

She asked, "Do paintings often engage you emotionally?"

"Yes, this one does, for instance."

"We're as old as the rivers, aren't we?"

It wasn't really a question. We looked again at the Philippe-Auguste painting that had forged the mood of her comment.

It was she who spoke next. "I think you know well enough the essentials of what you need to know about art. The academics of it are less important."

"Do animals like these live in Haiti?"

She smiled again. "No."

"Why are they represented in so many of the paintings?"

"Enslaved Haitians strove hard to remember the Africa from which they had been torn. They clung to their religion, Voudoun, which encouraged the belief that they would return home from bondage to Guinea when they died. The animals are images from a memory of their homeland."

I had, in the weeks since, played my impression of the encounter at the gallery over and over in my head in an effort to decode what I remembered of the words she had spoken to me. I was to see her again for dinner after I finished at the library. Walking across the Morgan quad toward the stone-clad building, I began to rehearse involuntarily what I would say when I saw her at seven.

Chapter Fourteen

The damp, cold morning air tore about the square in blustery fits. I pulled the hood of my unlined nylon rain shell over my head and hunched against the blade of the wind. The two cement walkways that crossed at the center of the campus quad were laden with the traffic of students making their way to early-morning classes. Voices caught and died in the sharp gusts. Head bent low, I felt very much a stranger negotiating a forest of communing shadows. I set as swift a pace as I could and made it to the library without noticing a face that I recognized.

I had chosen the Harlem Renaissance poets to study and write about chiefly because they were black writers of a bygone era whose work was profoundly artistic, soft-shelled, and emotionally comprehensible to me. Indeed, they wrote with lamentation and sorrow, with rage and protestation, but, always and ever, *well*, their exposed and infectious humanity the proof of it. In a sad, glorious time before the broad American celebration and commercialization of crudity hatched itself upon the tender arts, these were writers, first and foremost, whose verse declined quietly the full surrender of poignance to anger, craft to politics, and taste to coarseness.

Or so I saw what may simply have been just another refuge of mine in which to hide from remembering.

I was working on the appendices and notes to my thesis paper. Langston Hughes, the best known of the Harlem Renaissance poets, was far and away the most prolific of them, and thereby claimed the largest section of my annotated references. The New York–born Countee Cullen, who died in 1946 at the age of forty-three, however, was my critical preference.

I stretched out a yawn and reared against the back of my chair which was sandwiched between metal racks of books on the fifth floor of the library's stacks. I lolled my head and raised it in an arc to stare blankly into the industrial ceiling while remembering the lines of Cullen's "Heritage."

Women from whose loins I sprang
When the birds of Eden sang?

I smiled and reprised the exchange.

Eden, cradle of creation. Bordered by the Gihon River of Ethiopia. Genesis 2:13.

I'm impressed.

I'm impressed. I'm impressed. I'm impressed.

She had said this—and smiled. I hadn't felt so good in a long, long while.

I liked being alone in the stacks. Most of Morgan State's library users did their work in the main reading room, but I much preferred working at the little desk jammed against the wall cheek-by-jowl to books that spoke only when called upon. I had never particularly liked being alone before.

Geraldine Trice was a blurry character from that more normal, but now distant past life. As were my parents. From that time before, only my grandmother crossed over into the unsettled space of my open daily thoughts. And Gordon, who was relentlessly present.

Two books on black poetry rested on the little desk. I pushed them flush to the upper corners and checked the alignment with the palm of my hand, swiping it along the edge of the desk. I placed my ruled spiral notebook on the desk in the center, taking care to leave it parallel with the sides of the desk top. I then put two ballpoint pens and a sharpened pencil on the desk to the left of the notebook, lined them up, and spaced them equidistant from each other. I checked the arrangement of the items carefully and found it satisfactory. I did not know why, but I had developed in recent years a need to impose order upon the small objects with which I did my work. I needed to know where everything was, not only my research materials, my drafts, notes, monographs, books, and the like, but also my stapler, my paperclips, rubber bands, and three-hole punch. It seemed to me that I took excessive care of these inconsequential possessions and I did not know why, because I had had no early or natural penchant for neatness.

I was an obsessive believer in the usefulness of list making. In adolescence, I had been disorganized and irresponsible, but, perhaps as a consequence, largely happy. Since then, I had imposed upon myself the discipline that was not installed earlier. This was much like the body discovering the need of a skeleton after it had been fully formed, and then resorting to wearing the mislaid bones on the outside of the body's surface as a flexless cage. This made for considerable adult pain and smaller happiness, but in the last analysis, success, even though late-onset discipline was artificial and manifested itself in the obsessive making of, among other things, lists.

I wanted to be a writer. Why was that? Was I an artist, born to express, to create? Hardly. Had I then some perverse need to exert complete control over the tiniest of available disorders, over some little unit of something, at least: my notebooks, my pens, my pencil, my books, my excuses, my ineffectual explanations? Lists, for God's sake.

Before it happened, I had told Daddy that I wanted to be a writer. This was after I had told Grandma. My father said that no one knew any black—no, what he said was "colored"—writers except the people who wrote for the *Afro-American* and did not get paid anything to speak of. "Or somebody like that communist Richard Wright, who ran off to France with a white woman, or somebody like James Baldwin who is a homosexual. Who've you ever known who was colored, Gray, that was normal like everyday people who made a living from writing?" I couldn't answer this, and he gave me one of his *so there* looks. Had he heard of Zora Neale Hurston, who died penniless, he'd have thrown her in there too.

We knew a lot of black doctors. I don't know how many there were, but enough to see after the more than 100,000 black people who lived in Richmond. And practically all of these black doctors were rich, even Dr. Grimes, the speculum butcher who'd killed Heidi Parker, a sixteen-year-old schoolmate, and left more than a few others barren for life.

Gordon was going to be a doctor. He was going to do something that not only made a lot of sense, but made a lot of money. And I was going to be a writer. "That's crazy, boy, just plain crazy. When will you ever pull your head out of the clouds?"

I had put it in my graduation class yearbook anyhow. Although I had long ago lost track of the book, I knew the notation was there beneath my cap-and-gown picture in the 1963 *Rabza: Graylon March; Course, college preparatory; Activities, English club, drama club; Ambition, writer.*

I had been the only aspiring writer in my class, or in the whole high school, for that matter, if my science teacher, Mr. Garver, had it right. Certainly we'd heard of the famous black writers, but not one of our English teachers had required us to read anything that any of them had written.

For whatever the reason, I began as early as the eleventh grade to read their work on my own. I liked Richard Wright and identified strongly with his angry Bigger Thomas. I did not like Zora Neale Hurston, finding her Negro-dialect characters drawn more for the liking of white readers than black readers. I had been reassured to read that Richard Wright felt much the same way that I did about her. He was to write of her novel *Their Eyes Were Watching God*: "In the main, her novel is not addressed to the Negro, but to a white audience whose chauvinistic tastes she knows how to satisfy."

For many of the same reasons I disliked Paul Laurence Dunbar while the white folks praised him as they had the fawning Phillis Wheatley. I had been impatient with Charles W. Chesnutt and gave up on him, perhaps much too early. I thought that James Baldwin, the only living black writer I'd had a chance to read, was, with his broadly encompassing race perspectives, the most relevant of all of them to black folks' contemporary struggles.

I kept all of this to myself, however: whom I read, what I read, and what I thought about what I read. I did not share this with Mama and Daddy, who would both likely have been pleased that I was reading so much. I wanted to keep this for myself, an interest that I *owned* away from them, an incubating intellectual curiosity that I guarded as jealously as I did the Dogon dream notes in the plastic sleeve in the tin box at the back of the top shelf of my closet.

I read books I didn't even tell my grandmother about. I did not want to hear anyone tell me that they were happy I had found an "interest." I was having a one-way discussion with great black thinkers about matters more compelling than quantities and units, meters and measures, prospects and platitudes. I read on in small fear that I would be discovered by a caring person and subjected to a practical comment or a practical look or a practical anything. I had decided that I wanted to be a writer, the least *practical* career goal of any I had heard about. To have any chance at all of succeeding, I had to learn to think—that is, to think critically, to see from an imaginary space above, in one single sweep of vision, past and future, from the low, well-taught, mean ignorance of the present, in order to arrive at a voice that was mine, all mine, uncompromising to fools and concert-goers. Except for Grandma, who'd taught me to "look beyond the fence," I felt completely alone.

Footfalls resounded through the dark narrow cement halls of the stacks, growing louder with the sharp, short strike of a woman's heel. I turned from the wall to watch a tall, slender young woman I guessed to be eighteen or so approaching with two books under her arm. She wore a green dress and pumps that matched. Her hair was long and doctored to a brilliant sheen. Her makeup had been carefully applied over a tad-too-heavy base coat.

She said, "Hi." Pleasant. Not pretty. Cute. Taking the effect of this for granted.

I said, "Good morning."

"Are you Graylon March?"

"Yes." A little impatient, but curious.

"You left a reference material slip in the box downstairs."

"Oh, yes I did." Remembering that indeed I had done so.

"We found two books for you." She handed them to me.

"Thank you."

She smiled but made no move to leave. I waited.

"It says on the slip that you are a candidate for a master's degree in English."

"Yes, I am."

"If you don't mind my asking, what could books on dreams and reincarnation have to do with English?"

I expelled a small sibilant breath through my teeth, evidencing involuntarily that the question had annoyed me.

The smile fell. She turned and left, the click of her heels coming faster as she retreated down the long hall toward the service elevator. I sighed, disappointed with myself. The girl had merely tried to be friendly.

I looked at the books for a while without opening them, as if I were reluctant to be presented with discouraging news. The first book was entitled, *Dreams and Their Meaning*, and had been written by a Robert Melroy. The volume had a self-published font and feel to it. I read a few lines from the introduction, judged the writing unscholarly, and laid the book aside. The second book, *Reincarnation: Case Studies*, had been written by a Dr. Joyce Harris-Fulbright, a psychology professor on the faculty at the University of Southern California. The book had been published in 1964 by the Golden State University Press. The jacket notes featured three-line encomiums from Harry Grossman, a famous research psychologist, and five other professors from highly respected schools, including Dr. Broadus Benjamin, a pioneer in the field of paranormal phenomena.

I read first the table of contents and then leafed desultorily through the book, scanning a section here and there without much of a plan.

In the introduction, Dr. Harris-Fulbright gave a definition of reincarnation (*the transmigration of a soul from a dying body to a living body*) and listed religions and prominent people who either embraced reincarnation as a tenet of pietistic faith or as a simple nonreligious personal belief.

Among those who embraced a belief in reincarnation through their religions were the Hindus, Jains, Buddhists and Sikhs of India, the Theravada Buddhists of Burma, the Theravada Buddhists of Thailand, the Tamils and Sinhalese of Sri Lanka, the Igbo of Nigeria, the Haida and Tlingit of Alaska, the Alevis of Turkey, the Druze of Lebanon, Syria, Israel, and Jordan, the Buddhists of Tibet. It seemed a simpler and less taxing matter to list the world religions that did *not* embrace reincarnation (Christianity and Islam) than to delineate the much larger list of religions and cultures that did, a preponderance of faiths that may have prompted the philosopher Arthur Schopenhauer to remark that, "The best definition of Europe is that it is the part of the world that does not believe in reincarnation." But even in England, a *Sunday Telegraph* poll had shown that 28 percent of British adults believed in reincarnation, putting them on a believers list that included Napoleon Bonaparte, Henry Ford, Richard Wagner, Gustav Mahler, General George Patton, Virgil, Plato, and the ancient Egyptians who believed in reincarnation long before the establishment of Buddhism and Hinduism.

I weighed for a while what I had read. I tried, as always, without succeeding, to understand how people were able to girdle themselves with "beliefs" which were based upon little more than "faith" which was based circularly upon "beliefs" unsupported by any compelling remembered personal experience. Having never experienced either, try as I might, I was not able to understand how one could manage to *believe* in heaven or hell, either, as an eventual destination, or as an unending postlife condition. Thus, while I did not believe in reincarnation, with equal conviction I did not *not* believe in reincarnation. And I was not, in the least, uncomfortable about not knowing things that were inherently *un*knowable. Nor would I have believed the stories of people who were said to have testified to having remembered past lives any more than I believed that Oral Roberts was really healing people on television in Tulsa, Oklahoma.

But I *believed* my grandmother.

What's more, I *knew* that she had described to me things she could not have learned or known about within the very real mortal small realm of her life as a blind hand laundress living on Duvall Street in Richmond, Virginia.

She *knew* things about the heavens well before the scientific community even suspected them. She also *knew* things that even now cannot be conventionally explained. She *knew* that the Dogon people (of whom she had never heard) knew for at least 600 years about the orbit path of an unseeable star, and the general behavior of the stars and planets of the stellar world. How could the Dogon have known these things? How could my grandmother have known about the Dogon, or what they had known about for so long before everybody else?

My grandmother believed that she learned this from her Dogon father in a life that she was living in Mali in the year 1394, 149 years before the Polish astronomer Nicolaus Copernicus hypothesized in *De revolutionibus orbium coelestium* that the earth revolved around the sun.

The jacket notes said that Dr. Harris-Fulbright had investigated (presumably through the use of face-to-face interviews and story-matching historical research) more than 1,000 claims of remembered past lives, some of which were recalled via hypnotic regression and others that were remembered in dreams. The bulk of the book was devoted to case studies of claims investigated by her and others.

One such case, for instance, was the story of Laurel Dilmen (pseudonym) who was born in Chicago during the Depression years. Under hypnosis, Dilmen claimed to remember several past lives, one of which was the life of Antonia Michaela Maria Ruiz de Prado who was born November 15, 1555 on the Caribbean island of Hispaniola. The daughter of a Spanish officer and a German mother, Antonia's travels took her from Hispaniola to Germany, from Germany to England, from England to Spain during the time of the Spanish Inquisition.

While most hypnotic regressions produce recollections of a nebulous quality, the story Antonia (Dilmen) told to her hypnotist, Dr. Linda Tarazi, in thirty-six sessions over a two-year period was replete with the names, venues, events, and dates of the most obscure small-town transpirations. For example, Antonia (Dilmen) said that from 1584 to 1588 there were two, not the usual three, inquisitors for the town of Cuenca where she lived. She went on to name the two. When Dr. Tarazi headed to Cuenca to check this in the town's Episcopal archives, she discovered that Antonia (Dilmen) had been right, as was the case with every other trivial particular she had described, some of which were confirmable only from rare books in specialized Spanish libraries.

Dr. Harris-Fulbright concluded that Antonia's (Dilmen's) story was entirely too complex and detailed for her to have fashioned it out of whole cloth. In any case, why would she have done such, even had she the time, which did not appear to be the case? Dilmen was not seeking to sell her story, nor was she seeking publicity. Dr. Tarazi, who'd spent years verifying Antonia's (Dilmen's) story, in time came to believe it, and so in turn did Dr. Harris-Fulbright who presented the case in her book along with ten others she thought stood up under rigorous investigation.

I spent an hour taking down notes about the past life claims described in the book. I decided that I would try to reach Dr. Harris-Fulbright, either through her publisher or by telephone. The library kept in the reference section of the reading room a telephone directory for every major

American city. I looked in the Los Angeles directory and found a listing for a Dr. Joyce Harris-Fulbright on Mulholland Drive.

CHAPTER FIFTEEN

The Poinciana was located on a narrow elegant side street that led downhill toward the Baltimore harbor. The name of the upscale restaurant was painted on a façade in sweeping cursive characters of gilt superimposed upon a silhouette of a stylized trunk branching beneath the orange-red crown of a tropical Poinciana tree.

The restaurant's interior was compartmentalized tastefully into curving smoky-rose velour-upholstered booths and bench seats that softened voices and provided patrons the illusion of expensive privacy. The high-back booths were spaced and positioned by teak consoles that separated the dining parties and supported the exquisite African art that rested upon them in bottom-lit acrylic display cases. The warm indirect cove lighting was enhanced by old-style brass picture lights that illuminated the wall-mounted sepia daguerreotypes of well-dressed period Jamaicans and the etched-glass hurricane candles that rested on cream tablecloths in solid brass seats.

Jeanne had made the reservation for seven o'clock. I arrived fifteen minutes early and was seated by a maître d' dressed in a well-cut tuxedo. The retreating maître d's footfalls were quieted by sculpted carpeting marked with a muted exotic pattern I guessed to be of Far Eastern origin.

I had never been in such a restaurant before and feared that I could not afford it. The place had the feel of an art lover's home, a home in which the art was but an augmentation for the owner's family, and otherwise, though beautiful, without important value. I lived in a small apartment that was completely devoid of memento and ornament. I distinctly remember being struck by the contrast between my apartment and the restaurant which felt like an understated celebration, not of the art, of course, but of the lives of those who thought it somehow important to place the art there—in the company of someone's proudly posed forebears watching down from the walls.

I thought it was an arrestingly beautiful room—even as it awoke in me a feeling of mild despondency.

I saw Jeanne, tall and regal, speak to the maître d' at his podium which was bathed by a small yellow light directed low upon a reservation book. She smiled at the man familiarly. He returned her smile and began to lead her toward my table.

She walked with the long effortless stride of unassuming grace. It was as if she possessed, along with her more obvious gifts, a certain *savoir faire* of motor skills that allowed her to execute even the smallest movements with balletic originality. The gliding vision of her in long raw silk slacks and a white raw silk long-sleeved blouse created an illusion of elegant weightlessness. It was as if her secrets, unlike mine, were not ballasted with ugly experiences: those which influence even the least important of mannerisms, the eyes within the smile, the timbre of the voice, the uninformed and reflexive estimates one makes of both the intended and accidental new acquaintance. I was badly wounded and knew it, although I'd never confessed this to a living soul. I wore the manners of education like a bandage to hide an old sore that never seemed to heal.

Though I knew I had been comparing my insides to her outsides, it seemed, still, that little had marred her while so much had marred me. We had only talked about "race" enough for me to know that the subject was important to her, that *it* had happened to her as it had to us all, and that she had not rationalized it into an infected boil of self-hate, or at least nothing outside the ordinary. She had given every outward appearance of being generally unscathed. Of course, the experience of *race* is peculiarly different for each of us. Everything in my experience instructed me to believe that the world's nonblack people viewed blacks as little more than convenient postslavery devices to be placed between themselves and the bottom of global society. Having all of her life been afforded the armament of privilege, it was not likely that Jeanne's view of the world would be as sharply dismal as mine.

But it was not important to me that we agree on such things. It was only important that we both see ourselves as living in the world of ideas and, hopefully, in neighborhoods of view, not unsustainably distant from each other's. I was reasonably confident that her development had not been hindered by the privilege that seemed to have at least half-protected her. Indeed, the greater danger was that *my* development had been hobbled by the retrograde resentment I harbored toward those who possessed the privilege I had been made to muddle through without. Alongside infatuation, I felt a measure of this resentment toward Jeanne as well.

I rose to greet her. She smiled and offered a cheek to be kissed and then the other. I sat across from her and drank her in. Looking at her made me nervous, but she seemed not to be aware of this.

I may have overreported here my speculation about how her thoughts ran on the issue of race, but this was only a measure of how large she loomed, early on, in my regard. I hadn't, before, much cared what the women I had known thought, or even, for that matter, whether they thought about anything much at all. I cared, however, very much about what Jeanne thought. I cared even when I couldn't be sure that the caring was not largely stimulated by the curve of her neck, or the sculpture of her jaw, or the wedding of her features.

"I hope I wasn't late," she said.

"No. You weren't late. I got here a few minutes early."

"Have you been here before?"

"No. Never. It's a beautiful place. Who owns it?"

"An old family friend of ours. He's Jamaican. His name is Teofolo Hinton. He's about forty. Came to the U.S. fifteen years ago after he finished a degree at Cambridge University to go to Columbia Law School."

"Where did he get those?"

"Oh, the metal-plate portraits? They're all members of his family. The Hintons have been prominent in Jamaica since the end of slavery. Teo's the only person I know with a collection of family pictures like these."

"That one looks newer."

"It's the only one that's not copper-plate." It was a picture of a tall man in cricket whites standing beside a shorter man in a suit.

"The tall man is Teo's grandfather, Hector Hinton. He was a star bowler on the national team during the 1950s. The other man is Chief Minister Manley."

"I've heard of him. But he's not prime minister yet, is he?"

"You're thinking of Michael Manley, his son. The man in the picture is Norman Manley. He left office eight years ago."

We were drinking a dry white wine and talking easily. We hadn't yet looked at our menus.

A man with a Jamaican accent approached and offered to take our order.

"What do you recommend?" I asked Jeanne.

"Do you like crab cakes?"

"Very much."

"Well, these are special."

I ordered the West Indian curried crab cake with Madras curry; Jeanne, the coriander-dusted scallops.

It developed that I had no need to draw upon my preparations and rehearsals. There was periodic quiet, not dead quiet, but quiet mutually legible as lightly charged, binding us where language would only have cluttered.

As I knew next to nothing about the arcana of international economics, we talked about topics in the mainstream, where and how we had grown up, the civil rights movement, our common interest in literature, world events, Vietnam, my deferment, her immediate future and mine.

She asked if I wished to teach and I told her no, that I thought not, but that I wanted very much to try writing, to which she said, well give it a go, for regret is the saddest and most pathetic of all emotions, and then I knew that I knew her as well as anyone could know anyone in an hour.

"I'm trying to write something now."

"Your thesis on black poets?"

"No, something else."

"What about?"

"Have you ever heard the name Makeda?"

"Yes. It's an African name, isn't it? It's pretty. I like it. Why did you ask?"

Stumbling a bit, "I'm not sure. I . . ."

For the first time in my life, I wanted very much to tell someone about my grandmother, the über-remarkable channeler I loved more than anyone on Earth. All at once, with an all but irresistible urgency, it seemed important that I tell Jeanne about my grandmother and her Dogon pre-Columbian knowledge of the heavens. But my grandmother had asked me to tell no one for fear that she would be held up to public ridicule. After all, who would believe, in the prevailing social climate of America, that Africans had understood such things centuries before the invention of the telescope? Before Copernicus and his heliocentric model of the solar system? And, further, since my offer of proof would amount to nothing more than a dream had by a colored, blind laundress living in Richmond, Virginia, who would believe Grandma's story?

No. Grandma was right. Still, it seemed unfair.

Why shouldn't people believe her?

All they needed to do was ask the Dogon themselves.

The Dogon must have had some way of proving just when they'd come by this extraordinary knowledge of theirs. More proof, I would have wagered, than William Shakespeare could have massed to prove he had written the anonymously published plays credited to him—plays that were set in countries across a continental Europe of the sixteenth century that had never once been visited by Shakespeare, whose mother, father, and daughter were illiterate. The man reputed to be the greatest English-language writer of all time had possessed no library, willed no books, and lived virtually all of his life in Stratford, a provincial English town that was blessed with no literary culture to speak of. Where, possibly, could he have learned the craft of language and writing? No one knows.

Yet the entire Western world believed Shakespeare had written plays the extant evidence suggests he could not possibly, or at the very least likely, have written.

"Please don't tell Jeanne or anyone else about this, Gray," my grandmother had said to me from Ms. Grier's telephone just the night before. "The lady will think both of us are crazy. I would too, hearing something like this from someone else. You know how the world works, son."

I thought of my grandmother, looked at Jeanne, and retreated. I said to her, "Let me tell you in a month or so. I'm afraid talking about it out loud will scare me off course—that externalizing my idea will make it seem absurd, even to me."

She said, "I know exactly what you mean." And I thought, foolishly then and there, that I loved her.

I needed to tell her things and thought that I could. Without preamble, as if I had started speaking in the middle of a thought, I said, "I don't want to be a journalist. I want to write what I feel and think."

"Well, even journalists do that." She said this with lightly inflected irony.

"They're not supposed to."

"True enough, Gray, but how can they not? Yes? Nothing's objective after it's interpreted."

"I suppose." I felt good—well, nearly giddy, to tell the truth—looking at her in the small restful light of the restaurant. She peered very directly at me when I spoke, her eyes smiling a *knowing* that bore no relation to what we were saying with words that floated nervous and disembodied in the space between us. I turned away from her eyes in a half-hearted ineffectual effort to gain control over my thoughts. I could no longer hear the muffled tinkle of cutlery, the low weave of conversation from the neighboring tables. I could feel the gathering surf of pulse in my ears. I heard myself then making a speech about writing. It was likely intended for the most part to keep her eyes trained on me.

". . . But that's the hard part for me, you see? Because I live *inside* the feeling, and know it only because it is mine uniquely, I can never know that I am describing the real emotional color of it in words. I can think that I am doing this and fail badly. The writer is blind to himself. He can see the interior of his feelings, but cannot possibly see whether he is describing them to you with the emotional weight he feels and bears. As I cannot see myself from the outside, I cannot see what I write. It leaves me feeling insecure. Richard Wright called writing 'the sweet agony of uncertainty.'"

She continued to look at me for a long moment. Then she spoke, I thought, to demonstrate that she had been listening. "It's a bit scary, I know," she said, "when you write, you speak because you need to, but into empty space." *I must be natural. If I try to be clever, she will see through it. Easy. Natural. Stop screwing the top off the pepper shaker. Easy.* "It is a world that all artists brave, fearing rejection." *She looks so penetratingly at me when she speaks that mind I see turning behind those intelligent dark eyes. Try and not look away, boy. Hold it.* "But the moment a reader is engaged by your interpretation of things, your insecurities will lighten a bit." *I must stop looking at her like this or she'll think I'm the village idiot.* "You're a sensitive man . . ." *You're a sensitive man. You're a sensitive man.* ". . . and that is good . . ." *That is good.* ". . . so you will always have artistic insecurities. Or at least I hope so."

We ordered from the menu an ice cream confection called Pineapple Charlotte and talked more about our personal histories.

"My mother went to college in Paris at the Sorbonne. She began her writing career there and came to New York in 1941 to mount her first American production. She met my father in New York where he was studying medicine at NYU. I was born in New York. We moved to Chicago when I was three. My younger sister, Maryse, was born in Chicago. Now what about you? You grew up in the South, right?"

"Yes," I said, somewhat uncomfortably. She looked at me questioningly. "My father is an insurance salesman and my mother does not work." The words crowded out artlessly. "I guess my grandmother, my father's mother, is the person I'm closest to." I stopped there, abruptly it may have seemed. She peered at me as if she hadn't known what to say then. I flushed, I hoped, imperceptibly.

"Brothers? Sisters?" she asked.

"No," this said with a short edge that was unintended.

The distance between us lengthened. I felt a small stab of panic. I had not acknowledged as much, but I was lonely. Not alone, but needful of something she had in a short time made painfully apparent.

Her eyes signaled a small withdrawal. "Is something wrong, Gray?"

As she asked this, a man approached. He was clean-shaven and handsome with a neat salt-and-pepper Afro and skin the color of milk chocolate.

"Jeanne, dear, it's wonderful to see you." He smiled and held her slender hand in both of his.

"Hello, Teo. How have you been?"

"Never better. How are your parents? Your sister?" He spoke in the mellifluous song of upper-class Jamaicans.

"Everyone's fine, Teo. I want you to meet my friend Graylon March."

He clenched my hand firmly and smiled. "It's very nice to meet you, Mr. March. Welcome to the Poinciana. I hope everything has been to your liking."

I told him truthfully that everything had been wonder-ful—the food, the look of the place, the copper-plate fam-ily portraits, the music. Unobtrusively, in the background, Bob Marley sang his "Natural Mystic." I was grateful for Teo's intervention.

"Well, I won't disturb you further. Jeanne, please give your family my regards and come again soon."

He left us. We looked at each other. Settled back now

into our separate evaluations, sipping the Drambuie that warmed through us, calming the small unbidden apprehensions, finishing smoothly the occasion. Nice. Unclear. But still nice.

One of the things I liked most about her was that she was not one of those stupidly self-important mysterious types that hid themselves, either in some ludicrous effort to effect—what is it that it looks like?—some sort of tactical defensive bulwark, or to camouflage a deeper, more impressive shallowness. (Might this have been, however, how she could altogether reasonably have seen *me*?)

She did not leave things where they had left off. Helpfully, she reached across the unexplored social space between us and offered a small caring smile. "Families, Gray. Remind me someday to tell you stories about the Burgesses and Cesaires."

Reprieved.

"Thank you for a lovely evening. Call me tomorrow?"

"Yes."

I walked her to her car, a six-year-old Peugeot, surprisingly. We embraced lightly, tentatively. In the damp chill of the March night, I took in for the briefest instant the sweet special scent of her. And then the sensation ended, gone on the flutter of a dancing breeze.

CHAPTER SIXTEEN

Hello." It was the cultivated voice of a professional lecturer.

"My name is Graylon March. I'm calling from Morgan State University in Baltimore, Maryland. I am trying to reach Dr. Joyce Harris-Fulbright."

"Speaking." The voice sharp, curt, with a question in it.

"I read your book *Reincarnation* and found it fascinating—"

"Mr. . . . Pardon me, what did you say your name was?"

"March, Graylon March."

"Well, Mr. March, I really don't—"

"Please, Dr. Harris-Fulbright. I won't take much of your time, but my grandmother remembers a past life that is every bit as unbelievable as the life of Antonia—I'm sorry, I can't remember her full name."

"Antonia Michaela Maria Ruiz de Prado."

"Yes, well, my grandmother remembers a past life every bit as unbelievable as hers."

"Maybe, Mr. March, that is because your grandmother's story *is* unbelievable." This said resignedly, not rudely.

Still, although I knew that she did not know me and had no reason to believe anything that I was saying, I was becoming annoyed.

"Dr. Harris-Fulbright, please—" I drew in a long calming breath. "I can prove beyond a shadow of doubt that ten years ago, my grandmother dreamed about the existence of a star, invisible to the naked eye—its orbit, its weight,

its constituent materials—that only a month ago was con-
firmed by scientists to exist, at all." This wasn't quite the
truth, but I had to win her full respectful attention before
broaching the Dogon dream story that would fly in the
seedpod face of every Western prejudice about Africa that
she had ever been caused to inhale.

She said nothing for what seemed a long while. Then I
heard her breathe out in a labored push.

"Okay, Mr. March, you have my ear. Tell me what happened to your grandmother."

I told her about my grandmother's dream of being a
Dogon teenager in the year 1394. I told her my grandmother's father's name in the dream and what the old priest had
told her in the shady cliff-side courtyard that day about
the little star Po Tolo, as well as the path and period of
its orbit around the large bluish star in the low northern
sky.

"My grandmother told this to me ten years ago. This
was before the Western scientific community knew that
the little star existed. My grandmother is completely
blind, professor, yet she traced on paper the orbit path of
Po Tolo which she remembered from the map her father
had shown her in the dream. The drawing she made for
me ten years ago matches almost exactly the recent photograph made by Western astronomers that was shown on
the national news a month ago. Dr. Harris-Fulbright, my
grandmother has never been outside the state of Virginia.
She is a retired hand laundress who never reached high
school. She is blind. I have the map she drew and the notes
I took that day when I was fifteen. There must be a way
to forensically verify that the map and notes were made
ten years ago. Now, Dr. Harris-Fulbright, how possibly
could my grandmother have known these things had she
not dreamed them? I know this must sound like a lot to

take in at one time, but can you offer a plausible alternative explanation?"

Dr. Harris-Fulbright said nothing. I could hear her breathing. I waited six or seven seconds.

"Doctor . . ."

"Y-yes, well—I'm not sure what to say, Mr. March. Before your call, you see, I'd never even heard the word Doogon be—"

"Dogon."

"Pardon?"

"Dogon. The people are called Dogon."

"Yes, I see—"

"That's just my point, Dr. Harris-Fulbright. How likely is it that my grandmother, a retired blind laundress, could have even known of the Dogon people and precisely where they have lived in Mali, West Africa since the fourteenth century?"

"I think I see your point, Mr. March."

I looked around my tiny sitting room and was glad that Dr. Harris-Fulbright could not see it. The walls were an oil-based institutional gray and completely bare, save for the clean-paint rectangles where a previous tenant's pictures had once hung. The furniture had been thoughtlessly cobbled together from the distress auctions of departing graduate students. The threadbare divan listed leftward, signaling that I would likely be its last owner. Books and papers, aligned in neat rows, covered every flat surface in the apartment's three rooms. There were no personal effects, save the toiletries in the bathroom.

"What is it that you want of me, Mr. March?"

I hesitated. "I guess I hadn't thought it through. I read your book yesterday in one sitting. I wanted to get your reaction as soon as I could get you on the phone."

"Mr. March."

"Yes."

She started to speak, then stopped and took a measure of time to think. When she started again, she spoke more slowly than she had before, as if she were calculating in her head how she would meter her forward involvement. She had looked to be in her mid-fifties at the time that the picture was taken for the back flap of her book. She was a white woman with piercing cerebral blue eyes and long wiry gray hair in a high state of scholarly misrule. It was the picture of a woman who had little interest in adornment. She spoke much as she had looked in the picture. Without waste or varnish.

"Mr. March, if you have reported accurately on this star's recent discovery, and on your grandmother's description of it in her ten-year-old dream, your story would warrant further investigation. Most of the stories I come across, however, are found to be without merit. Yours, or rather your grandmother's, is, on its face, quite interesting."

Hers was the professional scholar's maddening habit of emotionless understatement. A near idiom unto itself.

"Here is how I propose we proceed, Mr. March. Give me a week to do some reading. There are things I would like to check out."

"Understood," I said with relief. I tried not to sound happy.

"If you give me your number, I will call you next Monday at eight p.m. your time and tell you what I think."

I gave her my number and agreed on the time of her call.

"Before we go, I have a couple of questions."

"Go ahead," I said.

"Please spell D-dogon for me."

I spelled it for her.

"And now, Mali." I did this. "You said *West* Africa, right?"

"Yes."

"And Po Tolo . . . Now, one last question—" I waited. "Is your grandmother black?"

"What, Dr. Harris-Fulbright, does that have to do with anything?" I asked wearily.

She spoke even more carefully then. "It happens that in virtually all authentically regressed past lives, the re-membered past life is of the same race as that of the living person being regressed."

"I see." Hackles quieting back into place. "The answer is yes, my grandmother is black."

"Mr. March, may I ask what your field is?"

"I will receive a master's in English in May."

"And what do you plan to do then?"

"I plan to write."

"I see."

I suddenly felt that I may have been rashly naïve and lacking a safe course forward.

CHAPTER SEVENTEEN

I spent the afternoon and evening at the little desk in the library stacks. On the way in, I had passed the young woman who had brought me the two books on reincarnation.

"I found another book for you," she said, and handed me the book while affording me a smile that, given my recent deportment, I didn't deserve.

"Thank you," I responded, and headed to the stacks where I planned to work on my thesis before opening the book that the young woman had given me. This would require a measure of discipline. The business of the dream and what I'd already begun to map out in the way of a literary piece based on it was claiming more and more of my time as my thesis deadline rushed toward me.

It was a thin volume, more a précis of sorts, as it turned out, than a book.

Two eminent French anthropologists, Marcel Griaule and Germaine Dieterlen, had written it eight years after my grandmother had her Dogon dream. The writers had traveled to Mali several times over a four-year period to study "the cosmological theories of the Dogon." Among the Dogon authorities they spoke with were a seventy-year-old *ammayana* (priestess of the Amma religion), a sixty-five-year-old patriarch, and two forty-five to fifty-year-old priests.

I used a yellow highlighter to underscore sections of the brief report in which Griaule and Dieterlen took care to quote the Dogon authorities directly.

The star (Po Tolo) which is considered to be the smallest thing in the sky is also the heaviest: "Digitaria (Po Tolo) is the smallest thing there is. It is the heaviest star." It consists of a metal called sagala which is a little brighter than iron and so heavy "that all earthly beings combined cannot lift it."

The four Dogon authorities described to the French anthropologists a third star in what is now known to the West as the Sirius System. They told Griaule and Dieterlen that relative to Po Tolo, the third star, Emme Ya, was:

Four times as light (in weight) and travels along a greater trajectory in the same direction and in the same time as it (fifty years). Their respective positions are such that the angle of their radii is at right angles.

Griaule and Dieterlen were shown a drawing by the Dogon of Jupiter and its moons:

This figure represents the planet—the circle—surrounded by its four satellites in the collateral directions and called Dana Tolo Unum, "Children of Dana Tolo" (Jupiter).

With respect to the planet Saturn, a Dogon drawing showed Saturn's halo, or ring, which can only be seen from Earth through a telescope.

The paper went on to establish that the Dogon had a vast knowledge of the cosmos for thousands of years, and that this knowledge held for the Dogon a great religious significance.

Every sixty years, the Dogon hold a ceremony called the Sigui (ceremony). Its purpose is the renovation of the world . . .

Since the beginning of this investigation, we were faced with the question of determining the method used to calculate the period separating two Sigui ceremonies. The common notion, which dates to the myth of creation, is that a fault in Yougo rock, situated at the center of the village of Yougo Dogorou, lights up with a red glow in the year preceding the ceremony . . .

I was tired and having difficulty concentrating on the section of the four-page writing that focused purely on the arcane religious beliefs of the Dogon for which I was equipped with no cultural frame of reference. The sections, however, that documented the Dogon's long mastery of the science of the cosmos were clear enough to me; even in the sleep-deprived state from which I had fruitlessly sought relief weeks ago from a doctor at the Johns Hopkins Sleep Disorders Center.

It was half past nine and growing late. I had promised Jeanne that I would call that day. Packing up my materials while reflecting upon what I had just read, I remembered a question that the author Robert K.G. Temple had raised in his new book from St. Martin's Press, *The Sirius Mystery*: "How did the Dogon know such extraordinary things and did it mean that the Earth had been visited by extraterrestrials?" To Temple, even the far-fetched infinitesimal possibility of an extraterrestrial visit to the Dogon was more likely than any notion that the Dogon people, 700 years in residence beneath Mali's Bandiagara escarpment, had developed a comprehensive knowledge of the existence and working of an interplanetary universe well in advance of the Western white world.

Then, of course, there was the further question of how my blind grandmother had come to know these things, again, well before the white scientists had made their "discoveries."

I only hoped that Dr. Harris-Fulbright, who understood more than conventional scientists did about the existence of alternative realms of knowledge, would be more successful than Robert K.G. Temple had been in overcoming what I saw to be the convenient impediment of unconscious prejudice.

The telephone rang for the second time that evening, startling me. I sat up, rested my hand on the receiver, and took a deep breath.

It was Jeanne.

"You promised to call." Said lightly. Sure of herself.

"I was just about to when my cousin called." I considered saying more but elected not to.

"Caught you at a bad time?"

"No, not at all. I can't tell you how good it is to hear your voice."

"What's your day like tomorrow?"

"Well, I have to listen to my poets in the morning. The deadline looms near." I sounded glib and was not proud of myself. She seemed to intuit that I was hiding something.

"Then let's spend the afternoon together. It's supposed to be warm and sunny. How about it?"

"That's the best idea I've heard since last night, which, by the way, was the best evening I've had in a long time."

"Tomorrow then. Pick me up?"

"Of course. Two o'clock?"

"Yes. À bientôt." And she was gone.

It occurred to me later that Jeanne had guessed that I was a poor graduate student whose furthered education was made possible by loans, grants, and a small work-study wage. I don't know how she came to know this, but I was sure she had learned, before our afternoon together, roughly what my financial circumstances were. This would have been easy enough for her to infer from the look of alarm on my face when I was presented with the check at the Poinciana. I suspected then that she had seen this and not known quite what to do, before finally deciding that it would only have made matters worse to try and help me.

I have been told by people close to me that my face remains impassive when I am feeling emotions like fear and anger. (I am not sure, however, how I look when merely alarmed, as opposed to being mortally frightened.) Thus, it may have been that she read nothing from my face when I learned that the check exceeded fifty dollars. All I know is that she knew I was all but penniless. After all, I had told her during dinner what my father, the sole March family breadwinner, did for a living.

I am certain it was for these reasons that she suggested we spend the afternoon "taking advantage of the glorious sunshine."

We drove downtown and walked to the water and along the quay. Afterward, we spent two hours in a public park, biding the afternoon hours, walking, sitting, talking—talking easily about a range of things, serious and frivolous.

I often found myself looking long at her when she could not see me doing so. I remember doing this as she was talking very smartly, I thought, about the relative merits of communism and capitalism for common people. "You know, Gray, no economic system, created by humans, can effectively rein in greed."

We talked about this for a while (as if it mattered what we talked about) before meandering into art, followed by the music of James Brown, the various foods we liked (Chinese, Indian, Caribbean, soul), religion (ritual Christians, but spiritual in the main), table games (we agreed they were crutches for the socially challenged), cross-cultural relationships (which we self-servingly thought could be made to work), sports (she pretended interest, I disinterest, both done feebly), smoking (the most repellent of personal habits), and, as it grew dark, Lorraine Hansberry (whose play-based movie *A Raisin in the Sun* we would see later that night at a small downtown art cinema).

She moved across subjects, large and piddling, with intelligent ease and without the hard leaden judgments usually born nonbiodegradable of incurious minds, sharp only to decide the inherently undecidable. I thought as I regarded her that her parents must have kissed her spirit often and unconditionally when she was very young; formed her, loved her to walk effortlessly in the smooth cocoa-brown skin she wore like the confidence that seemed for her an innate gift.

Whatever it was that she exuded was to a degree transferable. I felt better when I was around her. It was as if the war of negative mutually destructive reflex behaviors that had doomed the only serious relationship I'd had would not visit this one. Jeanne was *whole* with no need to reduce or excavate those who happened into her magnetic field.

I was wary, however, owing to a painful relationship I had endured with a decent respectable girl from Milwaukee, Wisconsin, named Derma Innis. Derma, a classmate at Morgan, was a big, gorgeous athletic type who did not relish a life in the world of ideas, and only viewed her disinterest in such as *incompleteness* upon coming into sustained contact with me, whom she claimed to love, but actually resented greatly for reminding her by example of what she was not. She required being rock certain about any number of things and people. To stay on top of this formidable responsibility, she dispensed with large groups of things and people with wild categorical verdicts, starting most of her sentences with *They are*, *Men are*, *Women are*, *Blacks are*, *Whites are*, and, finally, inevitably, *You are*.

She had once told me: "I bet you think you're smart enough to be the president of the United States," which was true enough, and a self-assessment I had counted as an important personal asset. She hated this sort of thing in me for reasons that made us, as a couple, a good deal less than the sum of our two quite different and fundamentally incompatible parts.

I was, for her, the funhouse mirror that I had not wished to be, and that which she hated, because its reflection of her distorted large her failings. Over time her affections became more and more extractive, demanding. But I had no expendable part of me available for sacrifice to her needs. I was in trouble all by myself and had been for years.

For me, there is nothing in the world more beautiful in a woman than an insatiably curious intellect accompanied by an elegant self-possession. Not only is the possessor of such traits worthy of admiration, but the gifted soul is also more fully free to return affection without compromising important interior defenses.

This is how I saw Jeanne. She was *free*. And without so much as trying. She was pretty, of course, and this, I confess, counted for something—well, a great deal in fact. But her physical appearance would have meant little to me had she not had the other qualities that were essential to sustaining one's interest.

By the time we reached the park in the mid-afternoon of April 3, 1970, the temperature had soared to an unseasonable eighty-two degrees. The buds on the giant oak trees had cracked but not yet opened. The sun, finding its strength, bore down with no relief to be found beneath the trees' naked boughs. We sat on a bench atop a knoll overlooking a small placid pond of gliding ducks quacking lazily as if they too had registered the dramatic change in weather. I wore a cotton windbreaker, and Jeanne a fashionable mauve sweatshirt that she took off and draped over the shoulders and back of her short-sleeved sport blouse. I threw my windbreaker across the back of the bench. We were quiet, watching the park's peace. Our upper arms came close to touching, and then slowly, searchingly drew themselves very lightly together in a way that stoked my nervous system and evacuated a thought I could not thereafter reconstruct. Our arms stayed together like that, unremarked, as if they had achieved safe docking from a perilous sea voyage.

I experienced then an emotion that was almost entirely foreign to me. It brought with it a surge of euphoria so intense that I became mildly dizzy, and may have been dumbstruck as well, had I, at the sensation's apex, attempted to speak. I knew, in that extrasensory way that one knows such things that Jeanne was feeling much the same. The outward indications of this were such that neither of us uttered so much as a word, or moved, even slightly, or looked away from the little pond that now held for us some great and enormous sentimental significance because it was what we were watching when our unclad arms touched for the first time.

In a nervously awkward motion, I moved the arm that had touched hers across the top of the slated bench. Looking still toward the lake, she nestled back into the cup of my shoulder. I rested my cheek against the soft, sculpted crown of her natural, unspoiled hair.

We stayed like this for an indeterminate time, speaking finally as if we had been transiting the same thought, however improbable that may have been.

"I want to go to Mali this summer," I said quietly.

She did not appear surprised or ask for an explanation. "Do you speak French?" she asked.

"Not a word."

"Well, then you'll need someone to translate for you, won't you?"

We looked at each other. Then we smiled and kissed. I had been shy about such displays for the whole of my life. This was the first time that I had ever kissed anyone in public.

It seemed the most natural thing.

CHAPTER EIGHTEEN

D r. Harris-Fulbright called me on Monday night at eight o'clock as she had said she would. She came swiftly to the point.

"Mr. March, have you talked to anyone else about your grandmother's dream?"

"No," I said.

"Has your grandmother talked to anyone about this besides you?"

"No."

"You're sure of that?"

"I'm positive."

"Good. Good."

"Why do you ask?"

"Well, until we can investigate this, we should keep it under wraps."

We? Investigate?

She seemed to sense nothing of the small dead space between us. No ear apparently for the language of silence.

"Has your grandmother had any other dreams of past lives like the one you described to me?"

I did not know quite what to say or do. I did not know how to advance my curiosity about my grandmother's experience, or whether I could do it at all without the help of someone like Dr. Harris-Fulbright. I was not even sure about why I hadn't been willing to let the whole matter drop, which, I'm sure, would have suited my grandmother well enough.

"Yes, two that she mentioned, one a few years ago, and another recently that she said she would tell me about when I got down to see her next."

"And when will that be?"

"Dr. Harris-Fulbright, I think we should back up for a minute."

"Yes?" Brusque. I decided that I wasn't going to like her, knowing that this would neither matter very much to her nor deter me.

"What is it that you have in mind? I think you should tell me now before asking any more questions."

"I am going to Washington for a meeting in June. I would like to make a day trip down to Richmond to meet your grandmother after I finish my business in Washington. Can you work that out for me?"

"I don't know. What would you talk to her about?" This sounded, I know, quite stupid and hadn't been at all what I wanted to say.

"Well," she said, pausing, "I wonder if your grandmother would allow herself to be hypnotized. Regressed?" It sounded less a question than a pro forma declaration. "It's the only way we can get to the bottom of this."

"W-well, I—"

"It's painless and won't take much of her time."

"That's not the—"

"You can be there, of course."

I wanted to be done with the conversation. I needed to regroup. I needed time to think.

"I'll talk to my grandmother about it when I see her two weeks from now."

"Good enough." Clipped. Dismissive. Suddenly so, as if the whole matter had fallen in importance to her. "Call me after you've spoken with her."

She hung up.

* * *

During the two weeks before I left Baltimore to spend a weekend with my grandmother in Richmond, Jeanne and I talked, either by telephone or face-to-face, every day. We were fast becoming all but inseparable, with the new habit of her presence in my life affording me a sense of growing well being. We would meet either at her office downtown at Johns Hopkins or at Morgan's library which was not far from her apartment complex in North Baltimore. On most evenings we carried out our dinner from Mr. Pei's Chinese or Negril's Jamaican or Tandoori Star's Indian restaurant. Twice we brought pizza home to the one-bedroom apartment she shared with the books that lined the walls and stranded her overmatched furniture in the middle of the apartment's three large rooms. She had a far-ranging music collection, a quarter of which comprised tapes of Haitian music for which I had small familiarity, but a surprising and immediate appreciation of the music's tonal idiom in which Africa, Brazil, and the Caribbean could easily be heard.

We kissed. We caressed. We played. We were silly one minute and serious the next. We talked about large global issues and small local ones. We went places, making spur-of-the-moment decisions: museums, bookstores, movies, a party, a walk. She even went with me to the funeral of the mother of a local college friend. I had confided to Jeanne how much I hated funerals, particularly those in which the families left the coffins open until the service began. I did not like looking at the dead bodies of people I had known. They seemed smaller than they had in life, shrunken, as if their departing souls had taken with them large sums of their former bodies' volume.

Things like this, things that I had never told anyone else, I told Jeanne. I loved her and thought she felt similarly. We had not, however, spoken the words. And we had not yet slept together. I had also not spoken to her of my demons.

Later that evening, while listening to a thirty-year-old recording of the composer-pianist and grand figure of Haitian classical music, Ludovic Lamothe, Jeanne filled in the spaces in her Haitian family's story, but said little of her American father's history. I assumed this was because there was less drama surrounding it. Her mother's parents, Giselle and Montas Cesaire, had come from Jacmel, a 300-year-old city on the south coast of Haiti. They had been born there poor. They were both black and, thus, not heirs to the privileges of mixed-race Haitians under the society's color caste system.

Though noted for his gifts as a painter, Montas Cesaire narrowly escaped death twice, once in 1916 during the American military occupation that claimed 15,000 Haitian lives, and again in 1937 when the Dominican dictator Rafael Trujillo invaded and massacred 35,000 Haitians. In 1916, an American Marine shot Cesaire once in his chest and twice in his right leg. In 1937, two of Trujillo's killers came within two feet of Cesaire who had taken refuge amongst the sharp clicking reeds of a sugarcane field. His two younger brothers and a nephew had been shot dead in the attacks.

Three generations of Cesaires believed to varying degrees that America had been hostile to Haiti, unrelentingly and for so long, because of Toussaint L'Ouverture's unprecedented humiliation of the slaveholding white world, that Americans believed only in white freedom, not in black freedom.

Montas Cesaire, in any case, made enough money from his paintings to send his gifted daughter Marie away to study writing and drama in Paris in the 1930s; after which she had come to the United States and met Jeanne's father, Dennis Burgess, in New York.

Driving home from Jeanne's apartment in the noisy old Corvair I had bought for $650 from a departing graduate student, I reflected upon how little I had volunteered to Jeanne about myself. Indeed, I had shared almost nothing she couldn't have learned from a public registry. She had not pried into why I'd been so close-mouthed. She had, however, on more than one occasion, looked at me worriedly, as if she liked well enough what she saw of me, but that the well-hidden parts concerned her. This entirely reasonable sentiment never caused her to ration her own disclosures about herself, her family, her view onto the world, or as you might well have come to expect, her defining *Haitianness*, which appeared to decant from its deep storied well a life-force energy of its own. She seemed, though, very much frustrated by this *gift*, as anyone would have been, I suppose, who owned, as she saw it, a rare, priceless treasure that had been viciously maligned by a smarting West and buried nearly 200 years beneath the smothering mass of an elaborately mistold account. She was laden with a wonderful, heavy, liberating truth that she could share in America with neither whites nor blacks. For it was the white world that had made her mute, and, in the same stroke, rendered the non-Haitian black world deaf. All of which had caused me to believe that she spoke out of an obsession which was uncharacteristic for one who was otherwise so levelheaded and patently intelligent.

She had said to me, mildly irritating me, "Gray, the Haitian Revolution is acknowledged by many respected historians to have been of greater hemispheric and global significance than the American Revolution. The world must be made to accept what these scholars have conceded." She had faltered slightly then before adding, "But it is very important to me that you believe this. First as a black man, but more importantly as the man I have begun to love."

None of what she said, including this last, did I return with any investment of emotion to match hers. She had to have wondered if her instincts about me had been wrong. Or maybe it was I who believed that this was the case. The truth is that I had always been slightly uncomfortable around people who deeply believed in anything. At least anyone save my grandmother and her dreams.

CHAPTER NINETEEN

Mindful of the young consumer advocate Ralph Nader's warning that the little biscuit-shaped rear-engine Corvair was "unsafe at any speed," I puttered south from Baltimore along Interstate 95 at a tortoise clip of fifty miles per hour. The trip to Richmond that would take an able car roughly three hours would require of mine a minimum of four.

I left my apartment at five on Saturday morning. It was dark when I crawled onto the interstate access ramp. Beside me on the passenger seat was the leather briefcase I had packed with my writing materials and a softcover copy of Dr. Harris-Fulbright's book. I had also brought with me an overnight bag. My plan was to drive directly home on Sunday morning after chauffeuring my grandmother to church.

I had written her to expect me between nine and ten. The sun peeked above the eastern horizon just as I exited the Washington-area beltway and headed south along the 100-mile leg to Richmond.

I had always liked driving alone on the highway in the dim early-morning quiet. It gave occasion to a rare real privacy, unthreatened by interruption, where one squandered time with no tax of guilt and mulled things carelessly in forgettable pieces of dissociated fleeting images.

I had not been to Richmond since I last saw my grandmother some months back.

I spent most of the long drive thinking about Grandma.

Makeda had always struck me as a hauntingly beautiful name. I knew that Grandma's mother had given it to her, and that she had never explained to her why, or from where she had gotten it. I don't think Grandma was being mysterious about this, either, though a lot about her may have seemed so. But it's not that she was trying to be mysterious or anything like that. It's just the way she was.

I believed that I knew her better than anyone did, but it's like I really *didn't* know her. But . . . well, it's hard to describe. It's like she was one person and several people at the same time. As if she was in places I couldn't be in, and so I couldn't understand much of what was going on inside her.

It did not help that I'm a literal sort of person, and not really religious. Daddy's not religious either. Mama claims to be, and she'd deny it, but I believe she's just pretending to be religious because she thinks that being religious, and believing she's believing in it, is how she is supposed to be. It was different with Grandma. She wouldn't talk about it much, but she believed the stuff. Yet that's not even quite it. She, I think, *is* the stuff.

I think maybe she was much like everybody else before she had the second dream, the Dogon dream (or was the Dogon dream the third dream now that I've learned from her of her twelfth-century life in Lalibela? No, I was just a little boy then, she said, so this must have come after the Dogon dream), which would probably make anybody religious—*spiritual* might be a better word for it—including me, maybe. I did not really know her before she had the dream, so I don't know how she was before that, but you'd think something like that would change anybody, wouldn't you? Maybe even me, after I saw what I saw on the news. Jesus! How can you explain something like that?

And there were those things Grandma wouldn't even

talk to me about. Like this business with Thursday being a day of rest. It's not that she was trying to hide anything. But this Thursday thing seemed to come from one of those places where no one else could go but her. The other thing was that big symbol with the clustered loops on the wall. I think she knew what it meant and would tell me if she could but she couldn't because there was a language for it in some other place that she had lived but not in the place where she and I lived together now. This sounds, I think, looney. Looney. Yes. Whatever the symbol meant, it went deep to her core. I thought it must have had something to do with religion because after the last two dreams, I had seen a change in Grandma.

I thought it must mean something that all three of the dreams that I knew about were from lives she had lived in West Africa. I thought this must have something to do with that symbol and some other things she did as well—like the Thursday thing.

I knew I'd read in the book that Grandma gave me when I left for Morgan—Professor Opoku's book—that West Africans, since before the time of Christ, generally believed in the immortality of the soul—I mean, really believed in it. I got the impression—and this may have caused the change in Grandma—that while Americans sort of visited their religion, Africans back then *lived* their religion. For the Africans—or the West Africans, at least—religion wasn't something you just observed, as if you existed outside of it. It was something you wore, as you would wear your own skin, without which you would not be able to get along in the world.

I think the three dreams may have deepened Grandma's faith—well, not so much her faith, but her scope of *knowledge.* I think she would still call herself a Christian, all right—she had been one in Lalibela—but she was these other people at the same time, people whose religious beliefs were different from those of the grandmother whose corporeal existence I shared.

In some ways, her religious beliefs from her earlier lives were compatible with her Sunday-morning Christian church worship. But in other ways, they seemed diametrically opposed to one another.

It seemed to me that where they were opposed, the contrasting beliefs very much mirrored the contrasting cultures that encompassed them. For instance, in America, *success* in life is to be found *up*, as in above, somewhere, just as heaven in the Christian afterlife is described as being *up* somewhere. Grandma may have truly believed there was such a place—that heaven was not only *up* there, but it was reserved for the Christian select. With the exception of Lalibela, in Grandma's three previous African lives, she had believed something altogether different. Her ancestors hadn't left in death to go *up* anywhere. From the spirit world, they had remained very much a functioning part of their families. They were all around her—in the earth, amongst the trees, on the wind. This just might explain why two African friends of mine at Morgan always seemed, to me, obsessed with doing favors for numberless relatives, immediate and distant. Grandma, since the dreams started, had changed her thinking, I believe in this direction, and people who knew her—especially people at the church—thought this was strange. Thought maybe Grandma was some kind of radical, which she wasn't. She was just Grandma.

I suspected that she had a few dreams of past lives—like the Lalibela dream she had reluctantly shared just recently on the phone—that she still hadn't told me about—wouldn't tell me about. I didn't know why this was so, but I believed there was more to be learned from her.

* * *

I took the Chamberlayne Avenue exit into the Jackson Ward section of Richmond where my grandmother lived. Much had changed since I'd left the city for college. A discrete downtown black community could no longer be located. The major new arteries that facilitated the city's daily white flight to the hinterlands had chopped and diced the old neighborhood into a hash of forlorn tenements, walk-up flats, and storefronts.

The city's retreating trench-cutting white fathers had called this vivisection of the old neighborhood *urban renewal*, while others called it urban *removal*, which it very much was.

First African Baptist had been all but destroyed by the city's assault upon the neighborhood my grandmother had never seen. Where homes once stood in close vicinity to the church's large gray stone edifice, sprawling flat weed-blighted vacant lots now reposed in wait of a faceless white city planner's next impetuous decision. The church congregation had broken out into warring camps over the crisis, with the old stagers wanting to stay put, come hell or high water, and the younger better-heeled and better-educated members wanting to pull away and buy Big Bethel, a newer bigger building in a leafy residential neighborhood on the far north side of town. Old, weary, and spent of caring, Reverend C.C. Boynton resigned his post as pastor and was replaced by the assistant pastor, Reverend James Cross, a young firebrand who Reverend Boynton never wanted in the first place, but was forced to hire by the savvy young Turks who were hell-bent on relocating the church to a distant neighborhood the old, the poor, the infirm, and the disabled would have trouble reaching. The deacons and deaconesses boards, packed by Reverend Boynton and dominated by old stagers, drew a line in the proverbial sand and took the young Reverend Cross and the church proper to court before the young Turks could manage to empty the church treasury to buy a building that had come on the market in just the right neighborhood for just the right price. As the internecine fighting within the church family worsened beyond recovery, tarnishing virtually everyone who was willing to risk an opinion, my grandmother had stopped attending services, with my mother and father (who attended through the years only infrequently in any case) following suit. It was a royal mess that mirrored sadly the dismembered state of the old neighborhood.

Roughly equivalent to what once had been six real city blocks from the marooned First African Baptist Church building, my grandmother's walk-up white clapboard row house, oblivious to its inevitable fate, took the gold morning sun on its face as I pulled up to the curb and turned off the Corvair. The little engine juddered and died.

CHAPTER TWENTY

Makeda! Makeda! It's Graylon! Come on in here, boy. Don' ya look a hansum sight. All grown up. Ya grandma tried to hide it, but she is excited as all get out to see ya. Look at ya, willya."

I had never heard anyone call my grandmother by the unusual first name that her mother had given her. Mrs. Grier, tittering and bustling about me, drew me into the vestibule and pulled off my flannel blazer. Mrs. Grier was quite elaborately overweight. When she laughed, which was often, she jiggled, and when she walked, she waddled and wheeled her girth. "My God, Makeda, he's a sight to see, I tell ya. She's so happy ya come home, son."

"Gray. Is that you Gray?" It was my grandmother's voice—softer and weaker than I remembered it—coming from the little parlor just off the tiny vestibule.

"Yes, Grandma, it's me." I walked into the room. She was sitting in her old upholstered rocker. The little armchair I sat in to take notes when I was a boy had been placed near her by Mrs. Grier at my grandmother's direction. The remembered and forgotten room registered with me as close and overstuffed, although there was, save for the wall hanging, nothing in it that had not been there for thirty years, and maybe even longer than that.

"Come over here, Gray, and let me hug you." I felt her cheek wet against mine as I bent to embrace her. The touch of her dispelled the shaming thought I'd had, upon entering the room, about Jeanne and not wanting her to see this place I had come from.

"How was your drive?"

"Fine, Grandma, fine."

"Have you eaten?" Not waiting for an answer: "Gertrude, get Gray some of those pastries he likes—you know, the apple ones—and bring some of that Welch's I use to give him to help us clean up after communion. You know where to find everything. Of course. Of course."

"Is it okay, Grandma, if I open the drapes?" I was feeling mildly claustrophobic. The dark drapes were heavy and lined and permitted no passage of light.

"Yes, yes. Go ahead. I tend to forget whether they're open or closed."

We spoke of small gossip for a while. Catching me up, she did most of the filling in. I had moved away and little about my new life would be of interest to her. She spoke at length about the church crisis and how it had brought out the worst in everyone involved. She said that before he resigned, Reverend Boynton had lost sway over much of the congregation and without it seemed a smaller and different man. She told me of weddings and deaths and births in a host of families, some I knew, or at least knew of, and others I did not.

"Does Daddy still come by every day at noon?" The room seemed then to slow and grow smaller.

"Yes. I expect he'll be along today before too long."

"D-does he ever talk about me?"

"Sometimes. Yes, sometimes he does, but it's very hard for him to do. Would you like to stay and see him when he comes?"

I sputtered a response: "I'm sorry, Grandma, I really can't. I'll come back later and stay the night."

"Gray, you and your father are the two people I love

most in the world. The two of you will have to one day deal with this thing, face it and put it behind you."

I did not respond to this.

"Do you hear from your mother?" she asked.

"She calls me on my birthday and Christmas. I haven't seen her since I left. I haven't seen or spoken to Daddy in seven years."

"That's a sad thing, son, a sad, sad thing."

"Well, it wasn't my fault, Grandma." My voice shook and was louder than it should have been. "He doesn't know me. He doesn't know anything about me." The seldom spoken words fed upon the anger I had long stowed.

She answered mildly, "It could be that you, through no fault of your own, don't know him either."

"He never liked me, Grandma, and he never loved me."

"That's not true, Gray." I started to interrupt her and she held up her hand, palm forward. "Hold on a minute, son. I think maybe I should tell you some things about your father that you may not know."

She heard me inhale in a long draw to gain control of myself. She lowered her hand and laid it gently folded into her other hand upon her lap. Her hair, nearly white by then, was drawn back from her prominent forehead in a low bun that rested against the nape of her neck. She wore an elaborately embroidered white gown that had been selected for her by her Nigerian friend who served for years with her on the First African Baptist Church deaconess board. Although she was in her early seventies, her dark rich skin was unwrinkled and free of blemish. Her erect bearing was marked not by hauteur, but by an ineffable kindliness. When listening, she endeared with a subtle tilt of her head and ear in the direction of the speaker. She never hurried her own speech. Nor did she unnaturally slow it down in an affectation of vanity. She was, simply, what she was, and pleased enough with that, without dwelling upon it.

I was not gifted with my grandmother's remove from worry. She did not squander precious stores of energy against rocks that could not be moved. Nor was she given to puffy tautology, or to the love of her own voice or person. She did not grind away fruitlessly over what she knew would eventuate to a foreordained result that she saw with uncelebrated ease.

Unlike my grandmother, I had been *trained* to think, but only within the delimited Earth-bound space endowed naturally to me. Like the similarly privileged, I could affect with my training a certain cleverness to bedazzle those I would leave behind, but beyond the walls of my endowment, all was empty show. I worried about nonsense, I think, because I knew just enough to know how little I would ever know about the logic of human events. For instance, I could not escape the morose belief that we are born alone and will die alone, and, in the space of our quite separate awarenesses, live alone, never quite understanding what we see, what we do, or why we are doing it. Thus, we spend our lives only appearing to do something when there is no something to do but wait.

My grandmother saw the absurdity of such depressing school-house gobbledygook because she was produced of an immortality from which to know better. On the other hand, I had little choice but to accept the finite box of mortal experience as my lot. I could not hope to outlive the ugliness meted out to *us* in this world, but she could and would. I suspect that I was not unlike most contemporary black people. The world had acted upon us and we had no real workable conception of how it might be possible for us to act upon the world. Hence, I was bitter, while my grandmother, having seen better times and knowing more were to come, was serene. Living in this ageless light of hers, however, did indescribable wonders for me.

"I think you see your father to be a hard man who always wants things his own way." I gave a nod that she could not see. "He has been unfair to you and I have told him so. Deep down, I believe he knows this, but he is a weary and beat-down man who has been trapped by this life.

"You are young and the young tend to judge. They tend to judge without knowing much. When I was young I did the same. When you look at some folks, you see only what they are now, not what they once were. It's that way with your father. You've been alive for just half of his life. How's it you know what he has gone through and why he does and says the things that you see now. All you can do is *see* him. You cannot *know* him.

"You are young. You are not tired. You are not scared. And you are not ashamed of yourself *because* you are scared. A man and scared."

"What's he got to be scared of?"

She took the full meaning of what I'd asked with a measure of scorn. She sighed and said, "Oh son, oh son, please try your best to grow up a little today. In life *why* is bigger than *what*."

I decided it best to say nothing and hear her out.

"I know you thought less of him when he didn't want you and Gordon gettin' involved in the sit-ins and demonstrations. He knew how you felt. He knew you didn't respect him. And it cut him, cut him deep." She heard me turn in my chair. "Come now, Graylon, if you owe me nothin' else, you owe me, at least, a little patience. He wasn't scared for himself. He was scared for you and Gordon."

"But that's a cop out, Grandma."

"You know I hate that common street talk. It has no place in my home."

"I'm sorry, Grandma, but—"

"Did you know that at the beginning of World War II, when your father was about your age now, he went to prison for a year for refusin' to fight in the war. He told the government that he would not fight over there for segregation over here. It was why he couldn't go to college. After he got out of prison, no one would loan him money and the government wouldn't help him. Did you know that, Gray? Over 2,000 Negro men went to jail for doin' what your father did before you were born—before you ever saw him. It changed him. God knows it changed him. He thought that Negroes would love him for the stand he took, but Negroes didn't love him for it, they ran away from him, even some of the church members. They stopped speakin' to him. They stopped speakin' to me. They stopped speakin' to your mother who had just married him. That was when your father stopped goin' to church and only began to go again a little when you and Gordon were small.

"Those were terrible times back then when the country started draftin' Negroes to fight the Germans. Even as soldiers on their way to die, they were treated as second-class citizens. They got second-class trainin' and even traveled over there segregated in the second-class parts of the ships. And the men that survived came home to face lynchings in the South and segregation in the North."

She started to rock slowly while humming a vaguely spiritual melody that was tonally foreign and belonged to no American black Baptist tradition that I knew of. She closed her sightless eyes and began speaking, it seemed, largely to herself.

"Those were terrible times, terrible times. I encouraged my David to stand up to them for what was right. Your mother Alma and I did. Although he didn't need us to tell him what was right. He was strong then. Young and strong and ready to stand up for somethin'. God, did they make him pay for it. Mashed him like an ant."

She was no longer reporting events, but reliving them in razor-sharp images replete with the racking emotions that the images roiled.

"If I remember it right, the summer of '43 was when it started. There were race riots in Detroit and Texas. Negroes in Harlem smashed near to every store that white folk owned on 125th Street after a Negro soldier was shot by a white policeman. In '46, after our boys came home from fighting for America, forty-five Negroes were lynched in the South. Paul Robeson, you know, was our hero then. The man spoke all kinda languages. He was a smart lawyer from a big school up North. He could sing. He could act. A giant of a man who could run like the blazes. And boy was he good lookin'. But mainly he stood up for his people. And that's when they come after him. Called him a communist. He was never a communist. Took his passport anyhow. Ole Truman, callin' himself a friend of the 'Negro.' But it was Truman who told the border police to shoot Paul Robeson on sight if they caught him tryin' to sneak into Canada to sing in order to make a livin'. And the Negroes ran away from Robeson like they did your father. Even the NAACP that gave Robeson that medal of theirs. No sooner than the white folk come after him, did the NAACP try to hide from ever givin' Robeson that medal."

She opened her eyes, including me again. "Black soldiers and white soldiers were fightin' each other on the troop ships goin' over there. Your father said he didn't mind dyin', but not in Italy, not in Germany, not for them, not for America. And they made my David and all the rest of them pay. And when they finally let him out of prison, they made it so he would continue to pay. Well, that was bad, but the black men who refused to fight the Germans and Italians could handle that, you know. What they couldn't handle was how they were treated by their own people who treated the men who shoulda been our heroes like traitors. Your father was never the same after that. He became bitter and suspicious. Lookin' out only for his own. He wanted you and Gordon to be safe. He wanted you to have a livin' they couldn't so easily take away from you."

A large dog growled a hoarse angry threat beneath the window my grandmother sat near. Her body convulsed in a sudden violent tremor. I rested my hand on her shoulder and looked through the glass.

"It's okay, Grandma. It ran down the hill by the Fountains' house. It's gone."

She trembled in lengthening waves. A line of tiny perspiration beads arced out across her brow. She breathed rapidly in short nervous grabs of air. I tried to calm her by gently rubbing her shoulders. She fought visibly to regain her balance. The episode then eased away and seemed not to have happened.

"Your father is a smart man who is disappointed with himself and with life because he did what he thought was right and paid with the future he thought he was gonna have. He doesn't trust people, not even Alma. That's why she's never worked and used her college education. He's all weighed down by duty and lonely under it. Lonely in a place that no one can reach, not even me. But he is cryin' in that deep dark place, cryin' like a little boy who is lost and can't find his way back to who he used to be. Do you understand what I'm tryin' to tell you, Gray?"

"Yes, I think so, Grandma." I was very much in a stunned state. I knew nothing of the man she was describing.

She smiled inside a reverie. "I wish you could have known him then; smart, full of fire, and ready to take on the world, he was. He would frighten me, even then, because he was ready to fight back. The chances didn't matter. I think it was me that led him wrong. I raised him up all by myself. I taught him right from wrong. I told him to stand up for right, even while I was washin' the rich white people's clothes. He did what I wouldn't a done, but it was me that told him to do it, you see, not directly, but told him just the same." Her eyes were full and near to spilling.

"He use to say to me, *Mama, the system*—black folk say that; like the system was some big giant thing that jumped on our backs and stayed there—*has destroyed our men, used our women, and made us all empty strangers to each other*. Then he would say that Negroes have been made into empty glass vials that white people filled with the flavors that suited *them*. I bet you find it hard to believe that your father used to talk like that, don't you?"

I wasn't certain that I *did* believe her, so different was her picture of my father from the methodical unrevealing man I had known all of my life. When I did not answer her, she said, "Soona or later, you'll have to talk to him and you'll have to talk about Gordon." I said nothing. The silence stretched out in the gray dimness of the small parlor.

Thinking back on what my grandmother had said to me about how my father was penalized for the stands he took on racial matters as a young man, it occurred to me later how painfully important what happened to him during those years had been to my grandmother.

I think that I knew this because my grandmother hardly ever spoke directly of racial matters. Later, in the same sitting after we'd sat silent for a length, she asked me with a light, almost offhanded curiosity, "Gray, what do white people look like?"

While my grandmother spoke often and proudly about her own people, and understood well enough the *event* of racial antagonism as evidenced by my father's harsh war-time experience, she all but never spoke of the way that she herself had experienced race, the emotional dynamics of which she seemed less tethered by than the rest of us were. If race seemed a battlement divide to all the other Negroes I knew, it never seemed such to her. Like the rest of us, she had been exposed to the ravaging social conta-gion, but she, unlike everyone else, Negro and white alike, had not contracted the disease. Thus, she bore none of its debilitating symptoms. For instance, I'd once told her that I felt *different*, unsure or sort of *un-myself* around white people, and she'd seemed not to have instinctively known what I was talking about. In some ancient neighborhood of her emotional space, race, or at least the angry implacable energy of its sundering power, seemed to her something of an abstraction.

Her social exposures had been very different from mine. I think that I knew this because when she asked me simply, "Gray, what do white people look like?"—race had seemed briefly like an abstraction even for me, as I hadn't known how to answer this question from a woman who'd been blind all of her life.

"I don't know how to make a picture for you, Grandma. Did you see a white person in any of the dreams?"

"No, there were only our people in the dreams—the only people I've ever actually seen."

I thought for a while and then asked, "Were there flow-ers in your Dogon dream?"

She answered almost immediately. "Yes, I remember that there were frangipani flowers. I loved them when I was a little girl. I had one in my hair in the dream."

"Did the flowers bloom?"

"Yes."

"What colors?"

"Pink and white—you don't mean to tell me that white people are the color of white frangipani, do you?"

"No."

"Then why are they called white people?"

"Well, actually, Grandma, none of the races, Negro, white, or yellow, are at all close in appearance to the colors they are called by."

"Why are they known by these colors then?"

"W-well, I'm not so sure, Grandma."

She shook her head in wonderment while I felt oddly silly—quite possibly as silly as my mother once told me she'd felt while trying to explain to me the difference between Negroes and whites when I was three or four years old.

CHAPTER TWENTY-ONE

The refreshments that Mrs. Grier brought into the parlor on a breeze of perky conviviality reprieved my grandmother and me from the inconstant shadow of a recurrent sorrow and installed in its space the welcome, though temporary, relief of small talk facilitated by the sweet, voluble, oblivious Mrs. Grier.

"So, Graylon, your grandmother tells me you're getting ya master's degree in a few weeks. That's wonderful, Gray, really, really wonderful. I know your mother and father are proud. Has your grandmother told you about the mess over at the church and Reverend Boynton quitting right in the middle of it. It's awful, isn't it, Gray? Just awful. Not like the old days, I tell you. No siree, not like the old days . . ."

Mrs. Grier went on chattering like this without need of reply for what seemed to me an age. My grandmother smiled at her good-hearted neighbor. I did as well—as much out of appreciation for her kindness to my grandmother as out of amusement at the sheer sight of a rare dear soul born with no trace of a sixth sense.

Mrs. Grier passed narrowly with the seesawing tray through the door leading toward my grandmother's kitchen, all the while talking, with the last of her words thrown jocularly over a retreating shoulder: "Gray, they tell me you got a girlfriend who's really something special. Hot dog!"

My grandmother laughed aloud, covering her mouth after I joined her, laughing louder than she had. She composed herself and said, "I can tell from your letters that this time is different. So she's the one, is she?"

"It's a little early to tell, but yes, Grandma, I think this time's different, real different, that's if . . ." I paused.

"Go on, go on."

"Well, that's if I don't mess it up."

"You mean by shuttin' her out?" She must have sensed the astonishment written on my face. She said, "You think your grandmother's a wizard, don't you?"

"Well, I . . ."

"You are a man, Graylon, a young man." She spoke lightly, "It's always a good guess that you wouldn't show yourself, especially in your case. Tell me, son: is she worth it?"

Bestirred, I answered, "Yes, Grandma, she is worth it. I'm pretty sure of that. I've never met anyone like her. I think that may be what . . ."

"What frightens you, Gray?" she asked softly.

"Yes, Grandma, what frightens me."

"Seeing what's at stake, son, you'll just have to risk it, won't you? So tell her who you are when the time is right. Tell her everything. It'll make things better for you. It'll make things better for the both of you."

I hesitated. Again she seemed to understand me. "She must be somethin', son. I never seen you so confused about a girl. Is it that what attracts you to her is also some of what scares you?"

I laughed. "You're not a witch, are you, Grandma?"

She chuckled and said, "Well, maybe I am and maybe I'm not. What is it? You 'fraid she's as smart as you, or maybe even smarter?"

"The other night we were talking about my work on the Harlem Renaissance poets. I told her that one great black writer had been harshly critical of them, saying they catered more to their white supporters than to regular black people. Jeanne said that my great black writer was only against white folk's rejection of *him*, that otherwise he was himself an *unconditional assimilationist*, to use her term for him."

"What is an assimilationist?"

"Well, what she meant by it was that the great black writer most wanted to be *like* white people."

"Who is this great black writer?"

"Richard Wright."

"Oh, him."

"You've heard of him, Grandma?"

"Of course, Gray. I've listened to him on the radio. Washing clothes was the work I did, not who I am. There's a difference, you know. Could your Jeanne be right?"

"Well, I suppose so."

"Then maybe you should think about marryin' her. You want smart children, marry a smart woman."

We talked on in this way for an hour or more with Mrs. Grier humming run-on hymns mournfully off-key from the kitchen.

I wanted to be out of the house before my father arrived. At eleven o'clock I asked her about the new dreams, the Lalibela dream we had briefly discussed awhile back on the telephone and another more recent one she hadn't described to me.

"You've been givin' all this some thought then?" she asked.

"Yes, I want to write about it eventually. I've been approved for a grant to go to Mali this summer to do some research on ancient African writers, but the Dogon dream is the real reason I'm going. Jeanne's going with me. I've also talked to a professor in the psychology department at the University of Southern California about this. She thinks maybe there's something to this." I saw her expression change. "Don't worry, Grandma. She's not going to do anything. She doesn't even know your name."

"Well I *know* there is somethin' to this."

"How do you mean that?"

"Well, the first three dreams and the one I had a few weeks ago are so different from any dreams I've ever had."

"Different how?"

"First, I can't remember ordinary dreams five minutes after I wake up. They feel like what they are, dreams— mixed up so you don't even know whether they're in color or black-and-white. The Dogon dream, the Lalibela dream, and this last one were different. They were so real to me that I couldn't tell them from real life, as real to me as sittin' here talkin' to you now. So real that when you woke me when you were seven from the Lalibela dream, I couldn't right away understand English. So real that wakin' up frightens me because I'm switchin' from one life to another, except the dream is better because in the dreams I can see. I know it sounds crazy but it has happened to me four times now. What does your professor person think of all this?"

"She believes there are people who have had past lives, people who, either under hypnosis or after a dream, describe events—names, dates, places—that occurred sometimes a thousand years ago with such accuracy that the people couldn't possibly have made them up."

I took from my briefcase Dr. Harris-Fulbright's book and put it in her hands. "This is her book. Have Mrs. Grier read to you the case of Laurel Dilmen on page 257."

"All right, I'll do that."

We then drew between us a silence which may have seemed, to an uninitiated observer, long and odd, but to my grandmother and me only the usual fashion in which we had sat and spoken together since I was a boy of five.

By now the sun had lifted from the floor the straight

edge of brilliant light that had scored the little room minutes before into matching triangles of past and future. I no longer looked across at her from light to shadow. We sat silent in one and the same small space of diffused late-morning light. I recall noticing the absence of bird sounds, as well as the new unbroken swooshing machine sound of flying motor traffic coming from the interstate bypass which had opened blocks away little more than a year before. The doilies had yellowed with age. The vase was empty. Bric-a-brac huddled about in dusty conflict. The brown pictures of long-dead kin seemed less than ever to have had anything to do with anything. Far and away, the most bothering of the gray room's forlorn relics was the picture of the spotted pony and the happy boy bestride it who was to become my father.

I looked up at the wall hanging with the strange symbol stamped on its coarse open weave. It lent a counterpoint of life to the gray little room in a way that was incomprehensible to me.

"Grandma, do you know what that is on the wall hanging?"

"Yes."

"Someone told you?"

"No."

"But you can't see it, Grandma."

"No."

"Then how could you—"

"I know, son."

"What is it, Grandma?"

"Adinkra."

"What is . . ."

"Please . . ." Leaving now. She was drifting away from me with us sitting there physically little more than a foot apart.

"Are you all right?"

She cast her face upward, as if to pray. The sunlight shining high through the window's upper sash relieved the deep darkness in which she endured the long waking hours. Her fingers played rhythmically back and forth across the book I had given her. I did not know whether this was a recently acquired habit born of her blindness, or an assignment by her of talismanic properties to the book in which kindred souls had been documented and called back to life.

As had always been the case with us, I would know from the language of her body when she was ready to speak of important matters, or to speak at all.

She said the word "Yes" quietly and won my undivided attention. Pronouncing the name properly, "Gray, have you heard of a city called Córdoba?"

"Yes. I think it's in either Spain or Portugal."

"It's in Spain. It was where I was living as a thirty-five-year-old woman in the year 953." The pauses lengthened. The breathing slowed and became difficult to detect. The body became utterly still. Her eyelids slowly dropped as she began to describe what she saw. "My name is Ez-ZahrÐ. My family is wealthy. The people are dark like me and control the whole of Spain. We are Berbers from North Africa. We are called Moors. Córdoba is the capital of a region called Andalusia. One of our generals named TÐrik captured it with 7,000 soldiers in the year 711 from Roderick, the king of Spain. By the time I was born, Córdoba had been built by my people into the most beautiful city in Europe, rivaled only by Byzantium."

I took from my overnight bag a pen and a small notebook. I began to write.

She spoke with the diction of universal humanity's cultured upper crust, and with an accent that was musically foreign to me.

"While the Saxons live far away to the north and west in wooden huts with only a few monks who can read and write, the buildings of Córdoba are fashioned from jasper and marble, and stand on splendid streets behind stone walls. The water for our public gardens is supplied via leaden pipes to lakes, reservoirs, fountains of marble, and basins of gold and silver. We are, of course, Mohammedans and our Great Mosque is the most astonishing structure of its kind in all the world.

"My husband is a doctor and our large marble house stands on the banks of the Guadalquivir near a bridge that spans it beside a lush public garden of delightful flowers which are irrigated. I have two children, a girl whom we have arranged to marry into a ruling-class family and a boy who will soon begin preparation to become an officer in the army. Today, I am reading in my flower garden behind the tall stone walls that surround our compound. It is July and warm still in the late afternoon. I have not felt well today and plan to speak to my husband about this when he returns to our compound this evening. My husband has three other wives that live in other sections of the compound. I am the first, the oldest, and the most revered."

I wrote furiously, trying to capture everything that she said. I did not own a tape recorder, but had reasoned, in any case, that she would have been unsettled by the caging of her voice. The drab little parlor contrasted so starkly with the opulence of her remembered past life that I saw her blindness for the first time as a benefit.

"I am hoping that I will feel better by the time my husband arrives. He has been invited to visit the Hall of the Khalifs this evening and has promised to take me with him. A few miles outside Córdoba stands the palace, which is the most magnificent building in a world in which Córdoba is all but unanimously recognized to be the cultural center.

"Thinking about seeing the great palace for the first time from the inside, I can no longer concentrate on the book that I am reading. I also no longer feel ill.

"I suspect that the deep malaise that has plagued me today stems from the exception my husband took so strongly this morning to what he calls my increasingly 'difficult temperament.' I am a woman, I know, and not expected to have such outbursts of opinion. I told him that it was my view that our people could not continue conquering and conquering from Carthage to Spain to Gaul and England. I told him that the people of the lands we have conquered do not like their low estate and will not tolerate forever existing in our thrall. I told him that despite the civilization we believe to be superior to all others, change will come as surely as the seasons follow one behind the other. I told him that while I know we are all-powerful and that we have the power to change even the vanquished's perception of reality, we have not the power to change reality itself. For only God can do such. He said that women should not talk of matters they cannot understand, and became angry. But I did not stop there and irritated him further on the prickly subject of our people's wealth by speaking of the term 'greed,' the evidence of which I will see in the palace tonight, the palace, I, like my husband, am quite proud of."

My grandmother's eyelids rose slowly. She shivered in a way that suggested that the shiver had bridged her back into the present. She took a deep breath and expelled the air slowly while allowing her shoulders to fall with the mannerism of a small sigh that I interpreted as a peace of sorts. Knowing nothing fitting to say, I remained silent. Her visage wore a mark of wonder her sightless eyes shone wide to complement.

She said with disbelief, "The people in the dream all

looked like *us*. I was told, or somehow knew, that they were called Moors and ruled most of Europe." She laughed, it seemed, at the absurdity of the idea. "My mother was the only person I'd ever heard say the word *Moor* about a group of people. Have you ever heard tell of it, Gray?"

"I've heard it, Grandma. I don't know much about it, but I've heard it. I heard it from you once long ago. In English literature, Shakespeare wrote a play, or was credited with writing a play, about a Venetian general who was a Moor. His name was Othello. He was black in the play, but it was just a play."

"Well, isn't that something? What do you s'pose this all means, dreamin' things I never heard about, but happened?"

"I don't know, Grandma. I know I asked you this once before, but I really don't know. Do the dreams scare you?"

"Lawd no, son. What scares me is wakin' up." She smiled to herself, savoring the dream she had only just recalled to me. "My, were the people rich, rich like you never seen before. Gray, will you read up on these Moors for me and tell me about them when next you come? Will you do that, son, for your grandmother?"

I had never tried to discover from her whether or not she believed that she had actually lived the lives she dreamed about, although she had said to me many times that the dreams were very real, very different. It then occurred to me just how profoundly the dreams had affected her, and that what had inspired the transcendent contentment that set her apart from her surroundings was not the mere knowledge of past lives she had lived, but rather the more renovating knowledge of the better worlds the dreams recalled. She lived, because of this, not with mortals in the rough contemporary moment, but in the long ages where the broad experience of events averaged down all suffering.

When I was ten, I had asked her in the parlor one late Saturday afternoon, "Why, Grandma, do you call yourself African, when everybody you know or ever hear talk on the radio calls us Negroes and colored people?"

With no trace of argument or prepossession, she had answered from shadow matter-of-factly and softly, "Well, son, it's that I've been African much longer than I've been anything else." She'd stopped there and remained silent for a time—as if she were mulling memories of far-off discrepant existences. "You like sardines, Gray?" Asked lightly.

With no idea where she was going with this, "Love 'em. You know that, Grandma," both of us smiling.

"Well, son, when they were fish swimmin' in the ocean, they weren't called sardines. Did you know that? They weren't called sardines until they were put in cans. And we weren't called *Negroes* until we were put in chains. Slavery's the reason why we're the only people in the world to be called by so many different names—and now, some not-so-nice ones we're calling each other. I've even heard you say the word, playing with your friends outside on the street, Gray. I'm just who I always was. Simple as that."

Recalling the talk I'd had with my grandmother all those many years before, I thought about what Dr. Harris-Fulbright had said, that *the remembered past life is of the same race as that of the living person being regressed.* My grandmother saw herself as the same person belonging to the same race of people. She was and had always remained African and black.

"Yes, Grandma," I now said lightly, "I will do the research and bring you a full report on the Moors sometime between my commencement in May and my departure for Mali in July."

"Good. Wonderful," enjoying herself, "I hope I'm not keepin' you too busy."

"There is one other thing, Grandma. The woman who wrote the book I gave you. Her name is Joyce Harris-Fulbright." I felt, as I spoke, a small inchoate twinge of guilt. "She would like to come and talk to you about your dreams."

She asked a flat uncolored, "Why?"

"As part of her research."

"I already know what I know. I know what I dreamed. I told you. You told her. Now she knows what I dreamed. Why would she come all the way here to hear me tell her what I told you?"

"Well . . . she thinks you might actually have lived before, you know . . ." I was floundering, "and that she could prove this if she could get from you more details about those past lives. I, I . . ." I stumbled, "She would like to hypnotize you."

Her sightless eyes seemed to lock onto mine. Her open countenance sagged in broad disappointment. "What has gotten into your head, Graylon March? Have you taken leave of your senses? I don't need to prove a thing. Why would I have some stranger come here and hypnotize me?"

I did not know what to say. I felt oddly soiled, as if I had been caught in a bath of molten light priming to trade my soul for small public notice. A smarmy novice thief, called out and scorned.

"My God, son. I don't want to be in nobody's book. I don't want people readin' what some stranger has to say about me." She sounded more grieved than angry. She stopped and swung her head in a woeful arc that took the place of the words she could not find to say. All she managed was, "Why? Why would you? Why would you betray my trust in you?"

"I—I thought—"

"You thought what, Gray?" Her voice had hardened.

"I told you that I wanted to write the story of your life and dreams. I told you a long time ago and you encouraged me, Grandma." Cold sweat trickled crookedly from my armpits down across my ribs. My voice floated high and plaintive. Broken thoughts strained to dance away in flight.

"Gray, I have loved you as much as any mother has ever loved a child. I never wanted to be in a book. But I was willin' to allow it because I thought it would help you to become what you wanted to become—a writer."

"Grandma, no one will believe it if I write it, no one will publish it either."

"Then let it not be published."

"Then no one will ever know about the dreams, Grandma."

"Do you think that has anything to do with my worth as a human being—or yours?"

"I don't understand."

"I don't *need* nobody to know me. I know me. That's more than enough knowin' for one person."

"Grandma, what has happened to you is a miracle the world should know about, our people should know about. You could expand the body of knowledge."

"College make you talk like that? Let me tell you somethin', son. Ambition is a good thing, but only if you really know yourself before ambition gets ahold of you and blows you about like wind in a kite. Let me make myself plain. I will not meet with your professor and I certainly will not let her or anybody else hypnotize me. You got that? Knowledge—or what is it you said, *the body of knowledge?*— will do well enough without me, I'm sure. Okay?"

"Yes, Grandma."

She made a dramatic gesture with her arm, punctuating her remonstrance. "You write it, son. Whether it gets published or not, *you* write it. But not to get you famous. And Lord knows, not me. Write it because you call yourself a writer, and that's reason enough. And maybe buy yourself a hat, and check from time to time to see that you can still fit your head under it." She winked a blind eye and made us both laugh.

I left my grandmother seated in the dark parlor and walked through to the vestibule. When I opened the front door to leave, so bright was the midday sun that I saw nothing at first except the featureless shape of a man standing there before me on the little wooden porch, motionless and silent. As my pupils adjusted, I saw that the man was my father. Discernible first were the weary eyes, rimmed with dessicated gray parchment skin. The eyes, a burning ruin of puzzled agony, shone wetly from deep sockets and conveyed a scourge of relentless melancholy. The shoulders sloped as if they had been borne down by the dead weight of harsh fortune.

He said only my name, "Gray," wedging with one word the choking inhibition of pride hard against the warring coequal truths of love and fury.

I said, "Hello, Daddy." Then he moved past me into the darkness of the house without saying anything more.

I did not return to the house until after dark that evening. Daddy had left for home hours before.

"Gray, I want you to promise me something."

"Sure, Grandma."

"Don't give me *sure*, boy. I'm serious."

"Yes, Grandma."

"I want you to promise me now."

"Yes, Grandma."

"Is this girl, this girl Jeanne, is she somethin' you're sure about?"

"Yes, Grandma. I'm just not so sure about *me*, you know?"

"Then you must do what you have to do to make things right, boy. Don't fool around and lose her, you hear me?"

"Yes, Grandma. I hear you."

"That means you have to do whatever it is you have to do to straighten things out with your father. He can't do it. He just doesn't have it in him. You'll have to show him, son. He's not a bad man. He's a good man. He just can't seem to find his way."

"I'll try, Grandma," I answered uncertainly.

"I've been a better mother to you than I was to him. You're stronger than he is. Help him, Gray. Help him find his way out. Do you understand what I'm asking you?"

"Yes, Grandma, but—"

"No buts. You do it!" She sounded afraid, and then continued, "My family is fallin' apart and I can't stop it. You know like nobody else will ever know what that means to somebody like me. Life is not worth living without family and mine is fallin' apart. Oh God! Oh Osanobua! Oh Onyame! Oh Allah! Please help me. Help me, please." She spoke these exhortations quietly, but with a tremulous robustness, as if she were warring against some defining weakness that characterized the dangerous new age that she neither liked nor understood. Then she began to weep. I moved by the side of her chair and knelt and put my arms around her and held her close to me.

"I'm with you, Grandma. I'll always be with you, Grandma. Do you understand me? Do you know what I mean?"

Her sightless eyes shone in the evening light like polished stones. "Yes, son. I understand."

We held on to each other for what felt a long while. Then she released me and for a moment seemed to see me.

"You go to that girl and you love her, hear me? And you marry her and you have children. And you let her and those children know your soul, and they will be safe because yours is a soul worth knowin'."

CHAPTER TWENTY-TWO

I did not attend the May commencement exercises. I told Jeanne that this was because I did not believe in the nonsense of pomp and ceremony. The truth was that I was ashamed of having no family to attend and I did not want Jeanne to witness this. I collected my master's diploma from the president's office on the following Monday and that was that.

I made calls on the same Monday to arrange a number of job interviews. Although I had already committed to begin work at the University of Pennsylvania toward a PhD in September, I had lately begun to think about working awhile first. Thus, I was seeking a college teaching position and was already under serious consideration by two English departments, one in western Maryland and another at Cheney State, a historically black school in Pennsylvania.

I then drove downtown to Blanton's Books, a used-book store with thousands of little-known titles. I bought a fairly recent softcover edition of a book that had been originally published in 1886: *The Story of the Moors in Spain* by the English writer Stanley Lane-Poole. The book's cover design had been taken from a painting by Eduard Charlemont that belonged to the Philadelphia Museum of Art. The painting was a full-length portrait of a bearded dark-skinned black man dressed in an elaborately embroidered white silk robe and headdress. The artist had entitled the painting, *The Moorish Chief*.

When I got back to my apartment I called Mrs. Grier

and asked her to get my grandmother to the phone.

"Grandma, I'm sending you a book about the Moorish civilization in Spain. Have Mrs. Grier over to read to you and don't let her stop until you've gotten through, at least, the first 131 pages. Oh—and also ask her to describe the man on the cover. Ask her who the man looks like. Don't tell her, just ask her, and I bet she says Daddy when he was young. Okay, Grandma?"

"Are you still coming home before you leave for Mali?"

I was glad to hear her ask this. "Yes, Grandma, I won't leave without seeing you."

Later that evening, I called Dr. Harris-Fulbright at home in Los Angeles and told her that my grandmother had decided against hypnosis, or even a meeting with her.

"Did you make clear to her the importance of this kind of research?" The question bore a tone of accusation.

"I did the best I could, Dr. Harris-Fulbright."

"Did you explain to her that she would be credited in any writings about her experiences?"

"Yes. But she doesn't want to be credited."

"She doesn't?" Incredulous.

"My grandmother sees the world differently from most people."

Jeanne and I, by then, had been seeing each other exclusively for just under three months and had yet to make love. In the matter of sex, we were both old-fashioned in very much the same way. We had become quite serious about each other, and while our separate florid chemistries gathered pace for release, we mutually understood that because of the serious character of our relationship, ill-timed sex would alter it irrevocably. Intuition told her that I needed healing first, thus making the closed, shrouded piece of my story all the more concerning to her. Generously she had decided to wait on me. Waiting was but another thing that she did well. She understood me, even the bruised, hidden parts of me she had yet been given leave to know. She was possessed of some intrinsic faith that I would survive whatever it was that was troubling me. Indeed, it was her faith, not mine, that gave me to believe that she may have been right.

I fantasized a great deal about having sex with Jeanne. Yet I was reluctant to press my case for it.

In early adulthood, I found my parents' teachings attacking me with surprising force in the literal verse of their very own brittle biblical morality on sex that makes the whole business of the dance so exciting on the one hand and so wrong on the other, both of which hands needed to applaud God's greatest gift to humankind, far and away.

Society had instructed me that sex was a bad thing to do, but not nearly as bad for guys as it was for the girls we begged to do *it* with us. While sex soiled us maybe a little, it soiled girls a lot. Although I am sure my parents never gave it much thought, they contributed significantly to our acceptance of this notorious double standard. I saw the relief and approval very much written on my mother's face as she worked hard to scold me after one of my condoms surfaced in the suds of her weekly clothes wash. Her son was safely heterosexual. I'm sure she told Daddy about the washtub rubber that very night. I'm just as sure that Daddy breathed a sigh of relief and crossed one of the bigger items from his long worry list.

It was that evening as we watched the sun set from her apartment balcony that I told Jeanne the story of my grandmother, Makeda Gee Florida Harris March, and her Homeric dream travels across the arc of time.

My mother called me on a Monday morning after my father

left the house for work. It was not my birthday. It was not Christmas.

My mother was fifty-two years old. She had once been a brilliant and beautiful young woman of formidable promise. But the years and terrible times, and indeed the men—her sons, her husband—in her life as well, had worn away all the colors of hope in her character, leaving in its gray open space only the dull daily mindless repetitions of the dutiful housebound wife and mother. She had submerged her once creative specialness and sacrificed herself all but wholly to the decorated shrine of my father's embattled ego. She had once loved him fiercely. But her ardor, like the rest of her unnoticed passions, had cooled over the years in its ritual mold. She knew that my father loved her. She also knew that he worshipped his mother, the woman who had given him everything with which he had scratched his way to manhood. Thus, my mother had no real grounded place in the world, except that of serving the men in her house, and doing so for neither glory nor praise. She, in truth, lived, or existed, between us, ever mediating, ever seeking a peace that was inherently unachievable.

"Virgil, you know how your father feels about your grandmother. He goes there every day. He worries about her constantly." I had no idea where she was going with this and thus elected to remain quiet. "He was there on the Saturday after you were there. With your father sitting there, your grandmother received a phone call from a professor in California that got her very upset. Your father said that your grandmother told the professor repeatedly, and then nearly shouted at the person, that she would not let the professor hypnotize her. Then your grandmother hung up on the woman. Your father got your grandmother to tell him the whole story about the professor and the strange dreams your grandmother's been having. Your father asked your grandmother how a professor in California would know about his mother's dreams, and your grandmother told your father that *you* had called the professor and told her all these things about your grandmother. Your father is beside himself with anger. He says that you're making his mother look like a lunatic."

Families reach a point where almost nothing can be explained rationally within them, where words are used but language is not formed and all reason is abandoned to the ghosts of forgotten wrong turns and fossilized hurts and misconstrued purposes.

I did not know what to say to my mother. Nothing I could say would have mattered to her, for it was I who'd have been doing the saying.

When I said nothing, my mother misinterpreted my silence and became uncharacteristically angry.

"If you have nothing to say for yourself, Virgil, just stop it, will you! Just stop whatever it is that you have been doing! Just stop it, do you hear me, boy? Just, just stop it!" Then she hung up.

CHAPTER TWENTY-THREE

The night following my grandmother's unpleasant telephone exchange with Dr. Harris-Fulbright, Mrs. Grier was startled awake at three in the morning by a loud crashing thud that shook the bedroom wall she and Mr. Grier shared with my grandmother, their next door neighbor. Mrs. Grier woke her deep-sleeping husband at almost the very moment the second crash arrived. She was frightened and urged her burly husband, a small building contractor, to call the police. Mr. Grier demurred, saying that he would handle the matter. He then took from the top drawer of their bedroom bureau a five-shot thirty-eight-caliber nickel-plated Rossi revolver he kept beneath his pillow. He told his wife to get the front door key to my grandmother's house that my father had entrusted to her for just such "suspicious occasions."

Mr. and Mrs. Grier opened the door and came immediately upon a darkened stair that was only lighted dimly by the yellowy sodium wash of a streetlamp.

Leading his wife by a good measure, Mr. Grier felt his way up the stairs of my grandmother's house just as the third crash arrived, followed by the sound of shattering glass. Mr. Grier turned at the top of the stairs and instructed his wife with authority to remain in the vestibule. With his gun drawn, Mr. Grier crept down the long black second-floor hallway toward the open door of my grandmother's bedroom where a glimmer from the streetlamp shone faintly upon a writhing figure that lay mummified in tangled bedding on the mattress of a mountainous mahogany bedstead standing fast against the common wall. With eyes that by then had adjusted to the dark, Mr. Grier noticed an end table that had been knocked over and a lamp that had once rested on it, in shards on the floor. On the bed, a lone figure's head lolled ensnared in a white bedspread that muffled screams of the most desperate sort. Though most of what he heard was unintelligible to him, he knew the figure to be screaming for help.

"Oh God! Osanobua! Somebody help me, please! Get away! G-get, get away from me!" All of this muffled, as the head appeared to be smothering itself in the twisted bedding while the bare legs kicked violently at some imaginary assailant from which the legs at the same time churned furiously to escape. Then the thrashing, entombed figure found purchase with its kicking feet and wheeled over the edge of the bed, landing in a heap on the shards of the shattered lamp, all the while screaming for help through the bedspread that had been sucked by then well into the figure's gaping mouth. "My baby! My baby! Oh God, please, not my baby!"

Mr. Grier recognized the top of my grandmother's snow-white head and called to his wife for help. As Mrs. Grier climbed the dark stairs, Mr. Grier drew closer to the flailing frenzied mass on the floor without knowing quite what to do.

Mrs. Grier then appeared in the doorway. "Oh my God, Makeda! What has happened to you?" She ran to my grandmother, threw herself upon the glass-strewn floor, tore away the bedding that was soaked with sweat and blood, and wrenched my struggling grandmother into her soft strong arms. My grandmother, bathed in sweat, awoke disoriented and in pain from a contusion on the shoulder that had struck the floor first and a badly lacerated lower calf and thigh.

Mrs. Grier rocked her slowly and said over and again, singsong, "I'm here, Makeda. I'm here. It's all right, I'm here." Standing three feet away, Mr. Grier watched, still not knowing what to do or say.

Mr. Grier brought a first-aid kit with which Mrs. Grier treated the cuts that my grandmother, until her mind had fully cleared, thought had been inflicted by the killer dogs in her dream.

In the dream, my husband and I had names, but we have somehow forgotten or lost them. This worries and alarms us because it means that we will not know what to call our child that is to come in three months' time. It is summer and the night is full of sounds and smells in the black of the moonless forest. We can only see clearly the star that we know can lead us to Canada and the Quakers and freedom. The night is so black that we have lost our faces too and have trouble finding each other in the wet swampy undergrowth. In the distance we hear the dogs closing on us from the south and the east. We stumble and fall in the muck, and Canada seems farther from Albemarle County, Virginia, than it ever did before. The howling dogs, that seem to incite each other's ferocity, grow louder and louder. My husband tries his best to remain brave-sounding, but I can hear the fear in the rising pitch of his voice. The turpentine we rubbed into our feet and onto our legs to throw off the dogs has washed away in the swamp. It is only a matter of time. My husband says that he is not going back under any circumstance, and that I am to go on without him if he can throw the slave hunters off the trail a bit. But the dogs catch both of us. My husband refuses to surrender and the men shoot him. When I run to him, two dogs, foaming with madness, lunge at me and bite my leg, my thigh, and then into my womb where my baby moves hard about, seeming to sense that something is wrong. I see the whitish swelling flesh of my insides soaked in blood. Then everything goes black as if I too have died.

The first thing my grandmother told Mr. and Mrs. Grier was: "Do not tell my son about this."

But Mrs. Grier said, "Makeda, this is too serious not to tell 'im, with you here at night all alone. Anyhow, he gon' see the cuts and know something bad happened."

Against that my grandmother argued, Mrs. Grier later said, desperately, "He won't see the cuts. My gowns will hide them. Now, Gertrude, I'm askin' you not to tell him. It'll cause more trouble than you know."

Mr. Grier stayed out of it. Mrs. Grier did not know what to do. My grandmother was her friend, but when she had first seen the bloodied old blind woman furled in a bedspread thrashing about on the floor at three in the morning, she quite understandably believed that my grandmother was well along toward losing her mind. In the end, she felt she had no choice but to tell my father, and did so the very next morning after she had slept the rest of the night in bed with my grandmother.

My father spoke with young Dr. Bakewell, an internist down at Richmond Community Hospital, the tiny colored hospital in which I was born on the street behind Virginia Union. Dr. Bakewell, who had done in his short new medical career all of a half-day of psychiatric rounds, told my father that my grandmother's episode might well have been "triggered by the stress engendered by that California professor who spoke to your mother just hours before she went to bed."

CHAPTER TWENTY-FOUR

The trip to Mali was to begin in just under a month. It loomed large before me as something of a consummation of sorts, intangible but important, no less so than the physical intimacy Jeanne and I were forestalled still to explore.

We had made plane reservations to fly from D.C.'s Dulles airport to Paris on Air France, and on to Bamako from Paris via Air Mali. We had still to make arrangements for travel from Bamako to Timbuktu, and from there to the land of the Dogon. We were to leave America on June 17 to arrive in Bamako late in the afternoon of the following day.

When I had first broached with Jeanne the idea of a trip to Mali, I was not entirely forthcoming about my reasons for wanting to go.

She had asked, "Have you been to Africa before?"

"No, I've never even been outside the United States."

"Why Mali? I mean—why just Mali?"

I lied, but only by omission. "I want to study the work of ancient African writers at the library in Timbuktu."

Jeanne had had a passport for some years. I had applied for mine at the passport office on K Street in Washington in early May. I was told that it would take a minimum of six weeks to process my application unless I were willing to pay an additional fee of seventy-five dollars to accelerate matters. So I wrote out a check for the larger amount. Although I could ill afford it, I paid for the two airfares and put Jeanne's ticket in the mail to her. While it may not have made perfect sense, I thought that buying and mailing the ticket to her would help me deflect the vigorous effort she would mount to pay her own way. The same day, I stopped at the Embassy of Mali on Massachusetts Avenue and collected from a friendly and solicitous cultural attaché an assortment of coated-paper color brochures and other materials about the culture, topography, history, and political system of Mali.

The next day, a Saturday, I called Jeanne to sort out our plans for the weekend.

"What do you want to do tonight?" I was feeling uncharacteristically good about nothing in particular.

"You choose this time. It's your turn. If it's a movie, you choose the movie. If it's dinner, you choose the food. It doesn't matter. I only want to be with you." Although she said this playfully, it caused in me an unmitigated spike of intense pleasure, literally thrilling me in some viscerally neurological way.

"Well then, I suggest, by the authority vested in me, that we eat in this evening and work through our plans for the trip."

"Okay. That's fine with me. Why don't I come to your place for a change?"

I hesitated before responding slightly less cheerfully, "Oh, Jeanne, you don't want to come here."

"Oh, but I do, sweet prince," her voice at once cheerful and serious. Soft metal in a silk sleeve.

"Come on, Jeanne, not here, please."

"Yes, Gray. *There*."

"My place is a disaster and I don't have time today to fix it. How about the next time?"

She was quiet for a moment and then decided not to push the point, although I could hear in her voice that my response had meant something more to her than I intended.

"O-okay, I'll see you here then at what? Seven?" Jeanne asked without light or lift.

"Seven is fine."

I spent the morning reading through the materials on Mali that the cultural attaché had given me. He was an engaging man who seemed genuinely pleased that I was planning to visit his country. I was somewhat embarrassed by the thought that I had relatives who decidedly were not. A great aunt on my father's side had called me and said, "I hear you're going to Africa," which to her was not a continent, but a country.

It wasn't a question, and I considered not responding at all, but thought better of it. "I'm going to Mali, Aunt Clarice."

"What's a Mali?"

"Mali is a country, Aunt Clarice. It's in Africa."

"Where in Africa?" This was asked skeptically as if she suspected I may have been trying to bamboozle her. For what reason I would do such a thing, I had no idea.

"It's in West Africa, Aunt Clarice, the part where we came from." My voice was flat. Unprovocative.

"I didn't come from no Africa," she had said, offended.

"Where *did* you come from, Aunt Clarice?" The barb flew wide of its mark and it was just as well.

Since I was fifteen, I had wanted to go to Mali—since that late afternoon my grandmother told me in her little parlor about the Dogon dream. I hadn't consciously realized before that day how much I needed to hear something good said about Africa, where our people (who were being treated so shabbily here in America) had come from. I'm embarrassed to confess that I did not know much of anything reliable about the land of our origin. The painful truth is that about all I'd been told, virtually from birth, was that we were a backward people from a backward place.

Given the intensity and the relentlessness of this line of attack, it was hard as hell not believing that Aunt Clarice may have been right in her estimate of us. Think about it for a moment. Willie Best, the bubble-eyed, slow-moving, dim-witted Negro handyman on *The Stu Erwin Show*, was a household name in the country, while Dr. Dubois, the giant Negro intellectual, could walk through most of our neighborhoods unnoticed, and although Daddy had told us that the Negro film director Oscar Micheaux had done his level best in the 1930s to have us appear like normal everyday people in his motion pictures, nobody I knew, knew anymore who Oscar Micheaux was. It was virtually impossible to deny that practically every image of us selected for broadcast to the whole country made us look dumb and worthless, while the vast majority of the Negroes I knew were just like my parents, but I almost never saw people like my parents on television or on the screen at the Hippodrome on Saturdays. What concerned me most was that we seemed to have begun acting like the hired idiots we'd been given no choice but to watch on the national broadcasts, which brings me back to my grandmother.

You may not believe this, but the Dogon dream she described to me that afternoon on Duvall Street when I was fifteen was the first positive thing I'd ever heard said about Africa, the place that had mothered, and like it or not, defined me, both from the outside in, as well as from the inside out. And no matter what Negroes said or had been caused to believe about Africa, we were all indissolubly bound up with her—Aunt Clarice, kicking and screaming, included.

I'd feel better, perhaps, saying that I decided to go to Mali for my grandmother, but that wouldn't be true. I was going to Mali for myself. My grandmother had been a living eyewitness to Africa *before* the age of slavery. She knew who she was. She had lived and experienced who we all once had been. She did not require repair. I did. I was infected with an insidious malady of the head and spirit that no mortal uninoculated Negro could avoid contracting while breathing in social America.

Thus, it was not that I had simply wished to go to Mali to document my grandmother's revelation. I *needed* to document her revelation in order to save myself.

The word *black*, the most recent peel-off label for our race (they were getting hard to keep track of), was just coming into vogue at that time, and Aunt Clarice threw that in, ". . . And I'm sick of all this *black* stuff, Gray. And where's it takin' us? Pullin' us down, I tell ya. Jest listen to 'em. Black dis. Black dat. Black, black, black. I tell ya, I'm sick of it . . ."

Thank goodness my parents were never like Aunt Clarice because this was a big big problem in the black community. Every other Saturday, Daddy sent Gordon and me to get our hair cut at Ace's Barbershop at the corner of Saint James and Leigh. The owner was called Pop, or at least that's all I can remember. Well, Pop would expel any patron heard using profanity, whether the patron was a regular or not. That was the rule and Pop applied it without exception. There was no rule, however, against stupid talk. I know this was so because once I heard Giant Turner arguing with Beverly Taylor (Beverly was a man and touchy about his name) about whether there was a pill that could turn black people into white people. Giant Turner said that he knew for sure that there was such a pill and Beverly kept saying that there wasn't. "Is." "Ain't." "Is." "Ain't." "Is." "Ain't." They just kept going around and around like this. Then Beverly said that he could prove that Giant was wrong. Well, Giant asked, "How?" It was then that Beverly said, "If there was a pill that could do that, there wouldn't be no black people." And Giant had no answer for that. Everybody in the barbershop laughed, even though nothing was really funny as I saw it, even though I was just a little boy.

When I was young, this problem of self-hate was a serious matter for black people in America. Aunt Clarice was only unusual in the extreme way that she appeared to truly enjoy hating herself and never ever taking no for an answer. The word *Africa*, whenever she heard it, was just one of the many panic buttons she pressed as hard and as many times as she could to submerge herself as deeply as possible in her very own well-tended acid bath of self-loathing.

From the very beginning, as everyone ought to have known, black folk have always had a hellacious time existing sanely in America. The place has saddled us with a gaggle of debilitating complexes. Just think what a nasty psychological business it is insisting to people who've treated you like vermin that you are equal to them. That alone is enough to make all of us as crazy as the dickens. Reverend King even had us saying that we *loved* them. I knew this was only a strategy. But, God, look at the cost to our heads. I think you can see now where people like Aunt Clarice came from. And were it not for Mama and Daddy, Gordon and I would have been just like them. As it was, truth be told, we were more like them than we cared to admit. Couldn't be helped, given the poisoned air we all had no choice but to inhale. So you see, because of Mama and Daddy, Gordon and I mostly loved ourselves a lot and hated ourselves only a little. Aunt Clarice, on the other hand, I suppose loved herself a little and hated herself a lot, which meant, laid end to end, Negroes were but mirror images of each other.

I *talked* about race pride, but found the genuine belief in such strangely irksome in Jeanne. It was like she was pulling at the edges of a scab covering an old and terrible wound. I must have reckoned unconsciously that I was safe under the scab even though I may have been drowning in pus there. How was that different from Aunt Clarice, except by degree? Perhaps it was because I shared this overlap with Aunt Clarice (an overlap she called mocking attention to with her ostentatiously celebrated self-loathing) that I resented her so profoundly.

So whenever off-campus parochial old Richmond kinds of black people asked me what my plans were for the summer, I'd tell them and brace for the Aunt Clarice response. Indeed, a lot of blacks I told were supportive, even envious. But, if I am remembering things correctly, the only one over fifty who thought I was on the verge of something wonderful and life-altering was my grandmother.

She seemed as excited about my plans as I was, and I don't believe for a minute that her enthusiasm stemmed from her Dogon dream alone, because owing to me, it was that dream that had plunged our family into its current state of confusion.

My grandmother had always had this way about her, and all she would say to me was that the "life of the spirit" was thousands of years long and things that were lost in one stage of that life could be recovered in another. When I asked her to explain this she'd demurred, saying only that I'd find out for myself soon enough. She had said one thing further that I thought may have been important, and that was that I'd be doing little more than traveling around in Africa "lookin' at stuff" unless I found a way, after "all that had happened," to open the eyes of my spirit. I troubled over what she had meant by this right up until the time I left Baltimore for Bamako.

By *all that had happened.*

The evening was warm and redolent with the renovating

scent of spring. The sliding glass balcony door at Jeanne's was fixed full open. The fragrant night air circulated through the apartment. The rustle of embryonic tree leaves made themselves heard in the clean night space. Jeanne looked casual and summery in a cotton tangerine tank top and faded denim jeans.

She embraced me and drew back, looking at me somewhat diffidently and less directly than usual. The small smile was marked by some new material question that I'd seen no evidence of before. She was armed with a finely tuned intuitive sensitivity with which she detected symptoms in me of a well-varnished ambivalence, symptoms, however, that she had diagnosed, I would later learn, wrongly. It wasn't that I lacked a passionate affection for her, as she might well have concluded, but that, unbeknownst to her, my soul bore some retrograde infection that stunted the expression of that affection.

"I brought all the materials that I picked up from the embassy."

I left a silence for her to fill but she only watched me under lightly knitted brows and said nothing.

I took the materials from my briefcase and spread them on the little coffee table. Her silence continued and extended well past the time it took me to make diversionary use of my hands. She simply watched me, not unpleasantly, but as if I were a dense puzzle, perhaps not worth the trouble required for solving.

"I've taken care of the tickets so we're all set."

"I didn't expect you to pay for my ticket. Let me do that."

"No. Absolutely not. In any case, it's done."

She lengthened her silence and looked down at her fingers which lay laced together on her lap. I stopped talking but could not hold the position. The widening spaces of quiet unsettled me, made me nervous.

I started again. "The man at the embassy was very nice. He said—" I stopped talking abruptly and looked at her watching her motionless hands. "Is something wrong, Jeanne? What is it?" She remained quiet. "What is it, Jeanne? Tell me, please?"

She continued to examine her hands then spoke strangely, in a flat voice, as if she were talking to herself.

"Why is it, Gray, that I have not been allowed to see all the places of your life?"

"I told you my place was a mess. I didn't want you to see it that way." My voice sounded querulous—whiny—and had risen an octave. Always with me a sign of anxiety.

"I was not talking about your apartment, Gray." She said this softly, sympathetically, as if to indicate her loyalty and that she would be on my side were she but informed well enough to locate it.

"When have you last spoken to your mother, Gray?"

I don't know why it is that my thinking processes addle when I am made the subject of even the mildest personal invasion.

"Not long ago. Maybe a week or so."

"When did you last see her?"

I did not answer. She looked at me and saw the change in my eyes.

"Gray?"

I was staring past her, over her shoulder, blankly into the black night.

"Gray?"

I did not shift my eyes but turned my head slightly, moving, with it, my eyes onto hers.

"Yes?" My voice alloyed resentment with grief.

"I love you."

She said this as a parent would say such to a small son who'd fallen on gravel and bloodied his knee. I wanted to cry and I hardly ever cried. Only twice had I cried since I was a little boy. I had not cried even when Luckbox, a schoolmate, drowned in Turner Lake the day I turned thirteen. But now, I would sigh upon Jeanne in sweet relief and feel curiously better, much better, and for no apparent reason at all.

"I know." I had trouble with my eyes and glanced down to hide them from her.

"We have never been alone together."

"I don't know what you mean."

"Some presence seems to always be with us, suspended somewhere between us. And you always talk to me as if it could hear us, and you don't want it to hear us, and so you don't talk much, except in conversation with yourself, even when I'm sitting in front of you, looking at you. It's like that now, right now. It's here, whatever it is, and you know this is so."

"That's . . ." I hadn't energy to invest a disclaimer with any real conviction. I couldn't, I just couldn't sell it. So I remained quiet.

"When did you last see or speak to your father?"

"I saw him and spoke to him when I went to see my grandmother." Of course this was only technically so, and my face must have told her as much.

The thoughts, the pictures on the screen of my mind took leave of her and the room, wafting off, transforming themselves, helter-skelter, into short-reel snapshots of momentless nonevents in my past. The eight-year-old ruining his brand-new white Easter Sunday suit with axle grease from the underside of an old abandoned Mack truck. The twelve-year-old ripping his gray flannel trousers at recess while scaling the anchor fence at Booker T. Washington Junior High School. Gordon and I walking that night along Brookland Park Boulevard harmonizing, *In the still of the night.* *Shoo dooby dooby do. Shoo dooby dooby do . . .*

"Gray?"

"Yes?" I said softly.

"You told me that you had no brothers or sisters."

"Yes."

"Did you once have a brother or a sister?"

"Yes."

"Which, Gray?"

"A brother."

"Tell me about him. Tell me how he died."

I looked vacantly at the brochures spread on the coffee table and then at Jeanne. Without uttering a word I got up and walked out of the apartment.

PART FOUR

CHAPTER TWENTY-FIVE

I have a bewildering penchant for absenting myself from situations I seem unable to understand or control. Life had acted upon me unsympathetically and complicated affairs I had much wanted to keep simple. Everything that mattered to me seemed broken, even to some extent my anchoring relationship with my grandmother. And now the tiff with Jeanne. Well, not even a tiff really. Presented with her first real disposition of intimacy, I had closed off from her like a frightened clam. The very thing my grandmother warned me against. As a result, I was going to Mali alone. I had given in to my worst traits. Without a moment of conscious consideration, I had within the space of an instant withdrawn to the painful comfort of an old and familiar despair. I had known the moment that I did this that I had made a serious mistake, a mistake I was temperamentally inclined to solemnize as virtue before preemptively imposing upon it a measure of sensible remedy.

I had never been on an airplane before, and such, when the big Air France Boeing 707 roared down the long concrete runway at Dulles, I discovered only then how little credence my nervous system placed in the physics of man-made flight. As the big aircraft lifted from the ground, the long wing, over which I sat, sagged disconcertingly under the great dangling weight of its two screaming engines. Not two weeks earlier, the port outboard engine had fallen off a 707 on takeoff from San Francisco, carrying half a wing with it, and causing the deaths of everyone on board. I kept my eyes trained through my window on the right-side wing's bobbing engines until long after the plane had reached its cruising altitude of 37,000 feet. On the ground I could construct an illusion of control. Six miles up, I had little choice but to accept that control over my life rested *ex post facto* in the hands of distractable assembly plant workers, component manufacturers, maintenance mechanics, and, for the present moment, the unseen hands of the three-person French-speaking crew up front.

Fear eclipsed wonderment. I did not like flying.

I was the only black person on the plane. The cabin had been darkened for sleeping. The night over the North Atlantic fell inky and featureless. The senses listened reluctantly to the shadowy stillness of the plane's dim hermetic space. All that reminded of human survival was the rise and fall of sleeping breasts against the ugly drone of the big Rolls-Royce jet engines.

I had begun to question the wisdom of the enterprise I was embarking upon. Jeanne had not come to the airport to see me off. I had not spoken to her since abruptly walking out of her apartment a month ago. I realized now that I all too often behaved as a stubborn and stupid man who acted against his very most essential interests for reasons broadly unknown to me and, I suspect, to the general male population of the species as well. It is as if I were captive of some primordial behavioral kink that evolution had omitted to remedy. Still, I believed the despondency resulting from my impetuous mistake with Jeanne would have been manageable were it not layered onto my lengthening estrangement from my parents. While I continued to love them, they and I seemed to have grown increasingly incompatible.

Now here I was, alone in every conceivable fashion, hurtling through a black abyss toward the unfamiliar, and doing so only because of an ill-conceived inertial idea fueled by an ambitious young would-be writer's curiosity.

I took a blanket and pillow down from the overhead luggage bin. I draped the blanket over my knees before doubling over the pillow and wedging it between my head and the plane's starboard window wall. I looked out at the inky blackness and soon drifted off to sleep.

The main concourse of the airport was dense with foot traffic. For the first time in my life, I heard only the sound of a language that was not English. The hall was full with the musical riffs of light bell chimes that called attention to flight announcements made in French for destinations like Lucerne, Dakar, Malta, and Moscow. If not racially more heterogeneous, the milling cosmopolitan herd of people was clearly more culturally diverse than any assemblage of people I had seen anywhere before in the United States. They were mostly French, of course, but amongst them could be heard a medley of other languages, none of which I recognized. It came as something of a comfort to me to see a number of very dark blacks, the men dressed in floor-length robes and fez-like hats, the women in brilliant primary colors that accentuated the richness of their complexions.

All that I saw seemed different from that which I had seen my whole life in America—the signage on restroom doors, the spare-line design of the lights and benches and floor coverings. The virtual *everything* was indeed somehow different, a measure less cushiony than America's lowercase architecturals, more sensible, serviceable, more industrial even, to a new eye accustomed to America's boastful surplusage.

CHAPTER TWENTY-SIX

The crowded lobby of the small French airport hotel was charged with the alienating energy of transiting strangers, strangers speaking too loudly, straining to make themselves understood above the clashing of dissonant and mutually incomprehensible tongues. With the exception of a small few, the travelers jostling for space and advantage were Europeans going assertively about their business in a manner of insouciant detachment.

There were the French, of course, but there were also high-pitched gatherings of Czechs, Swedes, Russians, Croatians, Pakistanis, Germans, Japanese, and five or more Francophone Africans. The unrelated languages spoken in unison formed into a cacophonous noise that made the small lobby smaller still.

"*Ça va?*"

"*Ça va.*"

The voices, textured and husky with color, carried robustly forward from directly behind me as I waited in line to check in. Air France had vouchered payments for a lunch, a dinner, and the small dayroom I was to use during the twelve-hour duration of my layover.

I looked behind me and saw two black men, one tall and rangy, the other quite short and corpulent. They wore festively embroidered robes. The tall man's robe was white. The round man's robe was an eye-catching periwinkle. They did not so much shake as clasp hands in an oddly gentle but nonetheless masculine way, with their left hands holding the right wrists of the hands with which they greeted each other. They seemed to know each other and to have bumped into one another quite by chance. I recognized that they were speaking French although I had no inkling of what they were saying. I had a fleeting impulse to say something to them in English, to ask, for instance, if they were going on, in the evening, to Bamako on the flight that I was booked for. They smiled and laughed together companionably. My courage began to ebb. I remained silent and turned back around to present the Air France voucher to the harried reception desk clerk.

The room was small and Spartan with a single glass aperture situated high on an antiseptic white-white wall through which only a heavy blue sky could be glimpsed. There were two single beds fastened as bunks, one against the window wall and the other against the wall adjacent to it. The room was almost completely devoid of decoration. Well-laundered white sheets wrapped the thin coil-less mattresses tightly like oversized bandages.

The bathroom plumbing was naked and visible. The carpet was wall-to-wall and coarse. The pillows and bedding suggested a military minimalism. The whole of the space registered the cold empty personality of a disinfected cloister.

I fell, fully clothed, splayed across the window-wall bed upon my back and stared vacantly into the tiny room's ceiling, hoping that sleep would arrive and rejoin me to a world that I knew.

I remained in this position and wide awake for the better part of the hour.

In the early afternoon, I called Mrs. Grier and asked her to bring my grandmother to the telephone. While I could scarcely afford the call, my grandmother had made me pledge to contact her the moment I had safely arrived in Paris.

"Gray? Is that you, son?" I heard relief in my grand-mother's voice. During the night of my long over-water flight, her colorful imagination had surely painted every possible horror that might have befallen me.

"It's me, Grandma. I'm fine."

"Where are you now? You haven't gotten to Mali yet, have you?"

"No. I leave for Mali this evening. I'm staying the day at a little airport hotel near Paris."

"I can't get over it. You being all the way over there. You sound like you right here in Richmond." She laughed, I thought, out of relief that I was safe for the moment.

"What's it look like over there?"

"I don't know, Grandma. Different, I suppose. Every-thing kinda looks and feels harder."

"What do you mean, *looks and feels harder*?"

"I know it seems a little strange to pick out something like that, but, you know, the benches in the airport, the seats on the bus I rode over here on, even the bed I'm lying on. The stuff is harder, that's all. Makes our cars and all feel like waterbeds."

"Waterbeds?" She said this worryingly, as if I had used profanity. I changed the subject.

"I've never heard so many languages spoken in my life."

"It must be really something, son. I'm so proud of you. And goin' to Africa. My grandson. What a thing! Makes me wish I was young."

"I know, Grandma. But it's like you're here with me. It's like when I get to Africa, you'll be there with me. That sounds strange, but . . ."

"No, not to me it doesn't. Not strange at all."

I did not know what more to say, and felt a little like a

faltering dancer who'd lost the step without knowing how to regain it unnoticed.

"Are you okay, Gray?"

"Oh, yes, Grandma. I'm fine, I'm fine." I felt that she did not believe me.

"Your mother called and asked about you. When you'd be arrivin' and everythin'. I'm sure your father wanted to know too."

"You really think so, Grandma?"

"I'm sure of it, son."

There was a second stretch of silence.

"Well, Grandma, I just called to let you know everything is okay."

She was silent for another moment, as if she were deciding something. When she spoke again, her tone was contemplative. Soft.

"Take care of yourself, Gray. Go on to Mali and bring it back for me, son."

"I will, Grandma. I will."

I had been sitting up to talk on the telephone. I lay back on the bed. Something nonspecific was bothering me.

It could have been that I was worried about Grandma. When I had visited her three days before my departure, she was less open with me than usual. When I asked her whether she'd had any new dreams, she tersely said no, closing off further discussion.

The words had been spoken wearily, resignedly.

I worried that she may have been poised to give up on a world that, by her measure of it, had been, for a long time, headed in the wrong direction. I think that she believed strongly that this was particularly the case for our people. She, after all, had been cursed or privileged to witness, firsthand, the long epochal downward trajectory of black folk's relative social circumstance near and far.

Before sensing her despondence, I had been at the time on the verge of raising with her the situation with Jeanne that haunted me much as an unshakable fever would. But seeing that Grandma at the time was of an uncharacteristically brittle temperament, I hadn't brought up Jeanne's name at all. I was sufficiently concerned about all this that I stopped next door to speak with Mrs. Grier about Grandma before leaving Richmond that day.

After some prodding, Mrs. Grier told me that on several occasions Grandma had *disappeared* (this was the word she used) for seconds while talking to her. What Mrs. Grier described was nothing so fantastic or supernatural as teleportation or such. What she said was, "Makeda would be in her body right there in front of me, but then she'd be gone to some other place. Then, in a few seconds, she'd be back again."

Mrs. Grier did not know about the dreams. She had thought only that Grandma was "gettin' old and slippin'."

"Have you noticed anything else different about her?" I asked.

She hesitated before answering. "Well, maybe that strange cross she has that was never around the house before. Leastways, I never saw it before."

"What cross?"

"It's a thick metal thing that's nearly the same whichever way you turn it."

"I don't understand."

"Well, the two pieces of it are the same, you know, about the same length. Like maybe it would fit inside a circle. It even had a circle inside it where the two pieces cross each other. And the cross had little birds on it. Did you ever hear of such a thing?"

"Was it very small? Small enough to keep in a jewelry box?" Save for the wall hanging with the symbol on it, nothing visible had changed in the house since I was a little boy.

"No, I'd guess it was somewheres near a foot anyway you looked at it." She frowned.

"What is it, Mrs. Grier?"

"The cross had these funny things on the three ends."

"Can you describe it?"

"I don't know. Alls I can say is what I was thinkin' when I saw it." She looked as if she thought there was something dishonorable in talking to me this way about her friend.

"What were you thinking, Mrs. Grier?"

"Well, I was thinkin' that three ends of the cross was bloomin' like iron roses."

It was 1:45 or thereabouts when a young African waiter delivered the ham and cheese sandwich I had ordered from room service. He told me that he was a thirty-six-year-old Badjara man from Senegal. His parents had given to him both a Wolof name and Wolof as his first language when he was very small. They had thought that this would help him along, inasmuch as the Wolof had been the dominant group in Senegal for centuries and still held most of the important positions in government and commerce.

Babukar had come to Paris from Dakar to attend university sixteen years earlier, but had dropped out before completing his degree in agriculture. While he had always intended to earn a diploma and return to his parents' village in Senegal, things hadn't worked out that way and he was losing confidence that they ever would.

Babukar told me all of this in response to the questions I began asking just after he'd put the sandwich down on a small table near the door.

He was half a head shorter than me, neat of build and feature, with deep brown skin that was clearer, but otherwise not unlike my own.

Although he had yet to marry, he said to me that he very much wanted to have a family because this was very important to the Badjara, in ways, I'd later learn, I had no cultural framework for fully appreciating at the time. He also said that his elderly parents still hoped he would return home soon and marry not a Wolof but a Badjara woman, and have many children who would then become part of an extended Badjara family network whose members—mothers, fathers, sons, daughters, aunts, uncles, sisters, brothers, cousins, grandsons, granddaughters—would share and share alike virtually everything that was sharable.

Babukar said with a measure of pride that this was "the African way," and because this was so centrally the case, he had never really adjusted to life in France where nobody seemed to care about anybody and certainly not about an African like him.

I remember thinking that the *African way* made *affordable* gentle personalities like his, and that his model of African man had not been made in America since the holocaust flagship docked at Jamestown in August 1619. By now I had been reared fifteen generations competitively selfish and callous by a million mothers and fathers, black, white, loving, hateful, voluntary, involuntary. Over the long estrangement, I had become different from Babukar in some fundamental way that did not flatter me.

Babukar looks at a glass and sees a window, a window unto a mother, a son, a sister, a cousin, a niece—nothing that he would *own*. I look at a glass and see a mirror, a mirror in which to see *myself*, *my* writing, *my* future, *my* this, *my* that, *my* place in the Great Acquisitor's running of the bulls.

Babukar, standing there in a white shirt and black bow tie, holding in his hand the rumpled bill to be signed by me, said that he'd never met a Negro American before and seemed excited at the prospect, having heard a great deal about us. And so I invited him to sit down on the room's only chair, a small wooden affair beside the shelf-desk that was affixed loosely to the masonry wall.

We talked for fifteen minutes or longer, long enough that I began to worry for his job. But by then he was well into telling me the story of his family, his village, his country. I did not know why he was talking to me like this. I think he believed that he *knew* me, that I was he. But I was not he and had not been for a long, long time. I tried to read him but could not, talking, as we were trying to, after so long a time, from so great a distance, after so much awful had happened. All that would appear to remain between us was race and how we both had been treated because of it.

It was then that I told him I would be leaving in a matter of hours for Timbuktu. He appeared pleased to hear this.

"Have you ever been to Timbuktu before?"

"No. I've never even been to Africa before."

Tossing tree leaves dappled the fresh sunspot on the wall across from the tiny window. For no particular reason, it occurred to me as I noticed this, that the self-effacing Babukar spoke at least four languages: Badjara, Wolof, French, and English.

"Mali is our neighbor. It is right next door to Senegal. Did you know that?"

I said yes when I wasn't sure that I *had* known that.

"They speak French in Mali. Do you speak French?"

"No, I'm sorry. I don't."

"Don't worry. You will do just fine."

"You know, we could be cousins," he added.

"Could we?"

"Yes. Yes. The Negro Americans when they were Africans came from all over Senegal, even from my village."

Looking at him smiling at me, I was unaccountably moved by what he had said. If Babukar noticed this, he did not let on.

"How long will you be in Timbuktu?"

"A week."

"Well then, you must go to Senegal. You must see Goree Island. It is where the slavers kept the Africans before they were taken across the sea to be slaves and, later, Negro Americans." It was not unlike, I remembered, how sardines were made.

"I will think about it," I said.

Babukar continued as if he had not heard me: "And you must visit my village and meet my family. They will take good care of you. Let me call to let them know that you will be coming to our village."

I didn't know what to say.

CHAPTER TWENTY-SEVEN

The moon shone huge and brilliant above a shimmering Mediterranean Sea.

Perhaps because I am my grandmother's spirit child, I believe in signs. The moon that night was larger than I'd ever witnessed it, a light as bright and soothing as God would mix to announce the resting countenance of a storied continent that was the embattled lovely mother of the black race.

I felt an involuntary stir as the northwest coastline resolved into view along the edge of waters that wrinkled white atop the obsidian depths. Ahead, the Sahara unveiled its vast curvilinear magnificence, delineated in soaring fawn sands and soft blue-shadowed valleys.

Never in my life had I felt as I did in those moments.

Adrift in the cold induced vacuum of the rich retired slaver's missing ledger, can there be an event more compelling in a victim's most private and troubled yearning than the long-awaited homecoming of a former African? Nameless. Homeless. Fifteen times removed. Unwell of spirit.

And there it was.

Africa.

In a solitary transformational moment, I owned it with breast and sinew as I'd never owned anything before, and with such surprising intensity that I shivered, deep within the night, all alone in a celebration that required to be shared.

I suppose it would not have mattered so much to the

actuary's issue, who angle unimaginatively only for solid work with regular hours and good benefits. But it mattered enormously to me that I was aboard that Air Mali flight, bound for the past, *alone*. Occasions like these were not to be forgone cheaply. For how often in life do they present themselves to those who would appreciate their value?

I *needed* Jeanne. I needed her here with me in Mali. I needed her together with me here to begin making our future, a future built importantly of memories in which we would figure almost symbiotically together; pedestrian memories of pedestrian experiences; small memories of being and doing and sharing and laughing and crying; sweeping memories of the years over which we would persist as distinct and different, yet inevitably become each other; cumulative memories lain down as affirming markers on the cold ground of time, units with which to measure how far we had come together and how well we had done. And this common transformational discovery experience, our presence here in Africa together, would be the benchmark from which to begin the taking of this measure.

This may sound (even somewhat to me) mawkishly sentimental. After all, I was alone, high above the Earth, in a foreign night with the moon outside my window and the stunning canvas of Africa beneath me. I will further confess that this may have influenced the language I have used to describe what I was feeling. But if I am certain of anything, it is that only the language can be viewed as sentimental, not the deepening conviction that inspired it. Not the feelings themselves.

The Air Mali Boeing 737 jet touched down on African soil at 6:37 in the morning. I pressed my face to the window the whole time it took the pilot to taxi into the terminal building area. An African ground worker waved up at me in a gesture I chose to interpret as a welcome. He was tall and lean, wearing wooden clogs, a wine-colored felt fez, and a long, white ground-length robe that shifted on the light morning breeze. Behind him, I could see far across the flat red-clay plain into the limitless distance.

The door opened and non–French speaking voices from the outside wafted into the plane's cabin. (I would later learn that it was Bambara that was being spoken. This was one of the three Mande languages spoken by half of Mali's population.)

It was the beginning of the rainy season and the air was cool and humid.

The plane's cabin itself underscored the first odd dichotomy that I would notice. All of the workers moving about outside the plane were Africans, while all who were onboard the plane—with the exception of me—the flight crew, and nine passengers that I assumed were Malians, were probably French nationals.

I took out the travel itinerary that I had handwritten in Baltimore and tucked into my shirt pocket. I had two hours to wait until my connecting flight left for Timbuktu which lay two thousand miles to the northeast along the Niger River in the central section of the country. I had more than enough time to clear immigration and customs before starting on the last leg of my journey.

I'd had difficulty reserving a room at a hotel in Timbuktu. So I'd arranged through the good offices of the Sofitel L'Amitié Bamako to stay at a small inexpensive guesthouse not far from Timbuktu's ancient libraries.

The flight attendants, both Malian women, put on light green six-button double-breasted blazers and began preparing the passengers to deplane. The attendant toward the front of the aircraft, a tiny woman in her early twenties, gave over the public address system a stream of announcements in French, only the first of which had I understood: *Bienvenue au Mali*.

I peered out toward the terminal which was a rudimentary ferroconcrete building decorated modestly along its top edge by a cornice from which protruded a flagstaff that supported a large version of the national flag. The flag was comprised of three wide vertical bars—green, yellow, and red, the borrowed colors of Ethiopian Pan-Africanism. Just beneath the swing of the flag were two lines painted in large letters on the façade of the building:

BIENVENUE
BAMAKO, MALI

Suddenly it started to rain, and with such torrential intensity that the water banging against the skin of the fuselage sounded like a shower of metal pellets. Within seconds, the rain stopped and the morning sun began quickly baking away all evidence of it having rained in the first place.

A mobile stairway was pushed against the side of the plane, and shortly afterward we were allowed to go down to the ground.

This altered in me an unstable balance of contesting emotions. This business, as it were, of going *down to the ground*. Nothing else would explain my calm state, inasmuch as I have never liked large new experiences.

As a child, I hated changing from my old elementary school to the junior high school on the same street six blocks away. I had been anxiety-logged about it, even when many of my friends transferred with me to the same new place. I had never liked crowds of strangers or meeting new people. My mother always had the hardest time getting me to try new foods. While I liked Chinese food, I had never once tried to maneuver any from plate to mouth with the two little wooden sticks. At Morgan, I'd never bothered learning to greet a Nigerian student in Yoruba, or a Liberian student in Kru or Krahn.

All my life, I had so invariably relied upon the security of habit that I was all but completely unaware of habit's own unremarked tenacity. I not only required neatness of space but also the meticulous preservation of small routine. In stores I'd search for brand names while knowing nothing at all about the brand-name products' serviceability.

I may or may not have known that everyone did such, or something very much like it, for the sake of preserving one's sanity. The modern age had become overcrowded with the exponential growth of the hungry little decisions that were increasingly laying claim to the peace and time necessary for making the big and important decisions. Habit was, at once, mind-saver and mind-killer—dumb, blind, salving. Opiate of the mindless masses. Indispensable friend to the anal-retentive. The glue that stuck marriages, democracies, dictatorships, and practically everything else together.

But I had, I thought, a worse case of *habit-clutch* than most.

This could have been due to growing up in a family unit headed by an overburdened insurance salesman and an overqualified homemaker. It could have been that we were so preoccupied with the numberless meannesses of the ugly awful South that we could not afford, at least for the moment, to go looking beyond. Rate tables, gray domesticity, and the ever ubiquitous humiliation of segregation summed up to a certain understandable *reduction* of us, I suppose. A certain unexamined, foreordained provincialism. It was much related to the race-business obsession of black people that coagulated in the spirit and blocked the light—the painful, mind-numbing, progress-retarding iron-weight that had been dragged around like a leg ball from slavery to freedom and beyond to wherever-the-hell-else we would ever, in a lifetime, be going.

The weight was there with me on the plane in Bamako, coloring assumptions, erecting inhibitions, accentuating the understandable perception of my own real and conspicuous isolation.

What would Gordon have felt and done here, all alone and as out of place as a goose in a phone booth? Gordon would never have come here, or even so much as thought about doing such.

But I was there and proud of myself.

Makeda's grandson. Makeda's spirit child. She had told me in so many words before I left home that I was "lookin' for something" that I would have to find before I would be able to write in my own voice. She told me that I would find something of what I needed to know in Mali and that it would "come from the past."

I was thinking about my grandmother's words to me as I went down the stairs and stepped upon the ground of Africa for the first time. I took a few steps from the plane in the direction of the terminal. I stopped and allowed the de-planed passengers behind me to go around while I turned full about to examine the details of the place carefully, to engrave permanently the picture of it on my memory—the ground, the sky, the massive old tree in the distance, the aromatic special smell of the vastness, the little Malian girl in the orange print dress boarding one of the smaller aircraft on the apron, the Arab man in a blue burnoose carrying a leather satchel through the terminal entrance, the boarding party of nineteen exotically dressed men and women politely making way for a very old woman with friable parchment skin and an arresting hand-wrapped headdress.

Just that quickly, something changed in me, something mysteriously renovating, but too new, too unfamiliar, however, to name. I felt slightly nervous, precariously euphoric.

I began walking toward the door of the terminal. A ground worker swinging a set of wheel chocks and wearing blue coveralls walked abreast of me and said, smiling, "American." That was all. *American.* Never in America, by a black or a white, had I ever been called an American. Never once. I thought, for reasons that escaped me at the moment, that this was, for all its ironic timing and meaning, hysterically funny. But the ground worker would not have understood this and I did not laugh.

Having uneventfully negotiated the immigration formalities, I exchanged at the airport currency-exchange kiosk some of my American dollars for Malian francs and took a seat in the lounge. Although I had declined to have breakfast on the plane, I still was not hungry.

There were few people in the lounge. A middle-aged scholarly-looking man sitting opposite of me caught my eye and nodded pleasantly. A tall, elegant very black woman in a chartreuse gown approached the desk agent to inquire about a flight. A gnarled old man squinched up rheumy milk-colored eyes to read the chalkboard on which flight information had been written in French. Two young men walked through the large room side-by-side, holding hands (or more precisely, fingers) in a practice I had not seen before in men who were not effeminate or homosexual. I was to see such male-to-male affection demonstrated frequently in Mali.

With no flights to arrive or depart before mine would, it remained intimate and quiet in the room, the peace broken only intermittently by the organic creak of the wooden benches and the occasionally audible exchange of people talking outside the building at a pace that seemed rapid only because I could not understand what was being said. I got up and walked over to one of the two public telephones that were semi-enclosed in partitioned spaces against the wall. The instructions appeared on the phone-housing in French. Even had I understood them, I could not have puzzled out which coins to use or where to insert them. I returned to the bench where I had been sitting.

"You are from America, aren't you?" said the scholarly-looking man sitting across from me.

"Yes." I was glad to hear words I could understand.

"I once lived in New York. I taught African history at Hunter College. I lived in New York for six years." He spoke with a heavy accent, but quite clearly, still.

"Are you from Mali?"

"Yes."

"This is my first time here."

"Then welcome to our country." He said this while slightly bowing his head in a courtly gesture.

"Thank you." I felt less alone and more sure of myself.

"If you need help with the phone, I'd be happy to assist you."

The suspicious American in me involuntarily inquired of itself why the man wanted to be helpful. Was it because this was simply the way his people behaved toward any stranger in need? Was it because I was an American? Was it because I was black? Was it because I was a black American? Was it in spite of one or all of the last three?

When Jeanne had been planning to come with me to Mali, she arranged for us the counsel of an anthropologist who was a colleague of hers at Johns Hopkins, a black Rhodes Scholar named Bern Spraggins. During a long meeting in her office, Dr. Spraggins said, among other things, "I'd suggest that you not wear on your sleeve to Africa the black American preoccupation with race. Africans outside of South Africa, Namibia, and Rhodesia don't understand why Negroes go on about it so much. They've been exploited by their Europeans rather more indirectly than we have by our Europeans. They're at a different stage of their time-release abuse than we are. They believe they've gotten back a country out of the deal and so they're in a bit of denial, but they'll get there in time. Just don't do what we do, and that is, talk about race all the time."

I wasn't sure that I agreed with her about the black American preoccupation with race. This she dismissed with little more than a small sniff, "Well, we don't consciously think about the air that we breathe but we breathe, nonetheless, with an intense subconscious consistency twenty-four hours a day."

This got us onto another subject that bore more directly on the solicitousness of the Malian Hunter College professor at the airport.

"I have this notion that I've yet to fully think through," Dr. Spraggins continued. "It's more shorthand thought than science. But when a black person travels abroad, he or she frequently discovers identities previously unexplored: the basic first-person identity, the basic interior *you*; the third-person identity, the effect on you of what you perceive others see you as being. When you meet Europeans abroad, what do you think they're seeing? An American? A black American? A placeless Negro? More importantly, when you meet a Malian in Mali, the homeland, will it bother you that you will not know what the Malian is thinking or seeing? Then, of course, there is the further complication of your *cultural* Americanness, which you may wish to deny, but will, in any case, bring you, a Negro, rejected by America, uncomfortably face to face with yourself for the first time in your life. You will learn, ironically enough, when you reach Africa, just how much you have been turned into both, a faux American and a Negro, by the very people who've rejected you. You, in the eyes of those you will encounter abroad, white and black, European and African, *are* and *are not* an American, all at the same time. The one thing that all who encounter us in the world would agree upon is that we are history's orphans— the American Negro, with that odd name coined for us by whites and intended to sound like a medical condition, a skin disorder, a name used to describe a refabricated people the world tacitly agrees now really belong nowhere."

I had instantly disliked Dr. Spraggins. Jeanne did not share this feeling, however, I think because she had always identified herself not so much with whites or America as with Haiti, a country, a culture unto itself that very much *belonged* to her. The Negro stranded in America would never know what such ownership felt like.

"Dr. Spraggins, how many black people, do you believe, think about such things?" I had asked, thinly irritated.

"Mr. March, the overwhelming majority of people, notwithstanding race, think very little about anything of abstract consequence. Day in and day out, they go vacantly about the banal business of their lives like mainstream lemmings. But they're not the point here, are they, Mr. March? People like you are the point. Black people like you who go all the way to Africa looking for themselves." She had looked unaccountably annoyed as she said this.

I put Dr. Spraggins out of my thoughts and looked at the Hunter College professor who had gotten up from his bench and started across the short patch of tiled floor that separated us.

"Bokhari! Bokhari!"

The professor turned in the direction of a man in a khaki epaulet shirt calling after him from behind the Air Mali counter.

"I *ni bara*," the man behind the counter said.

"*Ebede*," the Hunter College professor called back, waving at the man. "I am Bokhari," the professor then said to me. He was taller than I thought, an inch and a half or so taller than I was at six-foot-one. With his left hand, he redraped the sleeve of his ornately embroidered white robe to free the motion of his extended right hand. We shook hands. I noticed that he didn't hold his right wrist with his left hand as I had seen the two Africans doing at the Orly airport hotel. I wondered with mild disappointment whether he was shaking my hand this way because I was to him, firstly, an American.

I told him my name and that I would be teaching English literature on the college level in the fall. He had heard of Cheney State and seemed to know it was a predominantly black institution in Pennsylvania.

He had about him an attractive manner, a quiet completeness that seemed to afford him an ease of sorts. Unlike the veneer of charm, the pleasantness he exuded seemed to run convincingly through him.

Our bodies were turned in a manner that gave us a view through the open double wooden doors on the front side of the building. He spoke frugally of his experience in America as "memorable." He then showed surprise when I told him I had never been to New York.

Across the road from the terminal, a man stood beside a reddish earthen wall in the shimmering distance tending a dromedary. He wore great folds of a periwinkle-blue fabric that fell full to the ground. His face, polished coppery by the sun, was wrapped around and up with a long *shesh* of black cloth that tied back into a streamer resting against the small of his back. The tableau resembled a painting. Still. Timeless. Unself-conscious.

". . . One has to know where to place one's feet," the

professor was saying reflectively. "I didn't belong in New York."

I felt as if I were being guided; helped with answers to questions I had not consciously phrased. The pauses between us lengthened. Within them, I felt suspended above an open and endless natural space that acknowledged with its silence no requirement to answer for itself. The space, the tableau, the life was just what it simply was—*here*, as it had always likely been, time immemorial. I thought it hypnotically restful, and guessed that an unobstructed view of the horizon in all probability contributed to that most coveted of gifts: spiritual quietude.

As I have said, I am not a religious type, or at least in no doctrinal sense am I anyone's idea of a traditional believer. I do believe, however, that most of what has transpired in the cosmos from the beginning of time lies outside the reach of human understanding. I further believe that events are fated, and do not emerge as products of accident or happenstance. Ever. One has to believe something, and I have chosen to believe this. In fate. And in the eventual justice of fate. Or, is it more likely that I have not *chosen* anything? That things are what they are, and indeed have already happened in a future yet to disclose its decisions to me. With the scales of cosmic justice balancing back finally in favor of the long underfavored. Would that not explain the many ancient lives of my otherwise ordinary grandmother who has chosen me, of all people, to *see* for her, to foretell on her behalf the possibility of new glories inspired from the forgotten glories of the ancient past, her past, hence all of ours? And would this not explain the most unlikely meeting here in the Bamako airport waiting room with this man, Bokhari, the former Hunter College professor, who evinces both a path-lighting discernment and an encouraging kindness to me, a lost fresh victim of culture shock? A long way from home. But hadn't I always been, wherever I was and would ever be, and wasn't that the crux of the problem?

"I came home because it occurred to me that I belonged here with the large family that I missed. My wife was very unhappy in New York. Our two children were born there. My wife did not want them to grow up without knowing who they were and what they belonged to."

The easy candor with which he spoke might have seemed peculiar were we not talking in a milieu that encouraged such.

"In any case, I believe that you have come to Mali for a special reason. The least I can do is show you how to operate the telephone."

He looked at me as an avuncular figure might, and smiled. He did not ask me about my connecting flight. And for reasons I do not understand, I did not tell him, although I had an odd sense that he knew everything about what had brought me to Mali.

The coin box operated much as the American pay phones did. He showed me which coins to use and how to summon an international operator.

I thanked him.

He said simply, "I think much depends on you, young man. Do not be afraid to tell the world what you discover."

Before I could respond to this, he turned and walked back to where he had been sitting. He then took out a red pocket-sized hardback volume and began to read with concentration.

I sat down again and thought about what I would say. It was one a.m. in Baltimore. She would likely be asleep.

Jeanne would not be easy to persuade. I was sure that I had hurt her very badly, and not only by what I had done, but by how I had done it. Walking out like that. Cutting her off. Severing her with such unexplained, discourteous abruptness. While I was reasonably confident, at least at the time, that she still wished to be with me, I was equally and reasonably certain that she did not *need* to be with me. It was this very self-sufficiency of hers that I had found attractive in her from the beginning.

There is also this. Whatever it was that she had been well along toward thinking of me, she thought differently of me now, perhaps irrecoverably so.

The phone rang five times. Crestfallen, I began to take the receiver down from my ear when I heard her voice, small and hoarse with sleep.

"Hello . . . hello . . . who is it? Hello?"

"Jeanne." A long moment opened. Dawning.

"Gray? Is that you, Gray?" More incredulous than angry.

"I couldn't. I couldn't. I wanted to, but I couldn't tell you. I couldn't tell anyone. I never—I never."

"Gray?" She sounded frightened. "Where are you? Where are you calling from? Are you all right?"

"Gordon died because of me, Jeanne. My brother died because of me." I rested my forehead against the masonry wall of the open-faced phone stall.

"Gray, my darling, please tell me where you are. Please—"

"I'm in the airport in Bamako and little makes clear sense to me anymore."

Jeanne had never had reason to imprison herself in a protective shell. Her sunny spirit had always been allowed to breathe full by emotional strengths that made unnecessary for her the development of an ideology of the inevitability of universal human misbehavior. Thus, her opinion of me would not be shaped by predispositions she'd never found the need to develop about men in general.

I loved Jeanne, although I thought it somehow unethical to say this to her at that moment. Instead I said, "I can't explain this. I've only been in Mali a little while, but already there are signs that I am here because I am somehow supposed to be here, as if my coming for my grandmother were somehow foreordained."

I stopped and waited for her to say something. When she did not, I thought that I had lost the connection.

"Jeanne?"

"Yes, I'm here."

"I know this sounds crazy."

"I don't think it sounds crazy, Gray."

"I didn't realize how important this would be before I came here. It's hard to explain. You'd have to be here. What I mean is that there are some things that those who would have a life together—I mean a special life together—must do together. This is one of those things. I don't know how I know this but I do. I'm asking you to trust me in this. To believe me in this. Do you still have your ticket?"

"Yes, I have it."

"Will you come?"

She took awhile to answer. "Yes, Gray. Yes, I will come."

I told her that I would call again from Timbuktu to take down her flight schedule. Then I told her that I loved her and that I would be waiting for her at the airport in Timbuktu.

An hour later, I was bound for Timbuktu on a small Air Mali twin-engine Antonov 24B.

CHAPTER TWENTY-EIGHT

I had a second day to spend in Timbuktu awaiting Jeanne's arrival. The day before, I had walked around looking conspicuous in a faded yellow T-shirt and cotton twill khaki trousers.

The people of the town were virtually all Muslims, I was told.

Owing to that, I am guessing, the women did not look at me. At least not directly. The men and children, however, watched and smiled at me as if I were as large a curiosity to them as they were to me.

Someone who had no firsthand knowledge told me in Baltimore that all the women of Timbuktu hid their faces behind burqas. But this clearly was not the case. In fact, I saw more men covering their faces than women. The men turban-wrapped their colorful *sheshes* around their heads, and then either pulled them long below the waist across their bodies, or brought them across the lower half of their faces around and again. The women, as far as I could see, more often than not, wrapped their heads and not their faces. In all cases, however, the colors and patterns of their garments were stunning. The long robes shifted, sweeping and proud, frequently with white and periwinkle represented.

I should not have listened to anything that I was told before leaving America. For the little bit that I had been told quickly proved thin, if not flat wrong altogether upon my arrival. The Morgan library had had nothing of usefulness on Timbuktu, and nothing at all on the Dogon beyond the reference materials I'd read years before in my high school library.

The white reference desk librarian at the Baltimore city library had thought I was joking when I asked him for materials on Timbuktu.

"I always heard people say, you know, *From here to Timbuktu*, but it's not a real place, is it?"

I had said yes, it was a real place, and handed him the withdrawal slip I had completed from the lone card catalog entry the library had on Timbuktu. The librarian's search produced nothing of consequence, save his incredulous "I'll be damned" imprecation upon seeing the name *Timbuktu* printed on a card from his own card file.

Having seen no pictures, and having read virtually nothing about the city, may have been a good thing, inasmuch as the resultant void of expectation rendered my first glimpse of the place indelible.

It was literally like nothing I'd ever seen before.

I was first struck by how old and earthen the city was.

In America, the cityscape is young, mathematically perpendicular, relatively colorless, and massively nonbiodegradable, as if the sheer tonnage of it, the cold concrete fruit of its builders' will, had been violently, rudely piledriven into the naïve green earth, and imposed upon nature without nature's consent. In America, one could not look at the arrow-straight sheathing of the buildings and know the natural materials from which it had been derived. The Western cityscape, indeed, was nature's relentless enemy, an enemy that, whenever it took a mind to, caused nature to all but disappear.

In Timbuktu, the ancient irregular red-clay buildings *were* nature. Nature, reformulated into grand mosques and university buildings and homes and the like. The structures were not so much *on* the Earth as *of* the Earth. I found this harmony surprisingly settling, although I doubt this would be the assessed effect on most Americans, who are bred to appreciate slick, unforgiving exactness.

In any case, the much-fabled city was barely a shadow of its grand old self. Not long after it was established 900 years earlier by Tuareg nomads, it became the center of trade and scholarship for much of Africa and the Muslim world as well. When Europe was mired in the Dark Ages, Timbuktu, poised near the great northern turn in the Niger River, was, during the 1300s, one of the world's most advanced cities. Mansa Musa, king of the Mali empire, erected his royal residence, the Madugu, here. Gold and salt trade routes crossed here with caravans of heavily laden dromedaries that traveled from West Africa to Tripoli, Alexandria, Cairo, and beyond.

At its peak, as many as 100,000 people lived in Timbuktu. More than 25,000 students and scholars journeyed from the far reaches of the Muslim world to study and teach at its famous university, Sankore.

In 1354, the great explorer and writer Ibn Battuta, following his visit to Timbuktu, described the city as a marketplace of gold and great wealth, the African El Dorado.

By the time I arrived in June 1970, scarcely 19,000 people remained in what was then little more than a town. This was up from a low of 5,000 said to have been living there as recently as 1940.

In its ineluctable decline, the city was now much like a stubborn and aged night watchman defiantly peering into the face of death's final quiet summons.

Waiting patiently on fate at the parched southern edge of the Sahara desert's implacable approach, Timbuktu holds out as the misunderstood dying father would for the last long-anticipated visit of his wandered issue. To divulge to them an important and final bequest. To light forward their darkened paths from a bright past's failing stores before the ultimate and inevitable darkness arrives.

No trace remains of the Madugu, the king's royal palace. Now and again, in winter, a small salt caravan would arrive from Taoudenni. But trans-Saharan trade by way of the great Timbuktu was little more than ancient history. Gold was no longer the coin of commerce.

The city's greatness was done and would never return. But still, the city would not die. It had something yet to say. Something important. Particularly to those who had long before been stolen away.

"Jeanne will get here in the morning."

"Thank God," my grandmother said. This time, she sounded far away. The connection crackled and faded and then strengthened again. I had a passing vision that she was speaking to me from the deep well of the antiquity I had come all the way to Mali to explore.

"Grandma, you should see this place."

"Well. Maybe I can, son." She chuckled as she said this. "Tell me what it feels like."

"I don't know, Grandma. I know what it kinda makes *me* feel like. It's something I've never felt before. It's like the rest of the world no longer exists. Even though I know in my head it's out there, this world seems more natural. Close. Easy. Very easy. I don't know or care about what time it is, or what day or what year it is. It's as though I'm standing here a thousand years ago with funny-looking clothes on. Everything seems to be *living*—you know what I mean? The earth, the buildings—not just the people, but even the people's clothes. The people's talk in the streets, the shops. Everything's open and moving and mixing. Everything's touching. Everything's a part of everything else. I know I'm not making sense, but there are no separations

. . . wait a minute. Wait a minute, Grandma. Two elderly men in robes just walked by and greeted me. I did not know what I was supposed to say, so I just bowed and smiled . . . What did you say, Grandma?"

"I said, what is the weather like?"

"Warm. Sunny. In the middle of the day, the sun makes the orange-red earth look like it's on fire. In the evening, the Earth's color softens."

The connection crackled and hissed.

"When I was a girl, I worsh . . . sun."

"What did you say, Grandma?"

"I said I loved the sun on my skin."

"You'd be right at home here in your gowns. There are all kinds of people here. Of course, I can't tell them apart or know what they are saying, but right around Timbuktu, the Tamashek, Songhay, Moor, and Fulani people live."

"Have you met any Dogon people there yet?"

"No, but the Dogon live near here. Jeanne and I are going to visit an old library here first and then we'll go to the cliff that was in your dream."

"Tell me, Gray. Tell me what it looks like. I have this picture from my Dogon childhood in my mind. Tell me what the place looks like—the streets, the buildings. Do they have anything sticking out from them?"

I did not know at first what she meant by this, but then something occurred to me. "You mean the buildings?"

"Yes," she said expectantly.

Many of the sand-colored masonry buildings had timeworn wooden timbers protruding helter-skelter from them. One such building that had drawn my attention was sculpted in the shape of a pyramid, its four sides shot through with old beams that stuck out from the clay façades at odd angles and lengths. I thought of the timbers as heaven's handles put there by prescient builders to expedite the assistance of the gods in keeping the old structures standing right-side-up throughout eternity.

I described to her the beams that perforated many of the buildings in this way.

"I know—" And again, as if with swelling astonishment, "Gray, I know what it looks like!"

"You do?"

"Are the buildings the color of the ground? Like red sand?"

"Yes."

"I know what it looks like. In my dreams I have seen what you are seeing."

I did not try to test her further on this. For there was nothing that she wished to prove. She was interested mostly in having me describe to her the small details of everything I saw. Colors. Shapes. Structures. Smells. Sounds. The visuals of this timeless and different place.

"How are you being treated?"

"Fine. I feel a little guilty because I can't speak anything but English and people are struggling to speak to me in the few English words they know. But they've been very warm to me. Like they're trying to take care of me. I probably look lost."

"Where are you calling from?"

"There's this tea shop near the little guesthouse where I'm staying. The guesthouse doesn't have a telephone. The woman who runs it is Fulani. She speaks English pretty well."

For a while she said nothing.

"Grandma, are you still there?"

"Yes, I am still here, Gray." She changed the subject. "Do you have the old notes and drawings with you?"

"Yes, Grandma."

"And you remember what my name was in the dream, and what my father's name was?"

"Yes, Grandma, I brought everything with me."

CHAPTER TWENTY-NINE

The new sun rouged the rough plaster wall behind the small bed on which I had roused from a fitful sleep. Jeanne would be here in four hours or so. My first thoughts were addled and nervous. Not so much about the research Jeanne and I were to undertake together, as about the implication of her coming all this way for me, on the strength of what amounted to an unspoken vow that I had made to her. I knew now that she was the best thing that would ever happen to me, that I would have to take a risk, and open myself up to her.

I had to allow her to see most of the whole of me. This wouldn't be easy. I would struggle to face around to her. The tragedy of my brother's death may not have been the biggest part of the reason.

I do not mean to blame my father, but I believed he might figure in a problem that predated our current estrangement over Gordon's death.

I don't know that a child can inherit a tendency toward inwardness, but if not, the child, in all likelihood, can be socialized, I would think, in that direction.

I cannot recall that my father ever had any real friends. His family was his whole world, which included all of the few people he really trusted. Because of this, uncharacteristically, from time to time, when he was unbearably lonely, he would confide his troubles to Gordon and me, troubles that we were too young to hear, as if a child should ever be old enough to hear a parent's troubles.

Once when I was eleven, he told me, "Your mother is not happy." I had not wanted to hear this about my mother and asked him why, only as a nervous courtesy. He answered that he really didn't know why, but that he reckoned the problem was the result of an inherent incompatibility between all men and all women. He did not say this in so many words but I think this is what he meant.

What he actually said was this: "Men and women are different. We talk to each other with our top layers but the real differences are deeper. I don't know what your mother is thinking really, and she doesn't know what I'm thinking. We get along together but we're *alone* together because men and women are so different. I don't understand why this is so. I just know that it is."

I don't know what got into him and made him say such things, but they were devastating to a boy of eleven. I have always wished that he hadn't said anything, as was usually the case with him—that he hadn't dumped his awful pessimism so early at my doorstep. It may have been part of the consequence of him not having known his father. In any case, it had its effect on me. Among other things, it caused me to fear, even to accept, that my love for Jeanne would fade inevitably over time into the gray habit that, from all appearances, marked my parents' marriage, a marriage in which love was noticed, either by one or both of them, only when there was a crisis that threatened to uncouple them.

You see here that I have not mentioned my mother. This, I think, is because I had only observed the worn surface of her, her *goings-on*, the hard-governing rituals of her daily life—her habits. Because she was stronger than my father—where I had been able to witness, at least in him his pathos, his vulnerability—I'd only witnessed in her, her habits—a housedress on hard rounds, a once-fine but now long-unused mind in which chores had starved out abstraction—and her self-evident surrender, surrender to duty—housewifery duty, damnable, insatiable, life-eating, femininity-smothering, intellect-murdering, labor-intensive duty.

This was where I *came* from. This was what I feared I would promise to Jeanne.

I did have, however, at least two reasons to be hopeful about my prospects with her.

The first was my grandmother, Makeda Gee Florida Harris March who, as I saw it, lived above the plane of the known world. My parents had given me a formal education. But my grandmother had taught me to think, to dare, to imagine the possibility of unseen realms, and to paint them across the mind's eye in phantasmagoric colors. She was an instinctive teacher who taught using a method she, I'm sure, had never heard the formal name for, something my law school friends called the Socratic method where instruction was dialogical with more questions than answers. "What do you think about that, Gray?" which was her usual response to whatever it was that we were talking about. I couldn't remember either my father or mother asking me what I thought about something.

The second cause for hope was Jeanne herself, who would occupy with me a *world of ideas*, a world unavailable to the very parents who made it available to me as an unearned reward for their drudgery. My parents worked hard. My father peddling his company's gray policies, my mother slogging to "keep" house. Their work required them to leave themselves behind as they worked. Thus, they could not love each other when they worked, and because they worked so hard and most of the time, and worried the rest, they had little space left in which to love. Or at least this is how they seemed to Gordon and me. Just tired and worried-looking. And this was, as I have said, most of the time.

For Jeanne and me, it could be, indeed, I hoped it would be, very different than it had been for my parents. Jeanne and I should not be caused to leave ourselves behind when we worked because we would work together in the world of ideas, and the ideas were who we were, and moreover, the ideas were what we were to each other.

Now that I thought about it, I realized that she was not coming halfway around the world for me, but for *us*.

I recited this in my head. *I am not my father. I am not my mother. Jeanne is Jeanne and Jeanne alone, and like no other. Things are not how my father would see them. I am not so little as just a man and Jeanne is not so much as only a woman. We are not characteristic minions of some other or another faux science or determinism or popular gender prejudice. We are special, if not to the world, always, I am sure (it must be at least possible), to ourselves and to each other.*

She ducked through the low door of the plane, raised her head, and smiled brilliantly.

My heart raced with excitement.

She wore a ground-length orange dress of crinkly light cotton. The dress had a high, shallow V-shaped neckline and covered her shoulders and arms down to her elbows. Against the orange airy material of the dress, her deep chocolate skin glowed alive under the bright Malian sun.

She placed a sandaled foot carefully upon the metal tread of the stair.

My senses were keener than usual. Rapier-sharp.

I could hear the small *swish-clop* of the sandal-sole as she lifted it from the tread. I could hear the folds of the orange cotton crinkles shifting on the fresh warm breeze. I could see the ageless dance in her glistened eyes. I could sense the caution of her step giving way finally to the command of her heart.

Then she was on the ground, at home, and in my arms.

We spent the first day together walking the narrow unpaved streets of the old city. There was little in the way of motorized traffic to impede us. Save for the small wooden carts drawn by donkeys, the streets belonged almost entirely to people afoot, bantering and exchanging sentiments in a leisurely and attractive manner.

I pointed out to Jeanne a lady walking elegantly with a large wooden tray of bananas balanced upon her head. Jeanne said that this reminded her of scenes from her childhood stays in Port-au-Prince.

She expressed surprise that the women's faces were not veiled and cited as her somewhat dated authority Leo Africanus, the great Moorish writer from Granada, who chronicled from Timbuktu in 1526 that the "women of the city maintain their custom of veiling their faces."

Jeanne is naturally more outgoing than I, thus it was easy for her to ask a waiter in French what it was that was being eaten from a bowl at a restaurant whose entire front was open to the street along which we were strolling. The waiter said that porridge-like food was *to* and *na*, and when Jeanne asked what *to* and *na* was made from, the waiter said it was made from millet that had been pummeled and cooked first, and then cooled stiff before being dipped into a gravy made from okra. Then the waiter invited Jeanne to sample the dish, and she accepted without a moment's hesitation. I must have turned my body in such an attitude as to place myself safely beyond the kind waiter's courtesy, for Jeanne looked at me with an indulgent, somewhat sympathetic smile.

We moved carelessly back into the street.

"It was good!" Laughing at me. Teasing.

"I'm getting adjusted. It may take a little while."

"The world is waiting for you, darling. You've got to jump in." She laughed again. I did as well.

The muezzin's haunting call to prayer floated wide over the city above over heads. Children squealed in play. A hawker talked up from his stall the merits of his metal wares.

For us, it was true enough that the world we had left behind seem to no longer exist, and the world we had entered existed only for those of us who were there at that moment, a moment that had, in its exotic russet tone, apparently remained undisturbed for a thousand years. It was as though the moment, threadbare and tired, but beautiful still, had somehow been waiting for something. Perhaps only for a modest appreciation of its priceless treasures that lay about virtually in the open, unbothered.

Saying nothing, we stopped in what we thought must have been the middle of the city, and looked full around at it as one would a cycloramic painting. We held in our view a sight which no one that we knew had ever seen. The sight returned to us a curious emotion, the common memory of which would serve to sustain our tie to each other for years to come. Indeed, the two of us, standing upon the faded lost jewel of African glory, were jealous of a fortune the outside world had declined to acknowledge or scarcely even remember.

Had bona fide world historians been polled in the year 1200 on where the three major world regions would place 800 years thence, not one of them would likely have placed Europe first. Similarly, and with equal assurance, not one of them would likely have placed Africa last. For Europe, by the year 1200, had been by far the most backward of the three major world regions for 10,000 years.

The afternoon shadows stretched long. The streets and old buildings appeared redder than they had only moments before.

We reached the front gate of Sankore University, the last stop on our walking tour of the city.

The university's buildings were surrounded by a massive masonry wall which had been interlarded at ten-foot intervals by a series of tall obelisk columns. A towering pyramid-like structure behind the wall was visible from where we stood. The heavy wooden door in the wall was closed. There was no one within sight. The old door had something of a forbidding sacred aura about it. Discouraged by its evident antiquity, we did not try to push it open.

Before leaving the guesthouse for our walk, we had been told by a visiting historian from Belgium to "be sure that you visit Sankore University. It is older than Europe's first university, which is Salamanca in Spain, built by the Moors after they reached the Iberian Peninsula in 711 AD. There were three departments of the University of Timbuktu: Jingaray Ber, Sidi Yahya, and Sankore, perhaps the most important of the three. Students were introduced there to all of the branches of Islamic knowledge: physics, astronomy, mathematics, chemistry, medicine, law, philosophy. Modern surgery was pioneered and performed there behind those walls."

I looked at the walls of Sankore in the day's dying light and thought of what an African-American professor had said to our freshman literature class at college: "You cannot rightly consider yourselves educated persons until you have mastered the Bible and the complete works of William Shakespeare."

The ironic timing of the thought's arrival brought with it an emotion of considerable sadness and anger and private embarrassment. I had been forced to face the beast of my own inert ignorance. Ignorance of the world and of the ages, and of so much in the world that had happened completely unbeknownst to me. I knew not a jot more about anything than some unseen force or forces had allowed me to know.

Jeanne and I came down from the separate rooms we had taken to have dinner in the small meeting room on the first floor at the front of the building. There were four round wooden tables in the tiny room pushed inconveniently close to each other, requiring Jeanne and me to snake ourselves between them and into our chairs.

It was seven o'clock. Dinner for the guesthouse visitors was Western-style, modest, and palatable. Unless whispered, anything said could be heard by everyone.

Into Jeanne's ear I said in a low voice, "I'm prepared to talk about Gordon."

She awarded me a look of affording kindness. "Oh, Gray, I love you so much," whispering, "you tell me when you think the time is right."

"Okay." Relieved.

"Let's talk about tomorrow's work. What time do the libraries open?"

The libraries were the Mamma Haidara Commemorative Library and the Library of Cheick Zayni Baye of Boujbeha.

"I've made appointments for us in the morning and in the afternoon."

The solicitous man who was in charge of the Mamma Haidara Commemorative Library said, "Between the two libraries, there are over 700,000 manuscripts that survive from long ago. There were once many more. Some have disintegrated because of poor storage conditions. Some have been stolen because of their great value on the world market."

The man looked around the manuscript-laden room and then back at us as if he were gauging the good faith of our inquiry. Expecting astonishment to register on our faces, he said, "Most of the works here were authored by Africans between 600 A.D. and 1500 A.D." His expectations realized, he carried forward with heightened enthusiasm.

"They are not all here, of course, but African literatures from this period are virtually limitless. Epics, poetry, diaries, letters—written in our own African languages, many in Arabic, some now translated into French." His aspect teased with mild sardonic amusement. "Have no books been written in America about what is here—*has* been here, for what, more than a thousand years?"

We didn't know how to answer him. The librarian then smiled modestly and stopped to consider what more he would say to us. The government in Bamako was military and humorless. We were foreigners from a powerful country. One had to be careful.

"The documents are not organized as they would be in America. We are a poor country and have no resources for such." He then paused and reset the expression on his face to something somewhat less administrative.

"In these rooms rest the surviving literary evidence of Africa's golden age—our heritage." His tone changed as he said this.

The librarian had closed the main entrance door behind us after he ushered us in. The air in the large main room was cool and slightly scented with the odor of mildew that would dissipate with the arrival of the dry season.

"Was there something specific that you were looking for?" he asked in the French he'd begun to speak once he discovered that Jeanne spoke the language.

"No sir, not immediately. We'd like to read first and make inquiries of you in an hour or two."

"Please sit over here." He pointed to a long table on which some of the manuscripts were stacked.

"Thank you," Jeanne said, and bowed slightly in her long dress that was blue for the occasion, but otherwise not unlike the modest dress she had worn on her arrival the day before.

The man started to leave and then turned back, facing us. "You are Afro-Americans. Not so?"

"Yes," Jeanne said, welcoming the implied suggestion of a bond.

"We don't see many Afro-Americans here. Why is that? Do you know?" His voice bore no trace of accusation.

"I am not sure, sir, but I think it is because we have not been told about it."

"Well then, we shall have to do something about that, won't we?" And then for the second time, the librarian smiled. Before leaving the room, he placed on the table before us two newish-looking scholarly monographs that had been written in English. The first monograph focused on the Greek historian Herodotus and was authored by Gertrude Stryker, an antiquities specialist at the University of London. The second monograph was written by Khalid Said, an Egyptologist at Cairo University.

While Jeanne was deciding which of the French-translation documents to read first, I began paging through Stryker's monograph. I, of course, had read of the much-heralded Herodotus in my humanities courses at Morgan. He'd been described by my professors, and by the Western academy generally, as "the father of history."

On page 3 of the monograph, I came upon the following passage written by Herodotus himself:

The names of nearly all the gods came to Greece from Egypt . . .
These practices, then, and others I will speak of later, were
borrowed by the Greeks from Egypt.

At the foot of the same page, I saw the following con-
nective passage written in 50 B.C. by Diodorus Siculus:

They also say that the Egyptians are colonists sent out by the
Ethiopians . . . and the larger part of the customs of the Egyp-
tians are, they (i.e., the Greek historians) hold, Ethiopian, the
colonists still preserving their ancient manners.

After reading the first three pages of Said's monograph
on ancient Egypt, which incorporated photographs of ancient Egyptian statuary, I understood why the librarian had
wanted us to examine these two documents before delving
into the library's great trove. The Egyptians Herodotus had
referred to—Pharaoh Narmer of the first dynasty (3000
B.C.), Cheops, builder of the Great Pyramid, Mentuhotep,
founder of the eleventh dynasty, and others—were all very
unmistakably black.

The moldering ancient manuscripts that immediately
surrounded us had been originally written in Arabic and in
African languages by African scholars between the twelfth
and nineteenth centuries. Most had been translated into
French. Jeanne read from them aloud in English translating
for me as she went. The treatises touched on every imagin-
able area of scholarly study. The full run of the sciences.
Philosophy. Law. Religion. And medicine, as well, studied forward from the seminal work of the ancient Egyptian
physician Imhotep (circa 2300 B.C.), to whom the Greek,
Hippocrates, following more than 2,000 years behind,
owed a great debt.

Jeanne read to me like this deep into the morning. Giving me an overview of the general tenor of the works, she read a little from one manuscript, and rather more or less from others.

One document, for example, described the manufacture of pots in the Khartoum (Sudan) of 7000 B.C. Coming well before such had been accomplished in Jericho, the world's earliest known city. Another described the method used in implementing terraced hillside cultivation at Yeha in Ethiopia that Europeans would borrow and later claim to have invented.

She read from the writings of the eighteenth-century Timbuktu scholar El Hadj Oumar Tall, and indicated with a telling look her appreciation of the passage's modern application:

> *Tragedy is due to divergence and because of lack of tolerance . . .*
> *Glory to he who creates greatness from difference and makes*
> *peace and reconciliation.*

My grandmother liked summer mornings and she liked them best for the moments just after sunrise when she could feel the touch of the cool air's innocent promise upon her skin. Save for the sleepless crickets' song, the neighborhood, carved up by the city's fathers, was stock-still and quiet.

Jeanne and I, in the late Malian afternoon, were reading documents in the Mamma Haidara library in Timbuktu when my grandmother in the retreating darkness of early morning on Duvall Street made her way down the groaning stair and into the little parlor. She'd raised the window sash six inches and sat down in her padded rocker to breathe in the new day. While trying to envision us a world and eight time zones away, she'd fallen ever so seamlessly into the arms of Morpheus. With little to remind her of the time and place in which she was at present living, the space between the dream and her little parlor seemed to cover scarcely more than an instant. The dream itself may have begun the moment she'd slipped into sleep. It may have lasted little more than a second or two.

As she would later remember it to me, she as a young woman had been standing tiptoed in the orangish late-afternoon sun. She had been waiting—excited and expectant—amongst a crowd of thousands outside the colonnaded stone portico at the Great Hypostyle Hall in the monumental city of Thebes. The massive columns from base to capital measured some thirty feet in height and more than nine feet in diameter. There were 134 of the richly inscribed columns arranged in sixteen rows by the overwhelming structure's architect.

The crowd had then sent up a deafening roar. My grandmother had looked toward the hall of columns and seen what had caused the crowd to erupt. From between the towering columns, Pharaoh Mentuhotep, leader of the eleventh dynasty and uniter of two Egypts under one rule, strode out onto the great hall's tiled forecourt. The great pharaoh, now the ruler of all of Egypt, was tall and handsome and very very black. (His complexion, of course, was quite unremarkable and meant nothing to my grandmother at the time. Indeed, his color had been much the same as that of all the people she had ever seen.) My grandmother had looked then upon the mammoth stone structures that were evidence of Thebes' undisputed greatness and raised her arms to the sky in praise of the setting sun. All that she beheld that day was of her people's making and her people's making alone.

Emerging from the scales of her short dream back into the cramped drabness of her Duvall Street parlor, she'd said aloud into the tiny room's barren space, "We can only save ourselves from the inside out." She had uttered the words while passing through the space—a measureless metaphysical membrane—that separated the life in Thebes she had just visited from her waking contemporary life in the little walk-up on Duvall Street.

Jeanne was tired but did not feel so, and read further, until it became unmistakably clear how greatly advanced was Africa in the arts and sciences during the whole of the Middle Ages.

She leaned against me and continued to read. She rested her face on my arm. She read like this until she could read no further, having been overcome by the immensity of the experience that we were sharing. At some point she stopped reading and turned her face to mine. Only then did I realize that what I'd felt on my arm were her tears. I smiled at her, and with my fingertips scarcely brushing her skin, I wiped away her tears.

I thought about what my grandmother had said metaphorically to me when I was a boy about most people wasting their lives staring at fences. Thinking about her now—sense-messaging her from the marrow of my excited spirit: *We're not staring at a fence here, Grandma. Thanks to your exquisitely special soul, we're not staring at a fence. It's like I'm seeing myself whole for the first time.*

My thoughts wandered to Dr. Abana and how what he had said had shocked Morgan's students but not me. Not me, because of what my grandmother had read to me from the Book of Matthew in the Braille Bible of hers when I was scarcely more than ten. Words that Grandma told me were the words of Jesus:

The Queen of the South shall rise up in the judgment with this Generation, and shall condemn it: for she came from the

Uttermost parts of the Earth to hear the wisdom of Solomon.

And then, from the Book of Chronicles, she had read to me more than once:

And when the Queen of Sheba heard of the fame of Solomon,
She came to prove Solomon with hard questions in Jerusalem,
with a very great company, and camels that bare spices, and
gold in abundance, and precious stones: and when she was
come to Solomon, she communed with him of all that was in
her heart.

For some reason I'd never thought about, my grandmother read to me from the Bible more about Ethiopia than about anything else. Once I remember her reading to me about a Candace, queen of the Ethiopians; another time, about the wife of Moses—an Ethiopian woman named Zipporah; and just months ago, about an African ruler named Tirhakah, the king of Ethiopia and Egypt (689–664 B.C. twenty-fifth dynasty), who had fought to defend Palestine from domination by the Assyrians. Then, lastly, her reference on the phone to the queen of Sheba's son Menelik, who had taken the Ark of the Covenant from his father, King Solomon, and carried it home to Ethiopia; a story she had learned from her dreams of Lalibela, as it was not, I now knew, found in the Bible.

The day dying, I asked the librarian for manuscripts written by and about the Dogon people. He said he would try and find them for me.

I then, as an afterthought, asked for any manuscripts that had been written by scientists and religious scholars associated with Sankore University in the early 1400s. He said this would be easier to locate and returned ten minutes later with two manuscripts that had been translated into French from the original Arabic.

Jeanne began to read to me again. In the first of the two manuscripts, an African surgeon named Musa described a successful new surgery he had performed in 1405 at Sankore to remove "clouds from the lens of an elderly religious leader's eyes." The patient had been all but blind. Musa had restored the old man's sight.

I said to Jeanne that the clouds Musa described were cataracts. I then asked her, "What else does Musa's report say about the surgery?"

"Nothing, except the patient's name."

"What was it?"

"Ongnonlu."

I withdrew from the old plastic sleeve the notes I had taken at age fifteen from my grandmother's description of her Dogon life in the late 1300s. I gave it to Jeanne to read. Within moments, she gasped.

Ongnonlu was the name of my grandmother's Dogon father.

CHAPTER THIRTY

It was easily the most stunning natural formation that I had ever seen. It soared 600 feet above the baked ground like an undulating river-wall of marble red stone. The great Bandiagara escarpment that my grandmother described to me from her dream.

Three of us and a driver had traveled three hours by donkey cart from Bankass, a gateway village to Dogon country. Jeanne sat beside Douda, the driver, on the little wooden bench board. I sat in the load-bearing section of the cart beside a foreign-educated Dogon guide who had been introduced to us by the solicitous curator of the Mamma Haidara Commemorative Library.

The guide's name was Yéhéné. He looked to be in his mid-thirties and was otherwise unremarkable of appearance save for his eyes which were pacifistically quiet and inward-looking. I asked him a number of questions about the Dogon's Bado rites, how they were performed, their mystical meaning.

The rocky road, winding snugly along the base of the cliff, traveled noisily under the *crick-crack* of the steel-belted wooden wheels of the cart, making conversation all but impossible.

The sky was high and clear. The cliff ribboned ahead as far into the distance as the eye could see.

It was late afternoon and cool under the great cliff's canopy of shade. I watched the back of Jeanne's body rocking in lazy counterpoise over the irregularities of the bumpy trail. She turned and smiled toward me before looking up at the sculpted striated massiveness of the bluff. In a communion of discovery, she glanced back at me again and shook her head in marvel.

Impressively—since there was no telephone service to Teli at that time—Yéhéné had somehow managed to arrange a meeting for us in the little cliff-side village with a *hogon*, the highest of Dogon religious authorities.

Yéhéné told us that he did not normally make such arrangements, but he had done so in our case because it was plain to him that we were not conventional tourists, and that we knew a great deal about Dogon religious beliefs as well. This knowledge was uncommon, he said, particularly in Americans.

Before leaving Timbuktu in a weathered Renault station wagon, Jeanne had studied my ten-year-old handwritten record of my grandmother's dream, as well as her sketch of the elliptical orbits of Sirius A, Sirius B (Po Tolo), and Emme Ya (the Sorghum Female) around the bright star, Sirius.

On the morning of our departure, we had talked over both the notes and the drawing with Yéhéné. He affirmed to us their general accuracy and did not inquire into the provenance of either.

Yéhéné had briefly visited New York City for the first time the year before on diplomatic assignment to the Malian Mission at the United Nations. He half-jokingly told us that he had been "surprised" at the way Americans casually disparage their religious and political leaders publicly. He had not seen the practice as an expression of free speech, but rather as a show of "bad manners and a failure of human charity." When he spoke to us of his own local officials, his *hogon*, his elders, his priest, he used words ("peaceful . . . loving") that would strike most Americans as hagiographic. (He did not speak of the president in Bamako who was a military man.) Though he did not say it in so many words, our impression was that Americans appeared to him generally crude and overly aggressive.

Much of this had come out over a lunch of rice and vegetables that we had taken back at Bankass, the village in which we transferred from the Renault station wagon to the more terrain-appropriate donkey cart.

Onward, the little cart creaked.

I felt inexpressibly *free* beneath the cloudless sky, undisturbed, comforted even, by the unobtrusive salving sounds of nature—the small bray of the donkey, the caw of an unfamiliar fowl, the unintelligible quiet greeting of a passerby, nature's soothing rhythm unmarred.

Western civilization, wherever it could, had laid waste to the natural world, while forgetting the human animal's essential need of it.

Here was time passing without the metronomic measure of its relentlessly invasive tick. We were *here* at the base of the magnificent escarpment. That was all. Jeanne, Yéhéné, Douda, and I.

Being. Just. By itself sufficient. Time, neither enemy nor friend. Only *there*. As witness. Assigning value to life in its silent ration of it.

In the swirling high stone face of the escarpment, Yéhéné pointed out to us pockets where homes had been carved out and decorated with elaborately fashioned dark hardwood doors. The doors, Yéhéné told us, were displayed as works of art in homes around the world.

In centuries past, the cliff had provided a living refuge for the Dogon from slave hunters. Now it further served as a Dogon burial ground.

Approaching Teli, we heard the two-volume percussion music of women rhythmically striking millet against stone mortars with long-handled wooden pestles. Hard and sharp against the mortars' bottoms. Next, pulled soft and long against the side. Twenty or more mortars struck thus in concert. Syncopated. And then once in a while, the anomalous and wonderful offbeat blow for jazz.

Somewhere in the soft, sweetly timed swooshing drag-note, I sensed an elemental tug of kinship.

The male luminaries of the village, the elders and chiefs, were assembled on the *togu-na*, a gazebo-like structure of ideograms carved into pillars beneath an ornate roof.

Yéhéné made the introductions.

The men seemed to have been put on notice that we were coming. They were most gracious, presenting Jeanne with an array of well-crafted artifacts and a bouquet of pretty flowers. As Americans, it had not occurred to Jeanne and me that we should bring gifts.

The Dogon elders and chiefs at the *togu-na* spoke to us in Dogon, not in French. Thus, we were to rely upon Yéhéné to translate.

Jeanne said to Yéhéné in English, "Please express to them our gratitude for their hospitality."

When Yéhéné translated this, the tallest of the five men was looking at me, I guessed, with an expectation that I would speak first. He turned toward Jeanne and said, "We are honored to have you as guests of our village."

It may have been at this point that I began to know, for the first time, the limitations of language. The elders and chiefs had been effusively welcoming to us. At the time, owing to certain cultural presuppositions that were unfortunately wired into me, I embarrassingly mistook what was to them an obligatory courtesy for deference. The aggressive kindness of theirs that I had ascribed to our self-touted Americanness, I would later learn, they extended without exception to *all* visitors.

Yéhéné said, "They have asked you to join them for tea but I have explained to them that the *hogon* should not be kept waiting."

Yéhéné then drew us away amidst handshakes and warmly expressed pleasantries. As we were going, the youngest of the men spoke softly to Yéhéné in Dogon. Yéhéné smiled at the man and shook his head in sympathetic discouragement.

"What did he say to you?" I asked.

"He said to tell you that he's sorry."

"Sorry about what?"

Yéhéné looked uncomfortable. "He wanted me to tell you that he is sorry for what happened to you."

I said, "I don't understand."

Yéhéné averted his eyes. "My people possess a very old knowledge. For thousands of years we have known about the workings of the universe and we remember all."

Jeanne and I must have looked hopelessly confused, causing Yéhéné to breathe deeply before saying, "He wants to tell you that he is sorry that you were taken away."

CHAPTER THIRTY-ONE

We walked into the cool shade of a giant banyan tree that grew near the base of the escarpment. The tree was old and wide and appeared to require in support of its great weight the six huge trunk roots that muscled over and under the ground to a radius of sixty feet or more.

I read the recognition in Jeanne's expression.

"How long do these trees live?" she asked.

I smiled and did not answer as we sat with Yéhéné on the knees of the tree's gnarled buttress roots.

Moments later a dark, very small, very elderly man walked toward us alone. He was dressed simply in a long white robe and a cap not unlike that which my grandmother said that the Dogon priest who was her father had worn.

The small man looked directly at us as he walked. His face was long with well-cut features that were fixed in a grave arrangement.

"This is the *hogon*," Yéhéné said, as we rose to greet the high priest.

Yéhéné had said to us before leaving Timbuktu that the *hogon* we would be meeting was "special," that he was not only a spiritual leader but "carries the story of the Dogon people in his head." I had heard of such figures in Africa, as had Jeanne. I had been told that they were called *griots*, but Jeanne said that the term *griot* was a French coinage, and that the indigenous word *djeli* was more appropriate.

Four hand-carved chairs were brought from a nearby

ochre-colored masonry building and the *hogon*, whose name was not told to us, invited us to sit. A thick sweet tea was served by a pretty young girl in a long brilliant yellow dress.

The *hogon* was pleasant of mien, but enigmatically quiet, as if the exigencies of the moment were less important to him than the demands of Amma and the burden of remembered history.

Jeanne and I had talked at length the night before about how best to proceed. Besides the straight-forward questions that had to be asked, we were, for the most part, culturally very much at sea. Remembering that Haiti had remained culturally more African than black America— indeed, more so than any black society in the western hemisphere—Jeanne strongly advised that we not advance too quickly to the business at hand, as Americans were prone to do, but to pay, first, punctilious attention to the requirements of courtesy, requirements we'd already run afoul of by arriving without gifts.

Jeanne said, "No matter how anxious you feel about charging forward with the questions, hold yourself back or you'll seem—what is it the English-speaking Caribbeans say?—*broogoo* to him. Crude."

I followed Jeanne's advice although this was not easy to do.

We drank tea and spoke of inconsequential matters. The *hogon* asked what our impressions were thus far of Timbuktu, and Mali in general. He told us that he had heard much about America but did not think it likely that he would ever visit.

After a space in our talk, he said calmly, "What is it that you wish to ask me?"

He appeared possessed of a certain prescience and the suddenness of his question for a moment put me off my stride. I gathered resolve. Beginning then with this: "Was there ever a priest here named Ongnonlou?"

"There have been many priests here by that name."

Yéhéné, translating, seemed surprised by the question. It was foreign to any context that we'd discussed with him. If the *hogon* was surprised, he did not show it.

I drew a long breath and looked at Jeanne before going on. "In the year 1394, was there a priest here named Ongnonlou?"

"By your calendar?"

There are others?

"The Dogon have four calendars: a solar calendar, a Sirius calendar, a Venus calendar, and a lunar calendar."

"I mean 1394 years after the death of Christ." I feared that I may have offended him.

He smiled distantly. "Yes."

"There was a Dogon priest here by that name in 1394 A.D.?"

"Yes." The answer had come without hesitation.

I did not know quite how to continue. I had the odd feeling that he knew why we had come, that he—how else can one say it?—sympathized with us, and wanted to help.

"He was the blind priest who became a great *hogon*."

"Did he have a daughter?" I was growing nervous. Jeanne put the tips of her fingers on my forearm and touched me lightly, briefly.

"He had four daughters and five sons."

"Nine children?"

"Yes." Again the distant smile. Knowing. Terribly knowing.

"Who was the youngest child?"

This time he drew the smile between us. "The youngest child of the great *hogon* Ongnonlou was a girl. Her name was . . ."

He called the girl's name, but I could not hear it discerningly enough to lend to it the sounds and symbols of an English-language phonetic.

"Bright Light," said Yéhéné, completing the translation of what the *hogon* had said.

"It was known before she was born that she was to be a divine soul, a soul that had lived before and would live many times again. Thus the name Bright Light."

"How did she die?"

"I cannot tell you that."

This may have been a rebuke of some sort. I could not determine whether or not this was his intention.

"Late in the year of 1401," he smiled as he referred to our calendar, "Bright Light went with the women of the village, as she had always done, to wash clothes by the river. She became separated from the women and disappeared. She was never seen again." The knowing directness of the look. The eyes lambent, alive.

"What happened to Ongnonlou?"

"As a solace for the loss of his divine child, the creator god Amma gave him back his sight."

I picked up my cloth bag and removed from it the drawing which was protected by the clouded plastic sleeve. Passing the drawing to him, I did not say what it was, or that my grandmother had created it from a dream of a past life.

The *hogon* examined it without surprise and did not ask where it had come from. He spoke softly to Yéhéné, then rose and walked toward the rock face of the escarpment.

Yéhéné directed us to follow. The *hogon* entered a narrow cleft in the sandstone cliff that was screened from above by a huge knife-edged crag.

"Come. Come," he called in Dogon over his shoulder as we followed him deep into the face of the escarpment.

Forty feet in, the cleft widened into a cool stone-walled cavity that was lighted from above with golden supernal sunlight. In the center of the space stood a broad stone column of obvious great age measuring ten feet in height. The column had been impressed by a skilled stone artisan with intricate markings that were unmistakably Dogon.

"Come. Come."

As we drew closer, we saw that the engravings described the elliptical orbits of three small stars around Sirius. The drawing that my grandmother had made was virtually a perfect replica of the markings on the stone column. The orbit lines chiseled into the column, though old, had remained over the centuries easily discernible. First, there was Sirius, the bright blue star I had seen from my backyard on that cold night ten years before. Then, carved into the column was Sirius A, which had not been seen through a telescope by a Western astronomer before 1862. Then, Sirius B (Po Tolo) that the Dogon say is made of a metal they call *sagulu* which, according to them, is heavier than all of the iron on Earth. Lastly, scored into the ancient stone statue was the tiny star Emme Ya that Western astronomers had yet to see, or even identify as existing.

After allowing us time to examine the statue closely, the *hogon* spoke for the first time since entering the room. "The French scientist Dieterlen came here with a team of experts ten years ago to talk to us and look at the heavens carved into the stone. They said at the time that the carving was more than 400 years old. But they were wrong. The carving is much older than that. The Dogon have known about the movements of the stars and the planets for more than 5,000 years. Saturn with its rings. Jupiter and its moons. Sirius and its stars. The heavens all."

Jeanne said that a young American astronomer named Carl Sagan had explained that Europeans might have visited the Dogon in the 1920s and informed them of astronomical matters. The *hogon* merely smiled and moved his fingers across the effaced engravings on the ancient stone statue.

It was very still in the little rock-faced room. The smallest sound trailed around the smooth walls.

I sensed that the meeting had come to an end.

The *hogon* said, as if to settle the matter, "In time, they will find Emme Ya. What will they then say?"

With little or no thought, I reached into my rucksack and took out the picture I had taken of my grandmother the day before I left for college. Without comment, I handed it to the *hogon*.

"Oh yes, yes, yes," he murmured softly, almost as if to himself. "Our people recognized long ago that she was a special soul. What a great honor it is to finally see her in the flesh." His face alight with wonderment, he studied the small snapshot closely and, for long moments, remained quiet.

"Was she once an Akân woman?" When I was ten, I had heard that same question asked by the mysterious man at the 6th Street market.

"I think that, yes, she was."

I looked at Jeanne. The cool space in the cavity was silent and completely still. It felt as though we had ceased to breathe for fear that movement of any sort would distract the *hogon*.

Then he said almost inaudibly, "Adinkra."

I had hear the word before, from my grandmother.

"I'm sorry. I don't understand."

"The symbol there behind her. It is an Adinkra symbol. It is from the Ashanti of Ghana. *Nyame nwu na mawu*. The symbol represents to the living the immortality of the soul. The message behind the symbol comes to us from Amma or

Creator God. It has deep spiritual significance to Africans throughout this region."

I recalled the English translation of the same passage that I had read, on the flight across the Atlantic, in Professor Opoku's book.

> *"God does not die and I shall, therefore, not die" is an expression of the belief in the eternity of God and the immortality of the soul, which is the spark of God in man.*

The *hogon* knelt and took from his robe a small brown leather pouch. He filled the pouch with soil dug from the area of the engraved stone column's base.

He then rose and, with a formal gesture, presented me with the soil.

"The Dogon people would be honored if you would give this to her upon your return to America."

And then the old *hogon* was gone.

Jeanne, Yéhéné, and I sat for a while under the banyan tree before boarding the little donkey cart that would take us part of the way back to Timbuktu. The discussion with the *hogon* had had a disproportionate effect on Yéhéné, I think, because he had no notice of all that the discussion would involve.

We had been silent for a time, digesting things, when Yéhéné, looking at the ground musingly, said, "In your country, there is a great professor of our past. His name is John Henrik Clarke. A Negro American like yourselves. Do you know of him?"

Jeanne said that she did, though she had not read his work. I confessed to have never heard of him.

Yéhéné looked disappointed. "He was here many times."

I said nothing.

"He was blind also, you know. I met him in New York. He taught at one of the colleges there and would come to the UN to speak with the Africans there."

Yéhéné peered around musingly.

"He said to me once, 'I see the world clearly because I am blind. I am less distracted. I have the darkness in which to think and remember and know who I am. When I speak in America about the Dogon and their ancient knowledge of the cosmos, the *academy* works its collective authority to make me out as a lunatic. The first line of academic hostility to the notion of Africans having a past is to distract everyone in the world from searching for it. But I cannot see the distractions. All I do in here is think. Thinking in our people is somehow seen to be dangerous to the academy. When one does so by overrunning the rampart of glossy diversion, the West's first line of cultural hegemonic defense, the academy's centurions come out firing upon us like missiles from underground silos. Such is the West's hostility to the very notion that black people might have done something great as an outcome, not of individuals formed by *them*, but rather as products of great civilizations formed by their own people. The consequence of this, the consequence of the West's ceaseless cultural antipathy toward us, is that they have defeated us finally by causing us to think so little of ourselves. They have sought to guarantee our defeat by diverting us from even seeking to discover ourselves. But I am not distracted. I am blind.'

"Your Professor Clarke said these things to me. He is a great man and you, my dear Gray, have never heard of him. So sad. So sad."

We got back to the guesthouse in Timbuktu that evening after the dinner hour had ended and the two-person staff had left for home. The pendulum of our aroused emotions had swung back, with postadrenaline force, in the direction of hunger and fatigue. I accepted with no small gratitude Jeanne's offer to share the vendor-machine potato chips and sweets that she, before leaving Baltimore, had squirreled away in the pockets of her suitcase.

The evening sky was flecked brilliant with stars. The air was cool and dry. I stowed the leather pouch filled with soil in the bottom of the satchel in which I kept the notes and my grandmother's drawing of the Sirius star system. I had left the snapshot of my grandmother with the *hogon* as a token of appreciation, while fearing that I may have committed a faux pas of some sort. I bathed and changed into fresh clothes and headed for Jeanne's room, a thirty-foot walk along a narrow hall lighted by a single yellow bulb seated in the trunk of an ebony-wood elephant-head sconce.

Jeanne opened the door dressed in a white linen shift that augmented the rich bloom a day of sun had raised from her dark brown skin.

"This way, my Gray," playing with me now, seating me on the little bed with a thin mattress, serving the vendor-machine fare with cheery theatricality. She was anything but a brooder. She had a talent for happiness that I envied. Yet, I suspected, when she needed to be, she was as malleable as cast iron. God I loved her. Loved her silly. Especially tonight. This night. In this place. After today.

She was performing for me now. Walking about. Guileless. Funny. Very funny. Celebrating what had happened today without yet seeing the full stunning significance of it. Neither of us could possibly yet. Laughing. Laughing at me in that way that one only laughs when one is in love. And I laughed with her laughing at me. For I was celebrating not just the day, but us, and that she *knew* me—could and did know me, and was only the second person on Earth to do so. We had nothing to hide from each other anymore. Hence, we were not embarrassed by the giddiness that we shared toward the backside of now.

"You should have seen yourself, Gray." Giddiness subsiding. Laughter quieting. Recognition dawning. Belief lagging still. Eyes loving.

"You should have seen *yourself*, Jeanne."

"You walked into the mountain and found a lamp unto weary feet. Oh my God, who must your grandmother really be?"

"I don't know." Nearly whispering this.

Jeanne sat beside me on the bed. We were silent for an indeterminate period.

Jeanne asked, "Has she had other experiences like this?"

"Yes." I told her about my grandmother's life in Spain as a Moor, and then about her ill-fated flight with her husband from a Virginia slave plantation. "She has also had recent flashes of a sequel to a dream she had when I was a young boy. The flashes come not in dreams, but when she is awake. The dream itself is of a life she lived in the twelfth century in Lalibela, Abyssinia. In the dream, she is witnessing with her friend a procession of church members about to consecrate one of Lalibela's eleven interconnected stone mountainside churches. In the flashes, she is sitting alone underground in one of the churches which is carved in the shape of a cross from solid rock. Grandma said the cross, which is also carved into the stone roof of the church, is different from the cross we are used to seeing. The cross on the roof that follows the shape of the underground church has crossing members of equal length."

We were quiet again. Our bare arms touching lightly.

Loved skin feels quite like no other. With its special

properties and energies. Synergies that alter the heart rate. Blood pressure. Colors of the cosmos.

This business of man and woman and magic is not to be looked upon rationally anyhow, is it? Opposed counterparts of a troubled species. Counterparts that would seem so irremediably incompatible. Misfitting templates. One tissue, hard against the other, soft and aromatic. Outlooks hopelessly dissonant. Misinterpretations insanely inevitable. Yet whence comes the magic but from such fundamental and irreconcilable difference. The sweet frisson. Smooth flat surfaces do not bond fast to one another, nor do the saw-cut souls of man and woman join harmoniously when the alignment is ill-fated from the start. But when fortune smiles the perfect union, when kindness and magic can be mutual, all but a little of life's hard game is won.

I turned off the little lamp at the head of the bed. Jeanne and I embraced gently, saying nothing. We removed our clothes. Unhurriedly. We laid on the bed holding, caressing each other for a considerable period. Then we made love for the first time.

Tenderly.

CHAPTER THIRTY-TWO

Mrs. Grier seemed to have mislaid much of her composure.

"Lawd, ah'm so glad you home safe, boy. How was that Africa?"

"It was fine, Mrs. Grier. It was wonderful."

Bustling about the little parlor making ready, she glanced at me doubtfully.

"Ah'm jest glad, thas all. Ah'm jest glad you home safe and soun'."

It was nearly afternoon and my grandmother had been taking a nap when we arrived. Despite my discouragement, Mrs. Grier woke her and told her that I was sitting in the parlor with "the girlfrien'."

Dusting feverishly, Mrs. Grier sprouted tiny fresh beads of perspiration above her lip. "Thank you for taking such good care of 'im."

Jeanne smiled distractedly. She was nervous. Not frantic, as was the case with Mrs. Grier, no doubt, but nervous, still. I had never before seen her nervous.

We sat side-by-side bolt upright on a stiff little Victorian settee. I lifted from the coffee table an unusual antique bronze cross and examined it.

"You every bit as beautiful as Gray said you was."

"Thank you, ma'am."

"You sure I can't get ya'll somethin' whilst you waitin' for Makeda?"

"No thanks, Mrs. Grier. We're fine. Tell Grandma not

to hurry. We've got plenty of time."

Jeanne looked at the Adinkra symbol displayed in the middle of the wall hanging and then at the cross I had been studying.

"I've seen a cross like that somewhere before, but I can't remember where." She was quiet for a while, then she said, "I remember now. Oh yes, it's Ethiopian. It's a Lalibela cross. I couldn't place it at first because I had never seen one in the United States. A wealthy Ethiopian Christian friend I went to school with in Paris showed me one that she owned that was very similar to this one. Hers was an antique—hundreds of years old and very valuable. My friend's cross was almost identical to this. I'm almost sure this is from Lalibela."

We looked at each other.

"How did your grandmother come into possession of this?"

Before I could answer, we heard a footfall on the stairs above. Remembering my early training, I returned the cross precisely to its former position on the table. The old wooden stairs creaked with age. Jeanne gripped my hand and rose to her feet, pulling me up with her.

My grandmother turned through the vestibule and moved into a parlor that appeared just as it had when I was five. She paused in the afternoon sun shaft that must have felt warm on her skin.

"Welcome home, Gray." Sightless eyes agleam. Arms open. "So at last I get to meet your Miss Burgess. Hello, my dear. Welcome to my home. So glad to have you here."

Her voice had a rosy enveloping quality to it, causing Jeanne to visibly relax. My grandmother wore a generously draped, resplendently embroidered raw silk white gown with a head-wrap of the same fabric and color. Her uncovered eyes looked synchronously sightless and penetrating. It was as if she were seeing all and nothing.

I went to her and hugged her in silence for a long while. I led her to her red-velvet rocking chair, though she didn't need me to guide her. I then brought Jeanne by the hand around the little coffee table and over to where my grandmother was sitting.

"I-I've so looked forward to meeting you, Mrs. March." Jeanne grasped her hand and leaned down to embrace her.

"And I you, my dear. You'll never know how good you've been for Gray. I hear it in his voice."

"Thank you, ma'am."

"Gray, would you go to the kitchen and ask Gertrude to bring us—what would you like, dear, coffee, tea, juice?"

"Tea, thank you."

"Tea for Jeanne, and what about you, Gray?"

"Tea will be fine for me, Grandma. What can I bring you?"

"Tea as well."

After I left the room, my grandmother spoke to Jeanne: "I don't say this because he's my grandson, but he's a fine young man. He's had some tough things to handle. And he loves you very much. But I'm sure you already know that."

"Yes, ma'am. And I love *him* very much."

"I know, dear. I know. I can feel it. Now I can relax. Take good care of him. He's like a son to me."

"I will, Mrs. March."

The sun poked its beam through a V-shaped opening in the tall cumulus cloud. Its piercing ray seemed to arrest my grandmother's heed. She turned toward it and raised her face to its warming light.

She lowered her eyelids then, and appeared to relocate to and from somewhere in the far past, and then back again into the little room. She spoke very quietly—as if her words were offered not for us, but as a poultice, a salving rumination, a solace of sorts, to offset the man-made modern social condition; a modest celebration, perhaps, the reasons for which only she could know sufficient cause to understand or appreciate.

It was warm in the room. Across its deep shade, the sun seemed to choose her as its point of interest. She kept her face turned to it as she enunciated her words with meticulous care. Whispering meditatively as if to herself, "Here we are."

Was she speaking of a time or a place? I couldn't know.

Jeanne and I said nothing.

We waited.

Then drawing us in, she said, "I think that I remember most everything now. The grandest of times were of an ancient age in which our people worshipped this very sun. I think it must be those few things that are ageless—the sun, the soul, the universe—that join me from then to now, and to you.

"For our people, these present times are, without doubt, the worst of times—the self-destructiveness, the willing self-abasement—but know that this will pass and we will be restored of our health. I will die and live on among you to see this—and so shall you.

"Now, Gray," my grandmother continued, sounding more like herself again, "tell me what you have learned from the *hogon* about my father and the Dogon heavens.

"I want you to tell me everything that happened. First, what it looked like, and then what it felt like—the air, the rain, the wind—and the people, the earth, the night sky, the houses, and then the smells, the sounds—everything."

Despite these requests, I had the clearest conviction that my grandmother already knew everything that we were about to tell her.

"I need to know what they told you."

Later, I would come to believe that she had asked these questions more for our benefit than for hers.

I began as detailed an account as I could recall of all that had happened, starting with my encounter with the Senegalese room service waiter at the Orly airport hotel, and going virtually hour-by-hour through to the meeting Jeanne and I had with the *hogon*.

While I was talking she retrieved the bronze cross from the spot where I had replaced it on the table and began to move the palm of her hand slowly back and forth across its detailed surface.

I described to her the centuries-old banyan tree, which, I told her, was very like the one in her dream. She emitted just above a whisper, "Aah, aah," her sightless eyes moving from the sun and into the room, locking onto the location of my voice.

"Your name was Bright Light," I said to my grandmother. Eyes shining, she smiled a faraway smile.

She asked again about her father and I told her how he had become a great *hogon* and had lost his sight, only to regain it after the surgery at Sankore.

"Did the *hogon* know what happened to me?"

I told her how she had disappeared and she, of course, understood what this meant.

"Grandma, the *hogon* took us through an opening in the cliff to a chamber where an old engraved stone column stood with the Sirius stars carved into its face. What had been carved into the stone pillar was identical to the drawing you made."

"Aah. Aah." Pleased. Vindicated.

"Give me your hands, Grandma."

She put the cross down and extended her hands in front of her, palms up. I sprinkled on them a few grains of the soil that the *hogon* had asked me to give to her.

"Grandma, the *hogon* wanted you to have this."

She rolled the soil between the palms of her hands. Although I would further explain where the soil had come from, it would be unnecessary.

She raised her smooth unwrinkled face again to the afternoon sun in the window. Tears slipped slowly from her eyes and rolled in two slender lines across her cheeks.

All during this time, Jeanne sat beside me, silent, transfixed. My grandmother put her at ease by holding her hand while I told of our journey.

Though my grandmother had no history of making rash appraisals of people, she seemed to feel an immediate affinity for Jeanne and swept her unconditionally and uncharacteristically into her usually cautious confidence.

Jeanne's presence changed the chemistry of how Grandma and I customarily related to each other. She lent to the proceeding the cheerful ballast that a woman brings, a woman Grandma had pretty much already welcomed as *the* woman for her grandson.

With effervescent enthusiasm, Grandma asked question after question, requiring after each a detailed answer. She wanted to be told the story of our trip from beginning to end, with no particular omitted, small or large.

She pressed me for a description of Babukar, the Badjara room service waiter at the airport hotel in Senegal, who spoke Wolof and bore a Wolof name.

She asked, "What did he look like? Was he tall, with that beautiful dark skin the Senegal people have?"

I answered, "Yes, in fact he was shorter than I but tall and had the skin you like." I told her the story of Babukar's family with the detail of an intimate relation.

"The father worked as a carpenter six days a week, including Thursdays, although the family knew some faraway people—Akân people—Babukar said, who wouldn't till the soil on Thursdays because that was a day of rest for the Earth, and the Earth was a spirit, a deity that was second, as such, only to God."

With that, Grandma shook her head and hummed an exotic phrase of music that I had never heard before.

"Now tell me about the professor, Bokhari. What was he like?"

I described to her everything that I could remember, including the strange sense I'd had that Bokhari had materialized in the airport waiting room out of thin air, as manna born of some rare and protective astral alignment, and was placed there in the waiting room to serve as a shepherd to help me find my way *home*. At the time, the feeling hadn't seemed strange at all, but on the contrary, quite right and fitting.

Grandma then turned her face to Jeanne and said, "I want you to tell me about the *hogon* and everything he said to you. Gray is a man, and men leave out the little things that women know are important."

I suspected that she had made this invitation to Jeanne to have her feel that she was now one of us. That she was a trustee of our secret, Grandma's dreamt memories of her incredible astral journey across the ages.

Jeanne started to tell her about the *hogon* and how he'd led us through an opening in the great 600-foot Bandiagara escarpment.

"I felt as if I knew him," Jeanne said. "Even his title was familiar to me."

"What do you mean?" Grandma asked.

"When our guide said that he was taking us to meet the *hogon*, I knew then what a *hogon* was. That a *hogon* was a high priest."

Jeanne hesitated. Grandma said, "Go on. Go on, dear."

Jeanne began again: "My family is from Haiti. The religion of most Haitians is African in origin. It is called Vou-doun. A high priest in Voudoun is called a *hougan*."

Then Jeanne told Grandma everything that had happened with the *hogon* in the cool space inside the great cliff.

"Before we left, the *hogon* gave the soil of your birthplace to Gray to be given to you. Gray then gave the *hogon* a picture of you which he examined without speaking for a long time, as if he were looking upon the face of a great spirit."

All told, we stayed with my grandmother for more than three hours, talking, eventually, about the more mundane details of our lives and how they intersected and diverged.

As we were leaving to drive back to Baltimore, I remembered to ask Grandma about the metal cross with the elaborate crossbars of near equal length.

"A nice man with an accent gave it to me in church at the spring Lott Carey meeting." Lott Carey was a major national black Baptist association to which my grandmother had belonged for many years. "He said he thought it would mean somethin' to me. I have become attached to it."

"Do you know where it comes from, Grandma?"

"A deacon carried a cross like this high above his head in my Lalibela dream. It looks like the roofs of our stone churches. I was there. In Abyssinia. More than once. As different people. I was Jewish there once, I think, but I hadn't in that life been born into Judaism.

"Then once, in one of the flashes, I was sittin' in a church shaped like this." She ran her fingers over the cross. "I think it was the church consecrated in my Lalibela dream, the dream you woke me from when you were a little boy. We called it the Beta Medhane church and it was shaped just like this cross. That's all that comes to me."

I spoke by telephone with Dr. Quarles the following Monday to ask if he had ever heard of an underground church carved from rock in the form of a square cross, with a name beginning with the words *Beta* or *House*. He asked if he could call me back the following day. He wanted to speak with a colleague at Howard about what he thought could be the answer to my question.

I had consulted with Dr. Quarles before leaving for Mali. It was only the second time I had talked with him since completing my undergraduate work. Still, he had been very generous with his time when I had asked for his general counsel on traveling in Africa. He had also extracted from me a promise that I would come by and visit with him upon my return.

He reminded me of this when he called back the following afternoon.

"When can you get over to campus, Gray? I want to hear all about your trip. I've never been to Mali. I hear it's fascinating."

"I can do it anytime next week, professor. You tell me what's convenient for you."

"How is Thursday at one o'clock? We can have lunch."

"I'll be there."

He was an easy, unpretentious man who from all appearances was all but oblivious of his academic celebrity.

"Oh, by the way, I spoke to my friend. The church, or churches, are in Ethiopia at a place called Lalibela after King Lalibela who, in the twelfth century, had eleven of them hand-carved out of rock. The churches are said to be intricate in design with elaborate detail work. The churches are said to tower in height with tunnels and passageways chiseled through solid mountain rock connecting at least four, if not all of them. The name of one of the churches is Beta Medhane Alem, which means The House of the Savior of the World. My friend is certain that what you asked about is in Ethiopia because nothing like it exists anywhere else in the world."

"Did you mention the cross-shaped design?"

"Yes. He described an ornate work of ancient religious craftsmanship called the Lalibela Cross. The rock-hewn churches that incorporate this cross are Christian, which shouldn't surprise anyone who follows the evolution of Christianity. According to my colleague, Ethiopians have been Christians since 34 A.D., more than three centuries before whites converted to the faith. The oldest Christian church in the world was begun in Ethiopia. Does this help you?"

"Yes, it does, and thanks for all your trouble."

"No trouble at all. I'll see you next week then?"

"I'll be at your office next Thursday at one."

The following week, Dr. Quarles and I would have an hour-long talk in his campus office covering every important detail of my trip to Mali save, of course, any reference to my grandmother's dreams that had inspired the journey.

At the end of our meeting, Dr. Quarles, his features troubled by the unique isolation of the well-meaning but powerless learned, interlaced his fingers behind his head and vented a long and uncharacteristic sigh. "I have been fascinated for some time by Mali's long, storied history." He stopped his train of thought and looked vacantly into the ceiling, mulling something that appeared to disturb him. "I should have made some of it required reading for my students." Then, almost to himself he said tiredly, "So much we Negroes really ought to know about ourselves, we—God help us—well, Graylon, did you know that the Mali empire introduced a written governing constitution at a place called Kurukan Fuga in the year 1235 providing human rights to a population that covered a territory in

West Africa the size of Western Europe? Kurukan Fuga is now a UNESCO World Heritage Site . . ."

It was still another in an ever-growing list of things I thought I should have known about but didn't.

". . . and the French go on so incessantly about their Declaration of the Rights of Man and Citizen of 1789. You'd have thought that they were the first in the world to think about such things . . . I don't know, Graylon. I just don't know . . . the very French that colonized and enslaved Malians."

CHAPTER THIRTY-THREE

On August 25, 1970, Aunt Clarice died at home little more than two months following my return from Mali. She died alone in the early evening in the kitchen of a small rented frame shotgun house that backed onto a rail spur running along the northern industrial outskirts of the city.

On the death certificate, the Richmond city coroner's office listed the cause of death as "heart failure."

She was seventy-eight.

She had been dead for two days before her body was discovered by an overzealous water bill collector who, after receiving no response to his knock on the front door, went around to the rear of the dilapidated house, spotted through the kitchen window Aunt Clarice's motionless body on the floor, and called the police. The two white Richmond police patrolmen, upon arriving on the scene, concluded that Aunt Clarice, while collapsing, had pulled from the kitchen wall the large round clock that rested shattered on the linoleum-covered floor beside her body. From the stilled clock's hands, the two officers further concluded in a cursorily written police report that Aunt Clarice had died at 7:21 p.m., roughly the same time a twenty-six-car freight train was passing noisily behind her kitchen.

Aunt Clarice did not belong to a church and had no friends that we knew of. She had been retired from her job as a charwoman for thirteen years and lived on a tiny pension. During her life, her name only appeared in a newspaper once, that coming after a white reporter, interviewing sidewalk passersby for his paper's morning edition, asked her whether or not she supported the city's Negro civil rights leaders who had organized a surprisingly effective boycott of Thalhimers and Miller and Rhoads, two white-owned downtown department stores that were operating segregated lunch counters.

Aunt Clarice said to the reporter, "I do not."

Her comment appeared in the newspaper the following morning causing considerable embarrassment to the few blood relations she had left in the world.

Following her death, the *Afro-American*, in a brief death notice, reprised the comment and listed Clarice Miller's two surviving blood relations: *a nephew, David March, and a great nephew, Graylon March*. The notice said further that Aunt Clarice had completed the fifth grade at the Navy Hill School and had worked during her life as an office cleaner.

To her family's surprise, Aunt Clarice, six months to a day before her death, had prepared and dated a hand-written will that was found by my mother, who'd taken on the responsibility of gathering from my aunt's living quarters the few worldly goods she'd left behind. The will had been discovered in the kitchen rolled up and buried in a tin of tea bags. In the will, Aunt Clarice bequeathed to my father, her closest living relation, a death benefit of $2,000 payable from a small term-life policy issued by the Big Stone Life Insurance Company, a white company, with offices throughout the southeastern United States. Early in my father's insurance career, he had tried without success to sell Aunt Clarice a Bradford Life Insurance Company policy. She had turned him down explaining that Bradford was "owned by Negroes who would take my hard-earned money and keep it."

My father never received any money from Big Stone and paid from his own near-empty pocket for Aunt Clarice's burial expenses in twelve payments spread out over a year. Big Stone's agent, who over the years had collected small weekly premium payments in cash from Aunt Clarice at her front door, defended his company's refusal to pay the death benefit by explaining to my father that "the woman" had missed a payment resulting in the voiding of her policy. Because the premiums had always been paid in cash, my father was unable to challenge Big Stone's decision to deny payment of the benefit.

Grandma called me from Mrs. Grier's house and asked that I drive down from Baltimore with Jeanne to attend the funeral services which were to be held in the small nondenominational chapel room of the Bivens Funeral Home on Leigh Street.

I did not want to come but felt that I had little choice. My grandmother had requested my presence and that was that. On both my mother and father's sides, we were a very small family, and never is such felt more strikingly than in death. It would, nonetheless, not be easy for me to impersonate a mourner. I had not liked Aunt Clarice and had felt vaguely contaminated when in her company. She hated herself and her very existence weakened my own already compromised defenses against the infection that had caused her condition. I may have even *feared* her because of her exuberantly destructive honesty. Her cancerous idea of herself had been supplied to us all by a common nemesis, and having had no independent idea of herself to embrace, she embraced with lunatic passion the idea she'd been supplied with by those largely responsible for her low social station. Quaffing this poison seemed to have been the central point of her life. Inasmuch as she loathed herself because of her color, she'd had little choice but to loathe me and the rest of us for the much the same reason. Nonetheless, we were a family and appearances were, well, appearances.

I had not been to a funeral or inside a church, even, since Gordon's funeral seven years before.

Jeanne and I arrived late in the city and drove up to the funeral home just before the service was to begin. A young yet-to-be-ordained seminarian had been given by the family a small fee of twenty-five dollars to say a few generic words during the service. We were met at the door by a funeral home official in a black suit who handed us a short program and ushered us to seats in the middle of the little chapel's first row. Aside from the four March family members and Jeanne, the room, which could seat up to twenty-five people, was empty.

The five of us sat square on, eye level to the metallic-blue casket two feet in front of us. I sat to the left of my grandmother. Jeanne sat next to me. My father sat to my grandmother's right. My mother sat next to him on the end.

The seating juxtapositions represented well the health-less state of all the family I had left in the world—two sides linked together by a grandmother, who would serve as all the two camps of estrangers would share in common for the rest of their lives.

My mother and father never looked at me during the brief service, nor I at them. They were never formally introduced to Jeanne, to whom I had become engaged just four days before. By then, I had told Jeanne everything, as well as how difficult it would be to attend the service.

It was not long after Gordon notified Harvard that he would be coming to study there in the fall that he invited me to go with him on Friday night over to the north side of Richmond to a teenage hangout called

Stell Schell's which was located on the black side of Brooklyn Park Boulevard, the city's Mason-Dixon line.

My sight was blurring. It always did this when I was induced to reconstruct what happened that night. I had never spoken to anyone about this—doctor, friend, not even Jeanne, and, of course, not my parents—but some psychosomatic mechanism disturbed my sight, slightly warping objects like the chrome casket rail-handle reflecting light into my eyes which had begun to water inconveniently.

We took a city bus from Church Hill to Broad Street downtown where we transferred to the bus that would take us up to the north side.

We had been happy together that night, both of us more voluble than usual, Gordon going on about taking Harvard by storm, I in praise of him though nagged by an irritant envy, provoked by my parents' disproportionate and lightly veiled favor for him.

Still, I was very proud of him. Getting into Harvard was no small deal in our town, especially for one of us. I loved him and wished for a moment that I were more like him. But I wasn't, and couldn't be.

"As soon as I get control of my books, I want you to come up and see me. I can introduce everybody to my little brother. Okay? We'll be what's happening. The March brothers take Cambridge. What do ya say?"

"Sounds good to me." Daddy would never allow it. Gordon and I knew this, even though he had meant what he said.

"I am told that Sister Clarice was a good law-abiding woman, and deep down a . . ."

We were sitting just in front of the rear exit door, talking on about the future, and paying little attention to where we were. There were no other people on the bus and no one standing on the street by the bus stop signs trying to hail it. The bus was moving fast enough by then to cause the big heavy-duty tires to whine sonorously.

"I should be ashamed of myself for dragging you out on your ankle, but you need to get out more, man."

"It's okay. You know me. I just don't like a big crowd of people."

"You'll be fine. Cheryl and Essie said they'd be here. Wait. You'll see. It'll be great."

"Uh-uh. I can't halfway walk."

"I shouldn't be here myself. I haven't written my commencement speech yet. I got a thousand things, man . . ." Gordon looked out through the window and lunged across me reaching for the bell cord. "Shit."

The bus powered past Brooklyn Park Boulevard and into the white area.

"Although I cannot say that I knew Sister Clarice, I do know that God has opened his arms to her . . ."

Gordon had pulled the bell cord too late. The bus was rolling at a good clip, and in no time was well along into a dark, white residential section of cookie-cutter bungalows with patch-sized lawns decked out with Confederate flags and minstrel statuary. From the shadowy street, we could only have looked like unwitting subjects for human sacrifice standing alone behind the glass of the brightly illuminated bus. I was badly hobbled and Gordon had to help me down onto the street where we would have two overlong blocks to negotiate back to the demilitarized dividing line of Brooklyn Park Boulevard.

"While she may have stumbled during her life, she is in the arms of God now . . ."

I had turned my ankle in a freak accident while walking home from school a few days before. The pain had subsided but the ankle remained badly swollen. I could not put weight on it without limping. We walked slowly, and felt better when we reached the lighted square of the first intersection. Halfway to safety.

I was having a hard time maintaining that it was Aunt Clarice in the casket two feet in front of my face. My eyes were flooded.

From the intersection, we could see ahead of us the bright lights of Brooklyn Park Boulevard.

"How are you? Can you make it?"

"I'm okay. I can make it."

"Does it hurt?"

"Not so much anymore."

"Only one more block."

We were just boys. We were scared. Frightened stiff.

At the lighted intersection, the narrow streets that emptied into it looked as black as pitch. We saw no one before somebody—

From two round speakers in the room's acoustic tile ceiling intoned "The Old Rugged Cross," which I had always hated. Jeanne and my grandmother, not understanding, patted my hands consolingly.

—yelled, "What are you niggers doin' ova here?" the hateful voice drawling long the words.

They had come from the two sides and from the rear. We could not make out their faces. We had no idea how many of them there were. More than ten to be sure. Screaming at us from three separate gatherings in a chorus of profane and epithetic slurs mixed with promises of mortal violence.

We heard the scrape of metal.

"We gonna teach you fucking niggers somethin' tonight."

Silhouettes crept toward us in a pincer-like fashion. Emerging from the darkness, we saw that the silhouettes were not boys but men dressed in roughneck black leather vests and jeans, with angry florid tattoos marked on their shirtless chests and arms. Now we could make out their stormy fuming faces and they ours. The one shouting most of the imprecations carried a long open blade down by his thigh, stropping it as he walked. They were not so close that we would not have been able to flee along the open street behind us toward Brooklyn Park Boulevard had I been able to run even at quarter-speed, but I was not.

I was ashamed of my fear.

The worst of it was that the fear gripping me was felt for the very tormentors against whom bravery would have been the only available weapon with which to preserve that most important of indispensables: self-respect. The approaching faces could see my fear. My eyes shined with it. The faces delighted in what they saw.

I looked at my brother.

I could see that he was afraid too, but I could also see that he was in control of himself. He spoke to me quietly without removing his eyes from the faces.

"I want you to turn around and move away as fast as you can. I will delay them and catch up with you."

"No."

"Do what I tell you."

The faces had closed on three sides to within twenty feet of us. The traction of fear slowed time and prolonged its misery.

"You scared, niggers? We know you about to shit your pants."

"Move, Gray!"

"No."

"Move, Goddamnit. You get us both killed if you don't do what I tell you." Then he looked at me and screamed, "Mooove!"

I turned and took a step away. Only one. Jesus. I know it was only one.

Little more than a second elapsed before I heard an unusual sound, as if a viscid liquid had been pushed with great force through a puncture hole in a rubber tube.

"A-argh."

Then a low wet sucking sound and the rapid beating noise of receding footfalls.

I turned back around. Gordon lay on the tar pavement in the middle of the well-lighted intersection.

He saw me hobbling toward him and tried to cry the word "Run" but the blood welling from his mouth drowned out his speech. I knelt down and took him in my arms. His eyes, frantic with selfless alarm, implored me to run. The eyes darting in the direction that my retreat was to have taken. Then slowly the panic in them ebbed as his gaze swam away and his fingers lost their purchase on my shirt. His lifeless body sagged into mine.

He was eighteen years old.

The family rode to the cemetery behind the hearse bear-

ing Aunt Clarice's body in a black funeral home limousine.

"Daddy."

I held fast to Jeanne's hand. My father remained silent, looking straight ahead. Her course fixed for her years before, my mother said nothing and stared into the black pile floor of the car.

"David!" my grandmother said reproachfully, but it was of little use.

Life does to us things that life cannot fix.

EPILOGUE

Today, June 26, 2004, is my sixtieth birthday. Jeanne's birthday falls on August 21. She will be fifty-eight. In October, we will have been married for thirty-four years.

For the last twenty-five years, we have lived in a little town called Exmore located on Virginia's Eastern Shore, a finger-shaped peninsula that stretches southward 200 miles along the eastern side of the Chesapeake Bay from Delaware to the lower tip across the mouth of the bay from the mainland city of Virginia Beach.

Jeanne and I came here many years ago in response to a call from an old college friend of mine, Moses Boyd, who told me that he had a started a black weekly newspaper on the Shore and that he needed my help to get it going. Moses was a native of the area and felt strongly about the desperate situation of the black residents who comprise sixty percent of the Shore's population.

The Shore is an isolated place. Jeanne polled her students at the community college here and learned that fewer than half of them had ever ventured off the peninsula and across the bay to the foreign territory of mainland America.

Slavery, of course, ended here as it did everywhere else, but only nominally it would seem from the appalling appearance of things, where a consistent pittance of a salary can only be wrung from one of two chicken abattoirs, or from the convenience chain store that opened here in order to make capital of the locals' desperate scramble for work.

Our participation in Moses's project was to have been temporary, but once our newspaper, *The Bugle*, became effective in advancing the black community's social initiatives, we found the Shore hard to leave. By then, having worked for so long shoulder-to-shoulder with so many good people here, we were hooked.

Everyone says that the college and the newspaper have made a difference, and that things have improved. In any case, Jeanne and I have come to love it here and have no plans to go anywhere else.

Owing to complications with Jeanne's first pregnancy, the doctors advised us not to try and have more children after Michäelle was born.

Michäelle is twenty-eight now, and is in the last month of both her doctoral work at Columbia and her first pregnancy, which the newfangled technology tells us will produce a girl in about three weeks.

Michäelle is married to Charles Hobart, an accountant (of all unromantic things). Jeanne tells me lovingly, and not entirely facetiously, that I have been infected with a mild case of chronic asperity and that I, even though no longer young, must try to govern what I say. As usual, she is right. Charles is a good man and he has been a good husband to our daughter.

That is all that should matter.

But that's not all that matters, somehow, and I am a little disappointed with myself to have to admit such. I am spiritually put together much as my grandmother was. I seem to look for in people, quite involuntarily, that which I never found in my parents, or even Gordon. An elasticity of intellectual tolerance. A taste for the foreign, the unexplored, the unknown. A certain poetic inexactness. The sweet mess of unscripted creativity.

This is what I have looked for in people. What I have

found is that I, perish the insight, have become a little of what I so intensely disliked in my parents, that is intolerant, and sometimes self-righteously, judgmentally so.

I was as distant from them as they were from me. We were simply different, and there is little more that can be said about it.

But one recognizes and knows and, then, loves the *self* that one finds in another. How else could two people proceed, spiritually affirmed, except by mutual recognition? I found myself in Jeanne and, conversely, she in me. Thus could she *know* me and come to love me.

The tie of blood alone cannot engender love. Only the staged, ritualized form of it. One must really *know* another soul to really love that soul. I have known in my life only three, and here I count myself fortunate: Jeanne, Michäelle, and Makeda.

My father died of congestive heart failure just before Jeanne and I moved here to the Shore. I mourned him in form.

I am reasonably certain that he would not have thought much of what I have done with my life as the managing editor for a small little-known newspaper. It would not have meant success to him. Hence, he would not have understood the pure joy that Jeanne and I felt just recently when the struggling black farmers here, with *The Bugle's* support, prevailed in their suit against the United States Department of Agriculture on the grounds of racial lending discrimination. Nor could he have understood our despair when the government declined to honor the settlement that it had reached, in bad faith as it turns out, with the farmers. Or perhaps, remembering my grandmother's accounts, my father might have appreciated all of this as a young man. As it was, he seemed to have died twice, the first death a larger tragedy than the second.

The two of us, my father and I, were never to reconcile.

My mother died a year after my father. It was as if there were nothing else for her to do, my father being gone and all, which—all—was what he had been to her.

My grandmother, the great formative figure in my life, died in 1989 at the age of eighty-six. She lived long enough to example her immortal splendid spirit to our daughter, Michäelle, who was thirteen at the time of her great-grandmother's passing.

I am here on the Shore working hard for small wages and miniscule notice, clearly not only because of Jeanne, but because of my grandmother's lasting influence upon me as well. I am happy and fulfilled as I never imagined I could be.

Even now, I can recall, as if they had taken place yesterday, all of our Saturday and weekday talks, including one that took place during my last year of high school. My grandmother had been encouraging my embryonic confidence in the idea of trying to become a writer.

"Live where you are. Success can only be found in your heart. It's a very private thing, son. What everyone else calls success is usually not that at all, and the people who have what most people call success are often miserable. Don't be fooled by that. If it doesn't make you happy, it's not success."

Not long after my father's death, my grandmother would confide to me in the parlor of the house from which she would not, before her death, be budged, "My biggest failure in this life was with my own son. There were things I could not make him see even though he was a devoted son. It was just how he was after the war. Closed and afraid inside, fightin' so hard he couldn't afford to look around. Couldn't let his guard down. My poor David."

By most any standard, I cannot be remarked to have

been a productive writer. While over the years I've had several ideas for books, I've never been sufficiently motivated to act on any one of them owing to the ideas having been forced out and contrived. Any book based on them would have necessarily resulted in an empty uninspired exercise.

Over the fifteen years since my grandmother's death, I have, however, worked on and off, sometimes like a stuck stylus, on the book about her dreams of past lives.

Following the blow-up with my father, precipitated by Gordon's death and the ill-advised disclosures that I made to Dr. Harris-Fulbright of the University of Southern California, my grandmother requested that I not write anything about her experiences until after she, my mother, and my father were gone. She was adamant about this and there was nothing I could do to change her mind, including telling her that no major publisher would consider publishing such a book without her alive to verify its central thesis. Even under those circumstances, I told her, it would be unlikely that a publisher would agree to such a book. Still not moving from the position she had taken, she made a second request that appeared to fly in the face of the first.

"You must promise me that you will see to it that the book is published before these people find Emme Ya."

She was obsessive about this, and restated it to me with increasing frequency in the months before her death. Her last dischargeable duty on Earth, she held, was to make certain that "*these* people" not be allowed to take credit for astronomical discoveries that the Dogon people had made hundreds, if not thousands of years before. She would not listen to reason. Reality was of little concern to her. I told her that black Americans had almost no influence inside the American major publishing industry and that the industry would likely be little interested in Dogon proofs, even those that had been verified by white scientists like the French team of eminent anthropologists, Marcel Griaule and Germaine Dieterlen.

"You see to it, Gray, that this gets done."

"I'll do my best, Grandma," which did not satisfy her. That day, I'd sat where I had sat since I was five—in the side chair that I placed in front of her rocker that was hard, as always, by the sun-bathed front window.

She held lightly in her hands the Ethiopian Lalibela cross as one would an irreplaceable talisman. Though ill by then, she sat unusually high in the chair with her chin elevated as if she were an all-knowing shaman, looking back across the landscape of human experience.

"Gray." She spoke softly as if she had little time left.

"Yes, Grandma."

"I think you understand that you are the only person in the world, besides Jeanne, who knows who I am."

"Yes, Grandma."

"Your father would never have understood me. I never talked about any of this to your mother or Gordon. Only to you. You *must* tell the story. Some will laugh at you. You need to accept this. But many will listen. *Our* people. They're the ones that must be made to know what happened."

She paused to husband her strength.

"You are blessed, Gray. Not all of us have a larger destiny, but you do. Now, you must heed its command."

During the months that led up to my grandmother's death, she endured considerable pain—accompanied by a progressive erosion of strength, but with no corresponding deterioration of her mental faculties.

I made it my business to get from the Shore to Richmond to spend a day with her at least once every week.

We had long talks during these visits, talks about life and its elusive meaning. As often as she could manage, we held our talks in the little parlor at the front of the house. On those occasions when the stairs presented her with too insuperable an obstacle, we held our talks at her bedside.

Knowing full well what lay ahead, she appeared all but indifferent to the prospect of death. On those occasions when she did speak of it, she spoke of it dispassionately—as little more than a portal through which she would cross again from earthly life to the other side, the realm of the spirit world.

She talked to me more expansively than she had in the past about her many "journeys." She had, it seems, become a Jew when she converted to Judaism as a young woman living in Ethiopia nearly 3,000 years ago. Since then, she had lived several Christian lives, with an indeterminate number of them lived in Ethiopia. Two others—two American lives—had been lived as a slave on a Virginia plantation.

Another, her current life, had been lived as a blind laundress in the little house on Duvall Street in Richmond, Virginia.

She had also lived at least one life as a Muslim—a Moor—in southern Spain. So it was that, at one time or another, she had embraced all of the three large monotheistic Abrahamic faiths.

As my grandmother drew nearer to the earthly death that Christians seem to privately believe to be the end of everything, it became increasingly clear to me, from things she said, what overarching store she continued to place in the tenets of the West African traditional religions she had practiced during one or another of the several West African lives she had lived.

During our countless talks in the little front parlor, she'd once asked me long ago, "Gray, tell me, what do the pictures you've seen of Jesus look like? You know, the ones hanging on church walls?" When I hesitated, she'd added,

"You know, son, the fence Reverend Boynton and almost everybody else keep staring at."

Since she, as often as not, spoke in figurative terms, I hadn't immediately taken her point. I described to her the ubiquitous print of a painting I'd looked at most of my life, a print that hung on the wall of practically every church I'd ever been in.

"That's nothing like the image of Jesus I have in my head," she'd said. Then she'd found with her fingers the Book of Daniel. "Listen to this, son, *The hair of his head like pure wool*. Pure wool. Doesn't sound like the hair you saw in your picture, does it? The Bible has his hair more like mine, don't you think?"

Thus, because of what she had come to believe about who Jesus, in life, really had been, and the regard in which the Bible's Jesus had held the Ethiopians, she had little difficulty harmonizing her Christian faith with her several African faiths. She had come to see them all as virtually one and the same.

"The Akân people say, *If you want to speak to God, speak to the wind*. God is everywhere and not just in a church or some fancy building. Jesus believed the same thing. The first Christians never had a building."

My grandmother had the Apostle Paul as her biblical authority for this. She had read to me from the Book of Acts what Paul told the Athenians: *God who made the world and everything in it, since He is Lord of Heaven and Earth, does not dwell in temples made with hands.*

"So, son, you won't need to talk to my headstone in order to talk to me. I won't be there. I'll be in the air and the Earth. I'll be in the leaves of the trees. I'll be in the stars that light the African heavens. I'll be watchin' over you and your family. My spirit will always be close enough to touch and protect you all. So, do not grieve for me. My body will die, but my soul will live on. For my soul cannot die. Always remember that my soul is the spark of God in me."

Nine days later, she died at home in her sleep. I had been alone with her during the hours that wound quietly down. I sat by her bed in the dark and watched her smooth mahogany face. The lids of her eyes were closed. Her hair was dressed out in silvery whorls that sprayed like a rainbow across the bright white pillow that cradled her motionless head. Her visage under the moonlight bore the gentle mark of mystical insight.

Her soul poised to break from the failing flesh, I heard from her lips an expiry of small, faintly audible wordlike sounds.

"*Azudlozi lingayi ekhaya.*"

I moved close to her ear and whispered, "Grandma, I . . ."

She slowly opened her sightless eyes and spoke to me for the last time. "The spirit never forgets the way home."

I gently pressed my cheek to hers. At the touch of her warm skin, I experienced a sensation of karmic *envelopment*— her final gift to a grateful and loving grandson—the parting embrace of her immortal soul.

When I was a young man—even for a time after my grandmother first told me of her Dogon dream story—I believed that every life was finite and subject to nature's one merciless implacable equalizer: time. That all living things were termed to one birth, one passage, one death. That life was little more than a brief, occluded, misunderstood affair, spent forward on currents of mystery and hopeless illogic. I had fastened all focus upon what I believed to be the permanent wall of the impermanent flesh.

I no longer believe this. My grandmother lives—and I know this.

Six weeks ago, almost fifteen years after her death, I completed the manuscript and retained an agent in New

York to shop it around for me. It was sent to seven publishers. Within a month, four of them had rejected the book with a single-sentence form letter. A fifth wrote courteously that, *Though interesting, it is not the kind of work that our house publishes.* The sixth publisher answered, *While your grandmother's reincarnation dreams are believable generally, the idea that a tribe in Africa might know something about astronomy is not.*

The last publisher to be heard from, a small house in lower Manhattan, accepted the manuscript and agreed to publish it within the coming year.

Everyone in our family knew well how long I had labored to fulfill this final obligation to my grandmother. *The book*, as we had for years come to call it, had developed something of an ethereal presence in our home—a soft comforting awareness of some remembered ratifying greatness that gave us health and hope and foresight enough to understand the relative seasonality of our people's contemporary adversity.

Of what consequence is a brief mortal moment against the affirming weight of the ages?

When I called Michäelle to tell her the good news from the publisher, she became so excited that I worried for the health of my soon-to-arrive first grandchild. Michäelle told me then that the baby's middle name would be Giselle after Jeanne's mother, and that the baby's Christian first name would be Makeda.

CODA

In the ancient texts and holy books, the great black woman is referred to in many places and by several names.

In Matthew 12:42, Christ says of her, *The Queen of the South shall rise up in the judgment with this generation and shall condemn; for she came from the uttermost parts of the Earth to hear the wisdom of Solomon . . .*

The ancient Greeks called her the *Black Minerva*.

In the Koran, the Muslim writers made reference to her as *Bilqis*.

In I Kings 10:1-10 and II Chronicles 9:1-12 of the Bible, she is described as the *Queen of Sheba*.

In the Ethiopians' most sacred book, the *Kebra Nagast*, she is known to her own people as:

MAKEDA

AUTHOR'S NOTE

The Dogon people's millennia-old knowledge of the Sirius star system was first described to English-language readers in 1976 by Robert K.G. Temple in his book *The Sirius Mystery*, which was published in the United States by St. Martin's Press.

Wrote Temple, "The Dogon also know the actual orbital period of this invisible star (Sirius B), which is fifty years . . . The Dogon also say that Sirius B rotates on its axis, demonstrating that they know a star can do such a thing."

Robert Temple is an American-born writer who lives in England. He is a graduate of the University of Pennsylvania and a fellow of the Royal Astronomical Society.

In the thirty-five years since Temple's book was published, no credible challenge has been lodged to the Dogon people's age-old comprehensive understanding of the cosmos.

It wasn't until 1995 that Sirius C, the star that for countless centuries the Dogon people have called "Emme Ya, the sun of women," was detected by French astronomers Daniel Benest and J.L. Duvent.

Three significant real-life figures presented as fictional characters in Makeda's story have had over the years an important influence on my writing and sociopolitical thinking:

I met Kofi Asare Opoku at a conference on Paul Robeson held nine years ago at Lafayette College in Pennsylvania where he was, at the time, serving as a visiting professor. Professor Opoku, one of the world's preeminent authorities on African traditional religions, holds degrees from Yale

University Divinity School and the University of Ghana. Besides *West African Traditional Religion* (1978), Professor Opoku has authored several other important books on African religions and culture, including *Speak to the Winds: Proverbs from Africa* (1975) and *Hearing and Keeping: Akan Proverbs* (1997).

In 1970, Walter J. Leonard, a black assistant dean at Harvard Law School, persuaded the Ford Foundation to fund a small number of postgraduate research fellowships for African-Americans aspiring to work and study in Africa. I was fortunate enough to be one of the brand-new research program's fellows. Invited in the summer of 1970 to Ford's New York offices to brief us before our departures for several African countries (mine for Tanzania) was John Henrik Clarke, the compelling Pan-Africanist black American writer, historian, and Hunter College professor. The meeting that summer at Ford marked the beginning of a relationship between me and Professor Clarke that would last until his death in 1998 at the age of eighty-three.

In 1964, at the age of twenty-three, I read *The Negro in the Making of America* by Benjamin Quarles from cover to cover in two sittings. The book made an indelible impression on me, as did his *Blacks on John Brown* and the eight other black history books authored by the chairman of Morgan State University's history department. Professor Quarles died in 1996 at the age of ninety-two.

Acknowledgments

I am especially appreciative that *Makeda* has been chosen as the first book to bear Akashic Books' new Open Lens imprint. For this I owe a special thanks to Marva Allen, Marie Brown, Janet Hill Talbert, and Regina Brooks, as well as to the publisher, Johnny Temple, of Akashic Books. All of you have been unstintingly helpful in bringing this project to fruition. My thanks also to Jacqueline Bryan of St. Kitts who typed my handwritten manuscript.

My muse, my wife and dearest friend, Hazel, whom I've loved for twenty-eight years, I thank for caring so passionately, not only about *Makeda*, the book, but about the general social wellness of the entire African world family.

If you wish to contact Randall Robinson, write to him at rr@rosro.com.

RECOMMENDED READING

African Ark by Carol Beckwith and Angela Fisher

A History of Ethiopia by Harold G. Marcus

Blacks in Science: Ancient and Modern, edited by Ivan Van Sertima

General History of Africa: Ancient Civilizations of Africa by the UNESCO International Scientific Committee. Editor: G. Mokhtar

Past Lives: An Investigation into Reincarnation Memories by Peter and Elizabeth Fenwick

Precolonial Black Africa by Cheikh Anta Diop

Richard Wright: The Life and Times by Hazel Rowley

The Black Man's Burden: Africa and the Curse of the Nation-State by Basil Davidson

The Destruction of Black Civilization: Great Issues of Race from 4500 B.C. to 2000 A.D. by Chancellor Williams

The Secret Teachings of All Ages: An Encyclopedic Outline of Masonic, Hermetic, Qabbalistic and Rosicrucian Symbolical Philosophy by Manley P. Hall

The Sirius Mystery by Robert K.G. Temple

"Un Système Soudanais de Sirius," *Le Journal de la Société des Africanistes*, Volume 20, Part 1, by Marcel Griaule and Germaine Dieterlen

West African Traditional Religion by Kofi Asare Opoku

West Africa before the Colonial Era: A History to 1850 by Basil Davidson